Th

Joe Nobody

Edited by:
E. T. Ivester
D. Allen

www.joenobodybooks.com

This is a work of fiction. Characters and events are products of the author's imagination, and no relationship to any living person is implied. The locations, facilities, and geographical references are set in a fictional environment.

Other Books by Joe Nobody:

- Holding Your Ground: Preparing for Defense if it All Falls Apart
- The TEOTWAWKI Tuxedo: Formal Survival Attire
- Without Rule of Law: Advanced Skills to Help You Survive
- Holding Their Own: A Story of Survival
- Holding Their Own II: The Independents
- Holding Their Own III: Pedestals of Ash
- Holding Their Own IV: The Ascent
- Holding Their Own V: The Alpha Chronicles
- Holding Their Own VI: Bishop's Song
- Holding Their Own VII: Phoenix Star
- The Home Schooled Shootist: Training to Fight with a Carbine
- Apocalypse Drift
- The Olympus Device: Book One

Prologue

Lying on its side, the 600-foot long ship was a visual oddity that demanded the eye. With its stern aground 40 feet from the nearest water, the tanker appeared as a beached, primordial monster of gargantuan proportions.

At first glance, the carcass of the titan was being consumed by lesser creatures. An army of ant-like warriors swarmed the hull... scaling, climbing, and scuttling over the dead behemoth. A fleet of Matchbox® car-like vehicles surrounded the superstructure, their flashing lights engendering a colored sea of cobalt, crimson, and amber illumination.

To the careful observer, it was obvious that the giant hadn't given up without a struggle. A hedge of smashed vehicles, debris, and other flotsam surrounded the massive beast, evidence of the tsunami generated by its dying throes.

But the colossus wasn't dead.

A warning spread through the ant regiment, the multitude's movements accelerating with a vibration of panic and fear. The fleet of flashing lights began scurrying away, leaking from the goliath's shadow in a single file, like a lake being drained through a narrow channel. They seemed suddenly desperate to escape its proximity.

Screaming, terrified voices filled the airwaves, shouts of warning turning quickly into verbal mayhem. The initial armada of emergency response morphed into a riot of emergency retreat. The gas was leaking. Ethylene oxide was mixing with salt and water - the primary ingredients of a thermalbaric weapon.

Men, fire trucks, ambulances and police cars raced away, every second providing them precious distance – lifesaving space. On the nearby Hartman Bridge, the few remaining vehicles sought desperately to escape. Up and down the ship channel, radios blared with imminent crisis alerts, informing captains and crew to evacuate.

Law enforcement helicopters banked hard, abandoning their orbits, quickly followed by their news station counterparts.

The leviathan's bowels continued to hemorrhage, seemingly unaware or uncaring of the frantic exodus taking place. Tons of BTU-laced vapor spread from the vessel's primary storage tanks, filling passageways, vents, and cabins with a volatile cloud. It was only a matter of time before the explosive fog encountered a heat source and ignited.

Finally reaching the machinery spaces, the huge diesel's exhaust provided the necessary pyro-inducement. For a hundredth of a second, the gas only burned, the flame expanding rapidly in the confined spaces.

The ship's thick hull served as a containment vessel for the expanding gases - much like the iron casing of a bomb restrains the internal energy until it is overwhelmed. The crippled tanker and all that surrounded her were doomed.

The destruction was initiated by a wall of air traveling at over 700 mph as the keel surrendered. Compressed to the consistency of concrete, the blast wave expanded outward … shredding, tearing and crushing anything in its path. It was quickly followed by the fireball, a doorway to the sulfuric pits of hell opening for an ephemeral moment of time.

Hundreds of tons of concrete, composing one of the primary supports for the nearby ship channel bridge, were minced into powder. Sections of the expansive, connecting deck weighing over 50 tons were tossed into the air like dry, autumn leaves swirling in a seasonal gust.

Superheated, white-hot gases expanded from the epicenter, consuming oxygen and producing devastation in an ever-expanding ring of violence. The subsequent events were just as destructive, since the Port of Houston was lined with a kind of manmade kindling - chemical, refining, and manufacturing facilities. Secondary fires and explosions would rage for days. It was a target rich environment for catastrophe.

The expanding blast of condensed air and sound shattered windows for over 50 miles. The anchor of the ravaged tanker was discovered in a mall parking lot six miles away. Citizens as far away as Dallas and Austin called their local police departments to report an earthquake.

All of the ruin, death, and chaos were due to one small, shoulder-fired device - the rail gun.

Day One

Just over 12 miles south of the disaster and motoring along the shoreline of Galveston Bay, Dusty sensed a brilliant flash behind him. Spinning to peer over his shoulder, he witnessed a pillar-like fountain of flame, smoke, and debris rising in the atmosphere. "Get down!" he yelled at Grace, pulling her prone into the shallow bilge just as a hot, forceful gust of wind rocked their small craft. The commandeered inflatable nearly capsized, the couple saved from another drenching by the curvature of the earth and the fact that they were hugging the coast.

After their vessel had stabilized, Dusty turned to examine a column of scorched nautical fragments and smoldering ash rising into the air above the ship channel. He could guess what it was and whispered a small prayer that no one had been killed. "Oh Lord," exhaled Grace, staring at the ever-rising formation. "Did someone just nuke Houston?"

"I bet that tanker blew," Dusty replied in a low voice. "I hope they had time to evacuate everybody."

As their launch continued south, the thunder of secondary explosions sounded in the distance, the echoing rumblings and sharp claps reminding Dusty of a 4th of July fireworks display. He glanced down at the bag containing the rail gun and shook his head. "I should just toss that weapon overboard and be done with this. Let it sink into the bay's muddy bottom, never to be seen again."

"You could," replied Grace, unable to take her eyes away from the destruction. "But you promised Mitch you wouldn't, and besides, no one would believe you had simply thrown it away. At best, they would lock you up and throw away the key. At worst, they might even torture you until you told them where it was. You're damned if you do and damned if you don't at this point. You might as well hang onto it now – it's leverage. It may be your salvation."

Dusty shook his head in disgust, "I feel like I'm carrying around a bag full of evil... like doomsday in a suitcase."

Grace's posture changed, her sly grin reminding him of a cat that just cornered the rodent. Dusty had seen it before and braced for the overwhelming logic that was surely heading his way. He didn't have to wait long.

"What did you tell me once? Guns don't kill people, people kill people," she said.

"Now that's not fair," he protested. "I was talking about regular weapons, not something like the rail gun. That," he said pointing at the duffle, "is too much power for any one man to possess."

"Then don't shoot it anymore, Durham. Hide it, disable it, or just keep it unloaded – but don't shoot it. It can't do any harm just sitting somewhere."

The fact that she had reverted to using his formal name was a signal, a message that she wanted to leave no room for misinterpretation of her words.

"You do have a point," he eventually responded.

The couple continued in silence, plying the bay's waters and trying to remain unnoticed. It wasn't a serious concern - most eyes were glued to television news stations or toward the thunderous pyrotechnics on the horizon.

Eventually, Dusty glared down at the bag holding his invention. "Grace," he said, and then hesitated for a moment as if composing his thoughts. "I know I gave my word to my brother, but that was before I destroyed half of a city." He pointed with his head at the colossal columns of blazing flames over his shoulder, and continued, "Dozens, perhaps hundreds of people hadn't died yet."

"If you toss that overboard, you are throwing away the only hope you have of clearing your name and returning to your life back in Fort Davis. Do you ever want to see your ranch again? Do you ever

8

want to be able to walk around without checking over your shoulder?"

He pondered her questions. "We have several million dollars in that bag. We can live anywhere we like... Costa Rica, Thailand... you name it. It's not as if we'll spend our years in destitution. Now, we don't want to draw a lot of attention with a flashy lifestyle, but we don't have to live in a jungle shack either."

As was her habit, Grace took her time digesting his logic. "Are you sure that is what you want? You have lived in West Texas all your life. You live on land that was your father's and his father's before that. If you are 100% certain you don't care about returning to your home, then toss that thing over the side. But be sure, Dusty. Be very sure."

He continued maneuvering the craft, slowly proceeding a few hundred yards off the shore. They motored by bay houses, many equipped with wooden piers jutting into the blue-brown waters. Gorgeous manicured lawns sloped to the edge of the water, their emerald green hue a fitting contrast with the bay. The seaside real estate was prime and very expensive, the grounds boasting manor-sized homes and plentiful lots. On the horizon toward the east, beautiful multi-hued sails announced the presence of graceful wind-powered vessels. It was a landscape that inspired peace and contentment.

But not this morning.

Another chorus of detonations sounded from the north, riotous with the reverberations of destruction. He shook his head, an act that displayed regret and sadness while at the same time announcing his decision.

He pointed their craft toward deeper water, turning the small outboard's tiller and bracing it with his knee. Reaching for the duffle, he unzipped the entire length and pulled out the rail gun. He paused for a moment, gazing at what had been an innocent discovery and yet had changed so many lives.

The gleam of gold caught his attention. Attached to the rare earth magnets along the barrel was a tube of the gold coins provided by the Russian. A deep scowl crossed his face, the understanding immediate.

"What's wrong?" Grace asked, trying to read his expression.

"Gold isn't magnetic. Those coins shouldn't be attracted to the gun's magnets."

It took quite a bit of effort to pull the obviously iron-filled fakes from the weapon's barrel, so strong was the attraction. Ten minutes later, he'd verified every single tube was full of forgeries. The Russian had been trying to deceive him.

"But this is gold," Grace announced, holding a handful of the slugs and Dusty's pocketknife. Maybe not pure gold, but I can't scratch it off."

A thought then occurred to Dusty – if the coins weren't real, what about the cash?

He corrected their course back shoreward and began inspecting the wads of currency stuffed inside the bag. Pulling out a stack of what appeared to be $100 bills, Dusty inspected the top note. It contained the earmarks of the genuine article, complete with blue micro-strip that shimmered like a holographic image.

He flipped to the second note, and then the third. They were authentic as well, but the digitalized face staring at him was not that of Benjamin Franklin, but the nation's first president instead. One dollar bills! And so was the rest of the stack. He relented after checking five of the bundles. They all were the same, a big note on top followed by mostly George Washington's image on the rest.

"Shit," he mumbled, "That cheating Russian bastard. I should have known."

Grace, trying to lighten the mood and temper Dusty's anger observed, "Well, at least we're not broke. And the passport and other papers look genuine enough."

"So much for early retirement," he exhaled. "We'll have to put away the travel brochures and face the music here, Grace. I guess I have no choice but to hang onto that weapon. It's all I have left." The gunsmith paused for a moment, still processing his discovery. "I'm back to zero. We've got next to nothing. I can't provide for myself, let alone both of us. I've lost my family, ranch, and everything important to me. The media is rife with stories portraying me as some mad man, and half the world is looking to plant this old carcass six feet under the ground. What a mess."

Grace reached across the bag and touched his hand. "We'll be okay, Dusty. I promise. I know the truth, and I'm with you all the way."

For some reason, the weapon clutched so tightly in Dusty's hand switched personas. No longer was it a tool of destruction and the primary cause of his dire situation. He began looking at the device almost as if it were an heirloom, a cherished object that anchored him to the past... a happier time.

His impulse to toss the rail gun overboard passed. It was only a machine, not Lucifer in disguise. Without a human pulling the trigger, it wouldn't even make a good boat anchor.

"Maybe you're right," he said. "This little invention got me into this mess, maybe it's the only thing that can get me out."

Grace nodded and smiled, squeezing his hand with a warming gesture. "Whatever happens, Dusty, we're in this together."

And with that, he nestled the rail gun back in the duffle and resumed piloting their course.

The wind was picking up, blowing from the southeast and stirring up an uncomfortable chop. "We need to find civilization," Dusty announced. "This boat is too small for open water on a windy day."

His first mate pointed toward the distant shoreline with a nod, "Is that a Ferris wheel? You don't see too many of those out on the open sea."

Following her gaze, Dusty indeed observed the carnival ride on the horizon. He studied the scene for a moment and then remembered reading about a small amusement park in the area. He could also identify a string of pleasure boats exiting what appeared to be a channel of some sort. "Looks worthy of investigating. What started as a breezy morning is quickly building into quite the blustery day."

And with that, he turned the small craft toward the west.

Fifteen minutes later, the red and green markers of a navigation channel came into view. "Red, right, return," Dusty muttered, remembering an old novel he'd read years ago. The Ferris wheel loomed larger from his new perspective.

Before long, an extensive row of dockside restaurants and shops came into view, seemingly stretching to the horizon. A single, storm-weathered, wooden sign identified their location. "Welcome to the Kemah Boardwalk."

"I remember this place," Grace exhaled from the front of the boat, her eyes darting about the commercial area. "There's food, shopping and a hotel here. All the travel magazines rave about its variety of amusements and small town charm."

Dusty navigated their tiny craft along the edge of the main channel, the primary waterway bustling with early morning private yachts heading out to the bay for a day's recreation. Grace pointed toward the shoreline, "There's a place to tie up."

A few minutes later, they were securing the raft via a small dock line to the wharf-side cleat. After helping Grace onto the pier, the couple stood and studied their surroundings.

The boardwalk offered many of the amenities normally associated with an upscale shopping mall. Brick walkways and common areas led to a variety of small shops, large restaurants and an even larger amusement park. At the early hour, only a few of the shopkeepers had managed to open their establishments, but there were still a considerable number of people milling about.

"I need a fresh change of clothes and a shower, Dusty," Grace declared. She then threw him a glance and wrinkled her nose, "And so do you."

Dusty caught a reflection of himself in a nearby window and had to agree. If they expected to blend in with the tourists, it would probably help if they didn't look like they'd just survived a missile attack and tsunami.

"The shops will probably open at nine," he said, looking at his watch. "We've got about 20 minutes to kill."

They took a seat in a common area, people-watching and passing time. Dusty enjoyed observing a clever set of fountains, the nozzles flush with the brick walkway and firing random tubes of water through the air. Despite the early hour, a gaggle of little children was already darting in and out of the randomized, mechanical rainstorm.

They identified a small boutique offering beachwear for tourists. Bathing suits, sunglasses, and lotions dominated the retail space, but there were a few racks of street clothes. The teenage clerk was busy completing her opening checklist and didn't seem to notice that her first customers looked like hell.

After two trips to the changing room, Grace had selected a seaside outfit, complete with floppy hat and leather sandals. Dusty was having more difficulty, unaccustomed to anything but blue jeans and boots.

Grace finally helped him select a pair of khaki slacks and a polo shirt that wouldn't look out of place with his otherwise-western attire. A Panama style beach hat was, in his opinion, a poor substitute for his familiar western hat - traded to the now-dead Russian just a few hours ago.

"Let's eat," Dusty suggested as they paid for their purchases and headed out of the store. "I could swallow a buffalo whole, and more importantly, I need coffee... bad."

Grace shook her head. "How about we check into the hotel first, take a quick shower, and then go put on the feed bag?"

With a reluctant nod, he agreed.

They changed clothes in the public restroom, Grace having to remove a price tag from Dusty's new shirt to insure he fit in with the locals. Soon they were entering the hotel's lobby.

"I'm sorry, but we don't have any vacancies for the next few days," informed the pleasant clerk. "I'd be happy to check other nearby facilities."

"That would be great," Grace replied, the disappointment clear in her voice.

The young man working the desk tapped on the keyboard, and then looked up with a smile. "One of our sister properties, Southside Harbor has several rooms available. Their nightly rate is a little pricier than ours, but they offer a very nice environment."

"How far away is it?" Dusty inquired, and then added, "Does their 'nice environment' include fresh coffee?"

"Just over two miles up the lake. Less than five minutes by car, and I'm sure they'll have coffee."

Grace flashed him a troubled look, but he ignored it, instead continuing his conversation with the clerk, "Well, now that's the problem. Our car broke down on the road a few hours ago and was towed to the shop. For the rest of today, we're without transportation."

The kid considered the travelers' predicament for a minute before brightening. "How about a taxi?"

The cab arrived a short time later. While riding to the more ritzy accommodations, Dusty spied one of the huge box retailers. Nudging Grace, he observed, "I think a shopping trip is in our near future. Our supply list is going to contain more than just a change of clothes."

Southside Harbor was an impressive complex, the high-rise hotel surrounded by a large marina and numerous offices. Dusty paid for the cab, and the couple anxiously strolled into the lobby.

"We'd like a suite," he announced, reaching for his new ID and wad of cash.

The clerk shoved the registration form across the counter and said, "May I see the credit card you'll be using to secure the room?"

"I was going to pay cash," Dusty replied as he scratched in the information from his Canadian persona.

"I'm sorry, sir, but we require a credit card on file. You are welcome to pay cash at checkout, but I'm not allowed to reserve a room without it."

Dusty didn't miss a beat, "Son, with all of the credit card fraud, stolen identities and other shenanigans going on, I cut up all my plastic. Are you sure there isn't another option?" Dusty flashed the young man his roll of bills to emphasize his point.

"I'm very sorry, but the hotel is very strict where this policy is concerned, sir."

Both Grace and Dusty protested the requirement until the manager was summoned to the front desk. She was a middle-aged, attractive lady who obviously understood customer service and the needs of weary travelers.

After listening to the couple's tale of woe concerning lost luggage, rude airline employees, and a black cloud that seemed to be following them around, the manager's face brightened with an idea. "Have you considered a pre-loaded credit card? It takes only minutes to acquire one. It has to be safer than carrying around all of that cash anyway. You can easily purchase one right up the street."

Dusty thought about the new identity delivered by the Russian. "But I'm Canadian; I don't think I qualify for a U.S. credit card."

"Oh, there's no qualification," she assured him. "I buy them for gifts all the time. The credit card company won't even know your name or what country you're from."

Dusty turned to Grace and shrugged, "Can't hurt to try. Might come in handy."

She glanced toward the front door and frowned, "Our cab is already gone."

"No problem," chimed in the manager. "We have a shuttle service. I can have Danny run you down to the store right away. You'll be back in 15 minutes."

Grace stared longingly at the plush lounge chairs scattered around the lobby. "I'll stay here with our shopping bags and your duffle. Don't be too long."

Danny drove the courtesy car to the same retail giant Dusty had recognized during the cab ride. The gunsmith entered the massive space and was soon directed to the pre-paid card display. What he saw amazed him.

There were hundreds of options covering everything from coffeehouses to national fast food chains. He finally found the generic MasterCard and Visa section, quickly focusing on the brand recommended by the hotel's manager.

As he stood in line at the register, Dusty realized it was the first time the rail gun had been out of his possession since he'd left home to visit his brother in College Station. It was an odd feeling, almost as if he wasn't fully dressed. He didn't like the sensation.

When it was his turn, he handed the clerk three of the cards. As the small packages were scanned, the clerk inquired, "Do you want to load any funds onto these?"

"Sure. Is there any limit how much?"

"I can load a maximum of $500 per card, but you can go online and set them up just like a checking account and add more money whenever you choose."

"Hmmmm," he remarked while stroking his chin as if in deep thought. "Well, I have never actually bought one of these and am not sure what is best. Maybe you can give me a little advice. You see, I'm buying these as gifts. If I put funds onto these cards, will my nieces and nephews be able to access the money?"

"Anyone can use them. There's no name or ID required. They make great presents, and if they get lost, there's a toll-free number you can call to cancel and get a new card reissued."

"Splendid," Dusty replied. "Please load the maximum on each card."

The clerk's eyebrows shot up. "But sir, you do realize I can only do that with cash?" she questioned.

"No problem."

The lady laughed, "Could adopt me into your family? If you need any more nieces or nephews, that is."

A short time later, Grace and Dusty swiped a plastic keycard to enter the fifth floor room, the opulence of the accommodations immediately obvious, the space impressive and well designed for comfort. Plush carpeting, a huge master bed, expansive bathroom, and tasteful appointments made both of them smile and relax. The view of the marina added to the calming effect. Dusty noted the coffeemaker.

"I've got first dibs on the shower," Grace announced, balancing on her tiptoes to kiss him on the cheek, and then hustling off to close the bathroom door.

Dusty, with credit card on file at the front desk, wasted no time perusing the room service menu.

Agent Shultz checked his reflection, the mirrored interior of the elevator revealing a filthy, disheveled man. *It's no wonder*, he mused. *One hell of a morning.*

Were it not for the golden shield and official-looking photograph on the FBI credentials hanging around his neck, he doubted they would have let him in the hospital's front door. He'd originally tried to enter via the emergency room, but that entrance was inundated with incoming ambulances, emergency vehicles, and utter chaos.

The blue-haired ladies at the reception desk had kindly taken their time locating Agent Monroe's room number. They had shown mercy and manners, not commenting on his appearance. Given the bedlam back in the ER, he wasn't the only haggard-looking fellow walking the halls.

Still, he straightened himself out as best he could, tucking in an errant shirttail and dislodging a streak of mud from his pants. He wanted to present the best possible image to the boss.

He identified Monroe's room without any problem, entering quietly lest he disturb some procedure or consultation. There was only an aide present, a middle-aged Latino woman who appeared to be more involved in housekeeping than any medical task.

His boss was connected to a multitude of tubes, wires, machines and other associated life-preserving devices. The low background of beeping and hissing noises disturbed the otherwise quiet environment. The patient was perched in the middle of the bed, lying very still with his eyes closed.

Upon entering the room, Shultz stood and stared at his co-worker, mesmerized by the plethora of machinery attached to his body, wondering if the senior FBI man had any idea of how lucky he'd been. They had found him in a pile of debris at the edge of the parking lot, nearly drowned and suffering numerous injuries after being swept away by the tidal wave of water rushing onshore.

That entire sequence of events seemed like a lifetime ago. The pre-dawn assembly of the teams, the thrill of potentially apprehending the most wanted man in the world, the hope of finally being able to return home to College Station.

And then everything had gone wrong.

Strangers appeared in the midst of what was supposed to have been a relatively simple operation. Right in the middle of their takedown, a gunfight with unknown persons wearing FBI clothing convoluted the mission. In retrospect, that complication seemed like a minor annoyance once the military gunship collided with the tanker, followed by a Hellfire Missile exploding on the pier. Shultz could remember the radio waves being filled with excited, confused voices. And then the tanker heading directly for the bridge... a bridge full of snarled, gridlocked traffic.

Something had happened. It was all so quick, shrouded like the fog of war. One second, he thought Durham Weathers had been killed in the Apache's attack. A few moments later, a wall of water was sweeping away the converging law enforcement teams ... the mass of twisted, nautical wreckage eventually resting on their crime scene.

Shultz was beyond exhausted. He'd lost count of how many ambulances he had filled with co-workers and innocent bystanders. A mad scramble had ensued, the survivors rushing about to uncover the wounded and render aid. For over an hour, he'd dug through piles of debris and sloshed through muddy water, frantically rushing here and there, desperately searching for survivors of the tsunami.

All the while, first responders were pouring in. Exhausted, filthy and on the downslope of the adrenaline rush, Shultz had decided to stand back and let the professionals perform any remaining rescue work. He'd been loading colleagues into rescue units for what seemed like a lifetime when he realized the source of his own pounding headache was a rather large gash in the back of his head. He found a functioning FBI vehicle and began driving to the hospital – a decision that no doubt saved his life.

He was just over a mile away when the SUV's police radio carried voices of panic. The blast's shockwave almost knocked his heavy transport off the road. There were going to be more injured – a lot more. The bureau's crime scene was now a crater filling with ship channel water, any evidence not washed out to sea was most likely reduced to carbon by the inferno. There was nothing more he could do back at pier #19, so he continued his trek to the hospital.

Glancing again at his boss, Shultz knew the man was going to be disappointed. Durham (Dusty) Weathers had been the Houston office's primary focus for weeks. All of that work, all of the lost comrades, all of the man-hours, resources, and destruction – for naught. Nothing. Nada.

He needed to sit… take a load off. Pulling the nearby chair produced a vibrating scrape across the floor, as well as a grimace on the agent's face. "Damn it," he whispered, embarrassed by the racket.

"Hello, Tom," came a hoarse voice from the bed.

"How are you feeling, sir?"

"I've been better; that's for sure. Did we get him?"

The junior agent had dreaded the question, and for a variety of reasons. Special Agent in Charge Monroe hadn't asked how many men they'd lost. Nor was his first inquiry concerning the number of civilian casualties or collateral damage. No, nothing of the sort. Lying in critical condition with half of the nation's fourth largest city in ruins, the region's top FBI man wanted to know if the suspect was still loose on the streets. It revealed an obsession that had consumed all of their lives for the last two weeks. Shultz didn't know if he should be impressed with the man's dedication to the job, or worried about his mental state. It was easier to go with the former.

"Unknown at this time, sir. The crime scene has been... err... obliterated."

"What? What do you mean?"

"The tanker that washed up on the pier - it exploded, sir. A blast large enough to make a mushroom cloud."

Monroe didn't comment for several moments, the duration of the silence so long at one point that Shultz wondered if he'd slipped back into dreamland. The junior agent wasn't so lucky.

"And the aerial surveillance? The drones?"

"Those images and video are still being processed, sir. Right now the top priority is accounting for all of our men and putting out the fires."

"What about the rail gun? Surely we recovered at least some pieces of that damned weapon?"

"Sir, the tanker was lying directly on top of the spot where we last saw that damned thing. The explosion left a crater the size of a football field and then immediately filled with water. Frankly, the rescue effort has taken precedence, and retrieval of any evidence has not yet fully begun."

Something in the tone of his subordinate's voice made Monroe pull back and rethink his line of questioning. "How many dead and wounded, Tom?"

"A lot, sir. I don't have a final count, but a lot."

A grimace crossed the patient's face. "I'll recommend to the director that you take over the investigation, Tom, at least while I'm recovering. Until Durham Weathers is confirmed dead or captured, I don't want you to slow down our efforts… not one single bit. Is that clear?"

Shultz didn't tell his boss that the director had already called. He'd let the upper echelons work things out, such men often inflexible when it came to topics like chain of command. And then there was Weathers. "Yes, sir. It is clear. But you know there's very, very little chance he survived. Even if he did manage to make it through the missile attack and tidal wave, no one within an 800-meter radius of that ship is alive now."

Despite the tubes and wires, Monroe managed a curt nod. "No matter," he whispered. "We need confirmation."

You need confirmation, Shultz thought. *Weathers would have faded into oblivion or accepted a presidential pardon if you hadn't had a stick up your ass.*

Day Two

The couple spent the rest of the day napping, eating, and strolling through the marina. Grace visited the hotel's boutiques, informing her male traveling companion that she was a lady, and thus required more than one outfit for this little adventure. Dusty noted the bathroom counter had suddenly become crowded with a smorgasbord of powders, crèmes, and smell-wells. She also purchased a few items for him, including a razor and deodorant. "Give 'em an inch," he quietly mumbled, but then smiled at his reaction. She cared, and that made him feel good inside.

Dusty, living in West Texas for most of his life, was fascinated by the boats. He even toured a few vessels offered for sale by a local broker.

"Some of those yachts have everything you need," he informed Grace. "You can turn saltwater into fresh, generate your own electricity, and fish for food. Amazing. If the Russian hadn't ripped me off, I'd consider buying one and taking it to some remote island. We could live comfortably and no one would know we were there."

"The Russian left us with about $12,000 in cash. That's not enough money to last long, especially on a boat. We need to figure out what we're going to do."

He looked down with a grimace, her statement bringing back the harsh reality of the fugitive's world. "Let's go to the poolside bar and order a sandwich," he recommended. "We can hatch our plot there."

The pool was resort quality, with shining blue water, colorful lounge chairs, and a cascading waterfall. The oasis was nearly empty, so they selected two seats at the end of the bar. A smiling, young man appeared, offering the happy hour special margaritas. They chose iced tea instead, Dusty going with a ham and cheese, his lady selecting the spinach salad.

There was a television above the counter, a local news station showing footage of the recent disaster at the ship channel. The sound was muted, but it was clear that the reporter was interviewing survivors and first responders. The footage then switched to a different scene of mayhem and destruction, the medical center.

Dusty reached across the bar and picked up the remote, taking a moment to locate the volume button.

"Authorities are still seeking this man in connection with the explosions that rocked the medical center," the announcer stated as a picture of Dusty flashed on the screen. "KTWO news has learned that there may be a connection between the two incidents, but so far the FBI hasn't made any official announcement."

"Shit," Dusty whispered and then cast a worried glance at Grace.

"They don't know if you're dead or not, do they?" she observed.

"I wasn't counting on my picture being splashed all over the television again. I think we have to take that into consideration as we make our plans. Perhaps the Houston area isn't the place for us."

"It will die down," she said hopefully. "You saw those pictures of the pier. It will take months to sort that all out. This might have been just a one-time story."

Dusty was still digesting the new information when their meal arrived. He found himself taking note of the server's face when he set the plates down in front of them. *Did he study my features? Does he know who I am? Will he dial the police the minute he gets back into the kitchen?*

Paranoia was back in his life, and he didn't like it one single bit. They had been stupid, checking into the motel and shopping, lulled into the false security of believing they were in the clear.

"Of course the FBI isn't going to stop looking for me," he said after washing down a mouthful of potato chips. "They don't have a body,

24

DNA or any other proof of my demise. We were silly to assume they would give up."

Grace sat toying with her salad, the fork engaged more with rearranging than eating. "You don't know that, Durham. We have no facts, and that's the most troubling part of all of this. How can we make reasonable plans if we don't know what's going on?"

He nodded toward the now-muted weather report, "We know they're still looking for me... splashing my mug all over the airwaves. That's a pretty black and white fact right there."

She reached over and covered his hand with her own. "I'm with you, Dusty Weathers. I want to be. We'll figure it out."

"One thing is for certain; we can't stay around Houston. I've blown half of this city to hell, or at least people think I have. It wouldn't surprise me if the local cops have an order to shoot me on sight. Probably 90% of the civilians would too."

They finished the rest of their meal in silence. On the way back to the room, Dusty spied a sign advertising the hotel's business center. "Let's do some research," he suggested, nodding toward the threshold.

They entered a small room furnished with modern-looking computers, a printer, fax machine, and copier. Neither wasted any time, typing in various internet searches and scanning the results with intensity. Dusty browsed newspaper articles and the websites of local radio stations while Grace used her knowledge of the court systems and legal databases.

An hour later they both reclined back, disappointed in how little they had learned.

"That didn't help much," Grace admitted. "About the only thing I learned was that I appear to be no longer wanted by the authorities. All charges have been dropped and no new ones filed. You, on the other hand, are still the most wanted man in the world." Smiling coyly, she added, "My mom warned me about hanging around with bad boys. Why are you guys always so cute?"

Dusty grunted, "There are still federal officers in Fort Davis, and I doubt they're hanging out because the diner's blue-plate special is so tasty."

"How do you know that?"

"Because there aren't any rooms at the hotel. That place hasn't been 100% full since old man Smith died. Every Tom, Dick, and Harry with the same last name showed up claiming to be an heir."

Grace laughed, but didn't doubt the validity of his analysis.

When the humor had worn off, his expression became very serious, his voice sad. "Grace, we need to split up, and you know it."

"No."

"I don't want to either. It's actually next to the last thing I want, right after being in prison for 10 years and then being put to death via lethal injection. If we separate, you can work on clearing my name. You can go home and use that wonderfully powerful intellect of yours to end this the right way."

The lawyer in her knew what he was saying made sense, but the woman inside didn't want to acknowledge his logic. "I have waited years to feel this happy with someone. After my husband and daughter were killed, I thought I would never feel this way again. No," she sniffled.

Dusty reached over, gently lifting her chin. "Grace, you know it's best. We are both young; we can have a lot of happy years together, but not if I'm in jail... or worse."

They hugged, sobs racking her frame. Dusty held her tight for several minutes before the emotion worked out. "Okay. But we need to set up some way that I can contact you. I don't want to lie in bed every night wondering if you're dead or alive."

He thought that over for a bit, finally brightening with an idea. "I know a way... if we're careful."

The dust was finally beginning to settle, and it couldn't have happened fast enough for Agent Shultz. The hours following the ship channel incident had been a blur of status reports and forensic failures, all the while trying to recover from the loss of over a dozen federal agents in the explosion.

They had been lucky, with most of the Houston office personnel escaping death. To Shultz, in the role of leading the investigation, an injured agent was just as much of a manpower issue as a dead one.

Other regions had begun supplementing field personnel while those still able to report for duty began pulling all too familiar double shifts. Local agencies had been devastated as well. The number of official funerals would keep the local news stations busy for days. He shook his head, disgusted at the thought of having to watch the continuous coverage. The last thing the Houston law enforcement community needed was video of the processions, countless fire trucks and police cars following black hearses throughout the city. Shultz was sure he would attend more than his share.

Sitting down for what seemed like the first time in days, he noticed a stack of pink messages that had recently been delivered. He picked up the bundle, flipping through the records of incoming calls. He discovered that the administration group was now sending Agent Monroe's messages to his desk as well. *When it rains, it pours,* he mumbled.

Mid-way through the stack, he noticed one slip that was marked "Urgent!" in bright red ink. It was an internal call for the head of the digital technology group three floors below.

Sighing, he reached for the phone and dialed the extension, hoping it wasn't more bad news.

"We've processed the video images from the drones that were orbiting over the Houston Ship Channel. I think you'll want to see this right away," the nerdy-sounding tech informed him.

Shultz entered the lab ten minutes later, where he was led to a conference room equipped with a large screen monitor covering one entire wall. After everyone was seated, the department head clicked a few keys, and an overhead image of a bridge and waterway appeared on the screen. Shultz recognized it immediately as the area where they had hoped to arrest Durham Weathers just a few days ago.

The tech again tapped on the keyboard, and the image changed to show odd, glowing colors. "This is the infrared spectrum. You can see here… and here… and here are various law enforcement officers moving into position.

"Yes," Shultz replied, "I remember deploying men in that area."

"This hotspot here," the tech resumed, "we believe is the suspect. If I switch back to straight video, you can see he's hiding in what appears to be a pallet storage area."

Shultz nodded for the man to continue.

"Things get a little confusing during certain segments. The drone was in a high orbit to avoid the law enforcement helicopters in the area. As you can see, the video lacks clarity when the craft was at the edge of its range."

Shultz sat in silence, reliving the events of that morning. He saw the man they all thought was Durham Weathers appear, taking the bridge hostage with his super-weapon. Then the attack helicopters came into view, a large section of the display going pure white when the Hellfire Missile struck the shore. There were people running everywhere, some converging on the area while others, probably civilians, were trying to escape the violence.

Then something odd appeared on the screen. From the clutter of what he knew were the pallets, a thin black line appeared, stretching into the water directly ahead of the ship that was about to collide with the bridge. It appeared on the screen for only a fraction of a moment.

"What was that?" Shultz asked, sitting upright in his chair.

The tech waved him off, "We think that was a glitch in the binary stream being downloaded from the drone. It happens sometimes. The same line appears in the infrared spectrum, which is impossible, so we wrote it off as an anomaly in the data stream."

Another of the white-coated technicians was also curious. "Sir, could you back that up and show the black line again? I would like to see the time stamp."

The keyboard clicked a few times, and again the image showed the odd-looking black streak. In the lower right-hand corner was a date/time stamp. The newly interested tech pulled open a folder and began hastily shuffling through a stack of papers. Finally locating what he was looking for, his complexion flashed pale. He glanced up at the screen and back at the paper twice before announcing, "That was the rail gun!"

"What?" Shultz asked, almost bolting out of his chair.

Poking his finger into the paper, the tech announced, "Space Command in Colorado reported another of those odd EMP waves associated with the discharge of the rail-weapon. The time stamp matches exactly."

Shultz looked like someone had just dropkicked his new puppy. More mumbling than speaking, he observed, "So Weathers did survive all that. He wasn't blown to bits by the Apache's missile. I'll be damned."

The agent then brightened for a moment, glancing over at the department head. "But he couldn't have survived the tsunami? There's no way anyone got out of that alive!"

Hesitant and shaking his head, the tech didn't answer verbally, instead typing a new command and then nodding toward the screen. "We isolated this image, ten minutes after the tanker was washed up on shore."

The monitor presented what appeared to be a small raft traveling down a waterway. The picture didn't offer enough detail to enable identification of the occupants, but the outline of a large green duffle bag was clear against the white outline of the inflatable.

"That bag matches the dimensions of this bag perfectly," the tech said, the display changing to show a side-by-side picture. On the left was the raft; on the right was a shot of the pier, immediately before the black line appeared. "Whoever was standing there had an identical piece of luggage, and it appears as though they escaped."

Shultz's hand slammed into the tabletop, startling everyone in the room. "Fuck!" he grimaced, not caring about professionalism or offending the attendees. Then in a low, grumbling voice he added, "You lucky son of a bitch…. You got away…. I know you did."

Exhausted, angry and frustrated, Shultz made his way back to his office. Within minutes, he was preparing orders for every law enforcement agency along the Texas coast to be on the lookout for one Durham Weathers.

But then a thought occurred to the federal agent. Rising from his desk, he turned to the window with a southeast view from the federal building. The plumes of smoke and ash still rising over the ship channel were clearly visible. He then glanced down at the parking garage where Mr. Weathers' super-weapon had destroyed several vehicles in a fraction of a second.

"We've got to be smarter," he mumbled to the scene below. "We need to wise up and get a step ahead."

Returning to his desk, he added one last sentence to the FBI's alert. "Notify immediately – DO NOT APPROACH under any circumstances."

Shultz tapped the keyboard, distributing the message throughout the region. He returned his gaze to the distant horizon, content for the first time in days. "If we corner you again, you might do just about anything with that gun of yours, Mr. Weathers," he whispered. "This time, you're not going to know we're coming. You won't know we're there. One shot, one kill... Mr. Weathers."

Day Three – Morning

First thing the next morning, Dusty exited the hotel lobby and jumped in a waiting cab. The driver seemed disappointed to be called out for such a short fare, but cheered up when Dusty announced he was going shopping and wanted the man to wait, with the meter running, for his return.

"Might be a while," Dusty replied as he handed the hack a $100 bill. "This is a deposit. Is there a problem?"

The cabbie checked the currency and smiled. "No sir, take as much time as you want. I haven't had a chance to read the paper yet this morning."

He grabbed a cart, stopping first at a display of no-contract cell phones. He threw four of the base models into his buggy. Next came clothing, hygiene products, and finally a backpack. This was the third pack he'd purchased since that fateful day when he'd blown out the back of his workshop with the rail gun. When the gunsmith finally made it to the register, the checkout lady was impressed by the girth and variety of his selection. "My luggage was lost on the plane," Dusty explained. "You know the airlines; it might take them a week to find my bags."

She was sympathetic, having a sister who had recently suffered the same misfortune. When she'd finished scanning his purchase, she nodded toward his duffle bag and commented, "That looks like you brought it in with you – right?"

"Yes, ma'am. I didn't want to leave it outside."

He paid with cash, and then proceeded for the exit. A rather large man stepped in front of Dusty, forcing him to pull hard and stop the cart.

"Sir, I am with store security, and I need to look inside of that bag you've been carrying around."

Dusty was initially surprised by the guy's appearance. "There's nothing in there that I didn't bring with me," was the only response he could think of.

"Then you won't mind my checking inside," the fellow countered, clearly intent in performing his duty.

"I'm not an attorney, but I don't think you're allowed to do that unless you have reasonable suspicion. I just purchased several hundred dollars' worth of merchandise in your store. And now you think I am a crook? That doesn't seem to fit with any shoplifting profile I've ever heard of."

The security man shrugged, "No doubt, your behavior is atypical of most retail thieves. However, you arrived in a cab and paid cash for your purchases – not something we see every day. While you did spend some money here, you may have your big score in that duffle. Some of our smaller items carry hefty price tags. So, yes, sir. Those abnormalities fail my sniff test."

Dusty straightened to his full height, a rooster clearly readying for a confrontation. "I have personal affects in that bag. No one is going to stick their nose in there."

"Fine with me," the store goon sighed. "We'll call the local police, and let them do it."

"They can't search private property without proper cause either," he replied. "As it stands right now, it's my word against yours."

"This is just my part-time job," the gent stated with confidence. "I'm also a patrolman on the local force. Believe me. They'll take my word for it." The store-cop then lowered his voice, "Look pal, I don't care if you have dirty underwear, pornography, or pictures of yourself wearing women's clothing in that bag. I just have to make sure there's no store merchandise inside. Whatever else is in there is your business... as long as it's not illegal."

Dusty smiled at the guy, and then acted as though he was looking around for eavesdroppers. Leaning in as if he was going to confess the bag contained nefarious contents, he whispered, "Go fuck yourself."

The cop's eyebrows went up for just a moment. "Have it your way, sir. Please come with me back to the office. I'll call the officers from there."

Dusty had thoughts about just going around the guy, but then noticed two more muscular young men standing between him and the door. They looked to be praying he'd make a run for it.

Needing to buy time, Dusty shrugged. "Can I call my attorney while we're waiting?"

"Not on my phone. This isn't a police station, although I'm sure you will be seeing one soon."

Dusty, bookended by the store's security men, was led to the back of the facility. After leaving the retail space, they entered the warehouse. Continuing, they passed through an expanse populated with numerous rows of floor to ceiling metal racks, each stuffed with cardboard boxes and pallets of merchandise.

Dusty was getting very worried, the sick feeling of fear building in his stomach. At least these guys hadn't recognized him – yet.

There wasn't any doubt what would happen if someone looked inside of his duffle. Even if the cops didn't match his face to the bulletins and most wanted list, the rail gun and Glock .45 pistol would result in an inquiry. The weapons, combined with the wads of cash and fake gold would definitely cause his fingerprints and mug shot to be run on every law enforcement computer in the country.

His mind scrambled to figure a way out. He might chance pulling either the pistol or the rail gun, but both would require a significant amount of time to draw, load, and fire. All of these guys were armed, the outline of their sidearms now obvious under their shirts. Desperate to buy some time, he decided to try to stall. Pausing, he reached into his cart and pulled out a recently purchased pack of gum. As slow as possible, he fumbled with unwrapping a stick and popped it into his mouth.

The store-gumshoe frowned at the delay. "What are you doing?"

"My mouth is dry. Since you're obviously intent on locking me away for an extended period of time, I thought I'd better take advantage now before you throw me in the dungeon and forget I'm there."

"You can keep your possessions... at least the ones you paid for," informed the head guard. "Sometimes it takes the local cops a while to get here, so I hope you have some food in there."

They meandered through the bowels of the warehouse, eventually arriving at a room that was slightly larger than the average closet. Inside was a single chair. "Please wait inside," instructed Mr. Security Chief.

Peeking through the doorway, Dusty hesitated. "I'm claustrophobic," he protested.

"Not my problem," responded the guard, moving closer to intimidate. Dusty positioned himself as if he was thinking about running, the act complete with darting eyes and deep breaths. It was a distraction, giving him a moment to slip his wad of gum into the door lock's receptacle as his hand brushed against the frame. He finally went inside with a look of terror on his face.

One of the guards rolled the shopping cart full of packages inside the small room and then closed the door. Dusty heard the fellow check the knob, making sure the prisoner was secure.

Dropping immediately to the floor, Dusty listened to his captors through the gap between the linoleum tile and the bottom of the door. He heard the head man bark, "You two go back out and watch the store. I'll call the Kemah PD and get a car out here."

Following their orders, he listened as the two men stamped off. The boss hung around for a moment, and then his footsteps faded into the distance as well.

Dusty grabbed the door handle with both hands and pushed hard. It opened without much effort. The gum had done its job, blocking the lock's bolt from fully closing into the frame. He had learned the trick from an older boy in high school, sticking a mouthful of the sticky substance in the side door's lock so they could sneak in on weekends and play basketball in the gym.

He cautiously stuck his head out of the opening, finding the area empty of any store employees. He returned to the closet, rushing through his bags and packing his purchased items into the new backpack. Sticking the Glock and one of the new cell phones in his pocket, he exited the pseudo-cell and made for a far row of shelves.

The red light of an exit sign was visible up ahead, and it was tempting. His initial reaction was to make a rush for the back door, but something else drew his attention. There was a camera mounted on the wall. Glancing around, he noted the place was thick with the electronic eyes. That was a problem.

Even if he made a clean escape, there was little doubt his image resided on the store's security system – probably from multiple angles. That video, when analyzed, would confirm he was still alive, lead to the taxi, then the hotel, and finally an undeniable implication of Grace.

His hard-won new identity would be toast, the alias zipping through every law enforcement database in the country. Ducking between two large boxes, he hid in the shadows, trying to think things through.

He had to erase his tracks. The phones, pre-loaded credit cards and everything else he'd just purchased would be on the receipts. It wouldn't take the authorities long to tie it all together. That video tape had to go – it was the only solid proof that he was still among the living.

He pulled out one of the plastic-covered phones, making quick work of the packaging with his pocketknife. The setup screens seemed to take forever, but eventually he had service. He had made a shopping list on the hotel's stationery and found the phone number directly below the fancy letterhead.

"Southside Harbor, how may I direct your call?" A friendly voice answered.

"Room 515, please."

Grace answered on the second ring.

"It's me. You need to get out, and get out of there right now."

"Why? What's wrong?"

In as few sentences as possible, he explained what had happened.

"What are you going to do?"

"I don't know, but regardless, you have to get out of that room. Call a cab from the lobby or just start walking, but get out."

He could hear her breathing through the phone as her mind raced through the options. "Okay. Meet me by the fountains at the boardwalk as soon as you can. Our boat is probably still there – that might be the only way for us to skedaddle. That place will be busy this time of day, and I'll pretend to shop and lose myself in the crowd."

"Okay – I'll see you there."

Checking the aisle from both directions, Dusty crawled out of the nook and retraced his steps. Down the hall from his holding cell were a series of office windows, a few of them leaking light through the glass. Maybe he could find the recording equipment for the surveillance system.

The rumble of an approaching forklift caused a mad scramble for cover, the dockworker zipping past without seeing him. That heart-stopping event was closely followed by voices. Two employees, each carrying a brown lunch bag, entered one of the doors. *The employee break room*, he decided.

He bent low, duck-walking under the first window where several people were chowing down on their chosen meals. The next door was closed, the window dark. On the third door was a small sign, "Security Office."

He slowly peeked around the edge of the window, spying the security boss typing on a computer keyboard. Behind him, on a rack, were half a dozen video recording machines. *How do I get him out of there?*

New voices sounded behind him, and there wasn't anywhere to go. He spotted a large bulletin board nearby and moved quickly to stand as if he were reading the latest results from the company softball league. Two workers walked by, paying him no attention.

After they had passed, he strolled by the offices and found himself in another warehouse area. The place was huge. Again, he found a cubbyhole, crates of garden hoses on one side, racks of shovels, rakes and hoes on the other.

How could he get the security man out of his office long enough to remove the tapes?

He shifted positions to get more comfortable and almost knocked one of the long-handled shovels from its hanger. He caught it mid-fall, cursing under his breath at his clumsiness. *That thing would have made one hell of a racket banging up against the wall*, he chided himself. *Someone would have come to see what all the fuss was about.*

It was then that he noticed the wall-mounted fire station. Directly across from the rows of hanging tools was an alarm, hose and extinguisher. It was equipped with one of those "Break the glass in case of fire" devices.

Examining the shovel still in his hand, he whispered, "That is a stupid place to hang these tools... one of them could fall and set off the...." A mischievous smile crossing his lips, he suddenly had a plan.

Peeking out from his hide, he made sure there wasn't anyone nearby. He hefted the shovelhead and smashed the glass. Hooking the edge of the heavy tool on the handle, he pulled down the alarm and scurried behind a nearby soda machine.

Strobe lights flashed and claxons sounded throughout the area. He heard the security door fly open; the head guard's voice rumbling, "What the hell is going on," as footfalls raced away. Dusty popped his head around in time to spy the store cop rounding the far corner, being followed by the wide-eyed employees from the break room.

He was in the security office in seconds, taking a moment to study the complex-looking recording system. Shrugging his shoulders, he pressed a button labeled "Eject," and smiled when a tape cartridge appeared in the slot. Fifteen seconds later, he walked out with a backpack stuffed full of cassettes.

People were rushing everywhere. He spotted the elongated corridor with the exit sign and decided that was his best way out. Less than a minute later, he stepped into the bright sunlight, shielding his eyes while he got his bearings.

Walking casually, he made for the front of the store and his waiting taxi. The stroll was much longer than anticipated given the huge dimensions of the retail giant. When he finally arrived at the corner leading to the parking lot, he chanced a glance around the wall and noticed several people rushing for their vehicles. A police car was just arriving, the officer a little confused by all the commotion.

Dusty strolled right past the cop, his cab still waiting along the sidewalk.

"Sorry that took so long, the store was having electrical issues," he announced, opening the back door.

"I thought they'd arrested you for shoplifting or something," the cabbie teased. "Back to the hotel?"

"No, I feel like getting a bite to eat. How about that boardwalk place?"

"Sure enough," the guy replied, pulling the car into gear and rolling off.

"We've got him," sounded the excited voice through the cell phone's tiny speaker.

"Where?" asked Shultz, his heart already racing.

"Kemah. He was picked up via a patrol car's dash cam, walking out of a department store."

Kemah, thought Shultz, *it all made sense. An easy place to dock a boat and get lost in a thickly populated and touristy shoreline.* Then a scowl crossed the agent's face, his mind registering all of the landmarks in the area, everything from NASA's Johnson Space Center to the Kemah Boardwalk.

"Make absolutely sure the local cops don't try to be heroes. If they can keep an eye on him, then fine, but don't try to take him down under any circumstances. Houston's already suffered enough damage. I want a full tactical team, including the best sniper in Houston, at my parking spot in ten minutes."

"Yes, sir."

Twelve minutes later, a caravan of federal SUVs rolled out of the FBI's parking garage, Agent Shultz accompanied by one of the agency's elite hostage rescue units, which included some of the finest long distance shooters in the world.

He spotted Grace roaming the waterfront shopping area, staring through a storefront window, two large shopping bags filled with packages weighing down her arms.

"We're running out of money quick, darling," he teased, walking up behind her. "Do I need to cut up your credit cards?"

She glanced down at the overflowing bags and grinned. "This is the stuff we bought at the hotel. I didn't have a suitcase. I'm glad you're okay. What happened?"

They strolled together while he relayed his adventure, making for a secluded area not far from the amusement park.

"That was a smart move," she finally pronounced after he'd finished. "You were right – we've got to be more careful."

Taking a seat on a bench, Dusty scanned the area as if expecting to see SWAT teams maneuvering toward their perch. "I've got to get away from here. So do you," he finally announced.

It was obvious Grace didn't want to contemplate their separation. "They had to know I was at the ship channel. I'm assuming Agent Monroe let me go because he was hoping I would get in contact with you. I drove my own car to the pier, and they probably followed me there. So what's my story when I do resurface?"

Dusty kept scanning the crowd, half of his brain wondering what he would do if the cops did appear. Would he pull the rail gun? Should they try to run? After a minute of observing nothing but tourists, he refocused on Grace's dilemma. "You can't deny you were there, so why not play the stunned victim routine? You don't remember what happened and somehow found your way home."

"Home? Do you think going back to Fort Davis is a good idea?"

"You've lost your purse, ID, keys, car, and luggage. You're going to need money, access to a phone and internet. We need you functional and comfortable."

"They'll arrest me again as an accessory. I'll be back in jail before you can say 'Habeas Corpus.'"

Dusty pondered the statement for a bit, his eyes continuing to search the crowd. "Don't you have a right as an attorney to meet with your client? I mean, even if he's on the dodge?"

She nodded, trying to map it all out in her mind. "I do, but there's a gray area here. If I believe you're about to commit a crime, then as an officer of the court I must report any contact to the authorities. On the other hand, normally, I can't really be arrested as an accessory. But they've already proven that the rules can be completely rewritten when they arrested me over Hank's case. Assuming that they somehow did not slap me in irons, how would I get home? No car and no ID to rent one. I can't fly. And these new shoes are not exactly designed for power walking," she smiled weakly, attempting to lighten the mood, a small part of her clinging to the hope the two would not have to separate.

"How about a bus?"

Grace had never ridden on a bus before, the suggestion eliciting a grimace from her. "Really? That's the best way? Won't the police be monitoring the bus station?"

Dusty hadn't considered that, his mind trying to think of a better way. "Hey! Wait! I know. Come on."

Pulling her up by the hand, they headed for the hotel lobby where they'd initially tried to get a room. "I remember seeing something that might do the trick," he responded to her questioning look.

Inside, he made for a rack of brochures and pamphlets advertising local attractions. He scanned for a moment and then reached for one, handing it over to a puzzled Grace.

43

She read the heading, "Luxury Bus Tours to Las Vegas," flipping open the folder to scan the information inside.

"I've seen these busses at the truck stop at the I-10 exit north of Fort Davis. You could get off there and call Hank to come and give you a ride home."

Glancing up from the advertisement, she frowned. "And what if they don't stop there anymore?"

"Tell the driver you're getting sick and need to get off the bus. Pretend you've got a bomb. Hell, I don't know. Maybe they publish a schedule of stops?"

She pondered the suggestion, more questions than answers crossing her face. "How do you know they don't require an ID? How would we be sure the cops aren't monitoring their terminal... or wherever you board one of these things?"

Dusty led her out of the lobby, leaflet in hand. "I don't, but it's a private touring company. It can't hurt to call and find out. Besides, those busses look pretty comfortable, and I doubt law enforcement monitors them like they do the regular transportation hubs."

An hour later, they found themselves in one of the numerous restaurants occupying the waterfront. They had their choice of seating, the establishment just opening. After glancing around, Dusty asked their server for a seaside view in the corner, away from the main traffic flows. He sat with his back to the door.

Grace had been working with her new phone, speaking with the bus company's representative and pretending to be a tourist dying to see the Las Vegas strip. She had dialed Hank's home number, hanging up when he'd answered. She didn't know if FBI ears would be listening, the call serving to confirm her neighbors had returned home.

"I don't see why it won't work," she finally announced. "There's a tour leaving this afternoon. You board the bus at their office, which is a short cab ride away. They do indeed stop at that same exit you mentioned. Hank is home, so I wouldn't be stranded."

Dusty merely nodded as her tone indicated she still wasn't convinced the plan would work. Finally, after a sip of his coffee he ventured with a question, "So what's troubling you?"

Her eyes were moist when she looked up. "I want us to stay together."

He wasn't sure how to reply, fifty different responses flashing through his mind. Eventually, he chose the words. "I don't want to be away from you either, but we both know it's best in the long run."

Merely nodding, Grace didn't answer for a bit. "And what about you? Where are you going? How are you going to travel?"

"One problem at a time," he answered, "I can concentrate on my itinerary now that we've got you settled."

Their meal was served, a light brunch that both diners toyed with more than consumed. After a few bites of his sandwich, Dusty offered, "I think being close to Mexico is probably my best option. There are lots of towns down there that accommodate everything from transients to immigrants. If I get a sense that the cops are honing in on me, maybe I can scoot across the border and buy some time."

Conjuring up images of outlaws from old cowboy movies, Grace frowned. "I don't think you can just ride a horse across the Rio Grande anymore, Dusty. Have you ever been down there?"

He nodded, "When I was refurbishing my airplane, I drove down that way and bought some parts. It's actually very industrialized in some areas... the NAFTA agreement prompted the construction of big plants that otherwise would not be there. It seems like a good place for a bandit to remain anonymous."

The restaurant grew more crowded as the hour approached lunch. They were on their third refill of coffee when the manager stopped by, clearly wanted to recycle the table in the now full dining room. "Is everything okay?" he inquired, the third employee to ask the same question in the last four minutes.

"Everything has been wonderful," Dusty replied, "We were just leaving."

The couple sauntered outside after paying their bill, the bright sunlight and excitement of the growing crowd not helping their mood. "We need new luggage," Dusty announced. "You can't get on a tour bus with shopping bags without drawing attention, and I need to get rid of this duffle. The security guys at the store have no doubt filed a police report by now, including a description of my bag. The cops will be looking for a guy carrying such an unusual item around."

Grace nodded her agreement, a melancholy expression brought on by the task that advanced her departure.

"Let's get our luggage situation taken care of, and then I'll use one of these pre-loaded cards and my fake ID to rent a car. I'll take a separate cab to the agency, and turn it in after I find a spot to settle," he said gently.

They spent the next 30 minutes rushing into a shop, dividing the money and coordinating how they would communicate. The time flew by, both so intent on their last few moments together that there wasn't any opportunity for emotions to work their way in. Dusty spied his chauffeur pulling up along the access lane and announced, "Time to go." He took Grace by the shoulders and looked deep into her eyes, "I love you. We'll be together soon."

"Oh, Durham. I hate this... but... but you have to. I understand. And you have got to know that I love you too," she managed before the tears streamed down her cheek. "I will see you soon, Durham Weathers... of that you can be sure."

He stood motionless, watching as she entered the taxi. A thousand things flooded his mind as she drove away. Things he wished he'd said, feelings he hoped she understood. After a final wave goodbye, he watched until she was out of sight and then turned for the hotel lobby so the clerk could call him a cab.

Juanita stepped down from the Metro bus, her feet aching after the ten-hour shift at the hospital. Turning right without looking, she began the three-block adventure to her sister's apartment, her eyes tightly focused on the sidewalk directly ahead. She'd learned not to make eye contact or notice anyone or anything. *I'm just a lowly cleaning lady,* she told herself as she walked through the neighborhood. *Today isn't payday, so I don't have any money to steal.*

Despite the grueling hours, low wages and crime-ridden neighborhood, life on Houston's south side was still better than what she'd left in Juarez. Here the young boys might rob you – there they would rob, rape and then cut off your head.

She passed through a deceptively calm landscape. A group of tattooed young men congregated at the first corner, their sleeveless shirts advertising a significant investment in ink. She knew that much of what was engraved into their skin was a message of some sort, almost like a uniform worn by a soldier. Leaning against their older model sedan, she could hear their hushed voices and grunted laughter. They almost appeared friendly, but she knew it was a façade. The gang members could turn vicious without provocation or reason.

Out of her peripheral vision, she noticed one of them stretching his arms high into the air and revealing the shiny handle of a pistol in his belt. *Guns. What was the relationship between money and guns?*

She wondered. When one was around, the other surely followed. And then, almost inevitably, death joined the party.

Soon, she encountered a gaggle of small children chasing a soccer ball in the street. Three mothers stood talking nearby, projecting an image of suburban calm and relaxation. Juanita knew the real reason they were so diligent; a drive-by shooting had killed a 5-year old last week, less than a block away. *Guns and death.*

That train of thought reminded her of the new patient at the hospital. All of the staff had been talking about the FBI man and his visitors, rumors and concerns flying around the break room and nursing station. Juanita and her co-workers didn't like the fact that armed men had now invaded their once peaceful domain. She felt like guns were taking over her life.

Nodding as she passed the nervous mothers, Juanita entered the rundown apartment complex and sidestepped a scattered minefield of trash. The old man in 2C had set his garbage out three nights ago, confused in his mistaken belief that it was pickup day. The dogs had found the treasure trove of table scraps within hours. No one would clean it up, knowing the wind would eventually blow it to the abandoned lot next door.

With thoughts of soaking her feet in a hot tub, Juanita began her ascent up the three flights of stairs. The top floor units were cheaper and safer… somewhat. Guns. Armed men everywhere at the hospital. At least here, she could escape and soak her feet.

She inserted her key and entered the small unit, instantly greeted by the television blaring a soap opera in her native tongue. The volume was competing with her sister's hair dryer. Juanita glanced at the screen, only to spot an image of one man pointing a gun at another. *So much for sanctuary*, she sighed and then focused her attention on the crucifix hanging on a nearby wall.

Tessa switched off the blow dryer and smiled at her older sister, "How was work, Nita?"

"I'm exhausted. We had many new patients admitted today. It was chaos. The ambulances kept bringing in injured men from the accident at the ship channel."

"Oh, Nita, I'm so sorry. Just think; I'll finish school soon, and then you won't have to work like such a dog."

The statement struck the older sister the wrong way, but she quickly let it pass. *My work isn't so bad*, she decided, and then brightened at having something exciting to report. "We have some important Federale in my ward. He was injured in the ship channel explosion, and there has been a parade of men with guns and badges in his room all day."

Smiling, the younger woman teased, "Any cute, single ones?"

Always has her mind on men, Juanita thought. *She should focus more on that degree and less on hombres.* "I don't know, sissy. I don't pay attention to such things. I know he's very high ranking and receives many visitors. I had to return three times to finish his room."

"I heard a lot of them got hurt this morning."

A curt nod was Juanita's only response as she shuffled off to find the foot tub, her sister's reaction deflating her small, temporary bubble of esteem.

Tessa sensed she'd said the wrong thing and tried to recover. "So did you hear anything secret or new about the explosion? Any insider information?"

Juanita paused, trying to recall the snippets of conversation she'd overheard. "Not really. They were mainly talking about a man... a bandito who was involved with the whole affair. The patient... the honcho FBI man... was concerned about something called a 'rail gun.'"

"A what?"

"You know my English isn't that good, but I'm sure he called it a rail gun. The visiting federales were very nervous talking about the outlaw and how he might have escaped with that gun. I'm sick of hearing and seeing guns," she said, waving off the thought.

Tessa shrugged her shoulders, happy she'd drawn her sibling out of her shell, but not really all that interested.

Juanita watched as her sister returned to fussing with her makeup and hair, the purpose of the preparations finally dawning. "Are you going out?"

"Yes, I've got a date this evening. I'll probably be back late, so don't wait up for me," Tessa announced and then waited on the scolding she knew was about to be delivered.

Juanita pulled up, a disapproving look filling her face. "You're not going out with that Fredrick again, are you?"

"Yes, he's a nice guy and has a good job. He treats me very well," Tessa replied in a defensive voice.

"I don't like him," the older woman worried. "He's too flashy and became annoyed when I asked about his job. He makes my skin crawl. I wish you could find a nice man."

Tessa gently rested her palms on Juanita's shoulders, a warm smile on her face. "My sister. My dear overly protective sister. There are no nice men, according to you. Besides, I'm 26 years old, and while I love you with all my heart, I am capable of judging men. They are simple creatures with predictable habits. I'll be just fine."

The two women hugged, but the embrace was interrupted by the blare of a car horn. "There he is," Tessa announced with glee. "See you later," she added, moving toward the door and blowing her sister a kiss. And just like that, she disappeared through the threshold, a rush of whirling skirt, legs, heels, and hair.

Juanita ambled to the window and peered out through the crack in the drapes. She monitored disapprovingly as her sibling gracefully negotiated the steps, despite the heels. The scowl deepened as Tessa entered a large black German car. Shaking her head, Juanita whispered, "I hope you truly do understand the ways of hombres, Sissy. I pray you really are as much in control as you think you are."

Tessa loved the smell. The BMW's interior reeked of leather and fresh materials... of success and luxury. Fredrick's cologne merely added to the sensation. "You look absolutely gorgeous!" he smiled approvingly as she settled into the passenger seat.

"Why thank you, kind sir," she replied smoothly, barely managing to control the flush generated by the compliment. "You clean up pretty well yourself," she quickly added, glancing at his neat Dockers and Polo shirt.

"I'm sorry I was late," the driver continued, "business."

Tessa waved off the apology, "It's okay. My sister just got home and was telling me about her shift at the hospital. They had a big spike in new patients – due to that accident down at the ship channel. She's even got some important FBI guy in her ward."

"Really," Fredrick replied, his voice curious.

"Yeah... but her English isn't that good. She told me about a conversation she overheard about some sort of gun. What did she call it... a train gun? No! A rail gun. That was it!" Tessa laughed.

Fredrick chuckled as well, but it was shallow. When his date had mentioned the FBI, he'd naturally been curious. When the words 'rail gun' came from her lips, it had required concentration not to swerve the car.

Since the *Houston Post* had run the article entitled, "God's Gun," millions of men had visualized holding such a weapon. He had watched the local news as well, mentally connecting the implied-dots that somehow the medical center and ship channel were related.

"Do you think your sister would speak to me about this rail gun?" he asked, trying to sound shy.

Tessa's hesitation answered his question before the words left her throat. "She's not comfortable talking about her job," she lied. "I think she's embarrassed over being a cleaning lady."

Fredrick nodded his understanding, knowing better than to press the subject. Glancing over at Tessa's legs, he reminded himself that the woman next to him wasn't unintelligent. That wasn't his primary interest in her, but a factor nonetheless.

While he waited for the taxi, Dusty found the closest rental agency. It happened to be just down the street from the Johnson Space Center, one of NASA's main facilities. Years ago, he'd examined pictures of the massive Saturn V5 rocket displayed on the complex's grounds, and had often thought about visiting the popular tourist attraction. *At least I might get to see it as we drive by*, he mused. *Being an outlaw takes all the fun out of life.*

The cab finally arrived, and Dusty hopped in, handing the driver a small slip of paper with the address. The guy nodded and proceeded without further comment.

Across the parking lot, an unmarked Kemah police car watched the exchange, the nervous detective reaching for the radio. "He's just entered a taxi – destination unknown."

Agent Shultz's voice came back over the airwaves, "Good. I wasn't looking forward to operating around all those people down on the waterfront. Follow him. Don't let him out of your sight."

"Sir, wouldn't it be prudent to bring in aerial observation? Traffic is pretty heavy down here."

"No!" Shultz replied, his voice thick with frustration. "This guy isn't stupid. If he spotted a bird, it wouldn't end well. Maintain ground surveillance."

Dusty rode in silence as the cabbie maneuvered through the congestion along the north side of Clear Lake, hoping the Russian hadn't completely screwed him over by doing a poor job on the fake Canadian passport and driver's license. He had no idea he was being followed.

He paid the driver and entered the rental agency just as one of the police chasers pulled up across the street. "Suspect Weathers is renting a car," the officer radioed, quickly adding the address.

"We'll be there in less than 10 minutes. Continue your surveillance, but do not approach," Shultz responded.

Dusty filled out the paperwork and provided his passport and credit card. A few minutes later, the clerk handed him the keys to a subcompact and said, "It's in slot number 14. Thank you for using Alamo!"

He located the tiny car without issue, throwing his bag into the passenger side and then struggling to find the control to scoot the driver's seat back. A few minutes later, he was peeling out of the parking lot.

He reached up to adjust the rearview mirror and spied the black SUVs swerving around traffic less than a quarter mile behind him. "Shit!" he hissed, punching the accelerator and almost T-boning another car as he jumped the red light.

The rental's little 4-cylinder motor wasn't designed for high-speed pursuit, its weak, whining revs and short legs frustrating Dusty as he watched the police vehicles easily closing the gap.

He spotted the entrance to a residential neighborhood ahead, the oncoming traffic clogging the opposite lane. Without warning, Dusty cut hard left, shooting a gap that really didn't exist. Honking horns, squealing brakes and at least two rear-end collisions sounded as he barely managed to squeeze past.

Zipping into the subdivision, he worked the accelerator and brakes hard, maneuvering sharp left and right turns as the tires protested the abuse with screams and shrieks. "I may not be able to outrun you," he announced to the mirror, "but I might be able to gain some time."

Shultz's driver was desperately trying to manage the instant traffic jam caused by the suspect's crazy-ass stunt. Traffic going both directions had swerved, collided, and skidded to a halt. It was costing them valuable time. Picking up the radio, the FBI agent began issuing instructions to seal the neighborhood Weathers had just entered.

A minute later, Dusty was amazed to look up and see no one following him. His heart was racing faster than the tiny car's engine, so he decided to stop for a few moments and gather his wits. Checking up and down the street, he spied an open garage door just down the block. Both bays were empty, so he backed the rental into the opening and prayed no one was home.

Reaching for the Glock, he left the car running, and went to find the cord to pull down the overhead door. There wasn't one, but he quickly spied the electric control button on the wall. A few seconds later, he exhaled as the door rumbled down its tracks.

And then it stopped, jiggled up and down a few times, and began opening again.

"No wonder the garage was left open," Dusty mumbled. "The damn door is broken."

He climbed up on the rental's hood and found the electric opener's emergency release and pulled the handle. A few moments later, the garage was shut tight.

The door leading to the home was locked, and Dusty was glad. Any thought of entering a man's castle went against his grain. Someone might get hurt, and he'd already caused enough damage the last few days.

After turning off the engine, he perched on the hood of the rental, pondering his next move and listening for the sound of any street traffic. It was very quiet.

After his heart rate had finally slowed, Dusty took a moment to study his surroundings. The garage was tidy, furnished with a small workbench, a few storage boxes, and a nice chest freezer. A motorcycle rested on its kickstand along one wall.

"They'll be looking for this car," he whispered, gazing at the bike. "I wonder if I can hotwire that thing?"

The thought was interrupted by a noise inside the house. Or was it? Dusty couldn't be sure, but his mind started working overtime, visualizing a frightened homeowner dialing the police to report an intruder in the garage.

Being pinned down suddenly didn't seem like a good idea to the Texan. He glanced longingly at the now-closed door, wondering if it had been a mistake to pull inside. "Better to have room to move," he decided. He was reaching to hit the button again, when a set of keys hanging on a small hook caught his attention. The motorcycle! That might buy him some precious time.

He pulled the ring from the hook and sure enough, the key slid smoothly into the ignition. The tank was even full. After retrieving the rail gun and his bag, he secured them to the seat with a bungee cord from the workbench. He fired up the engine, its smooth purr reassuring.

It had been decades since he'd ridden a motorcycle, images of an old dirt bike and roaming the hills of West Texas filling his mind for a brief moment. "I hope it's like a bicycle, and you never forget," he whispered. Donning the helmet would even provide a bit of a disguise.

He stepped toward the controls, intending to hit the door's button when another thought occurred to him. Remembering the emergency release, he pulled the big door open and then pushed the idling bike into the driveway. A few seconds later, the garage was sealed up tight behind him. If no one were home, it would be a while before the cops found the rental. Time. Precious time.

He wobbled the handlebars a bit as he rolled down the driveway, almost letting the machine fall over before he got the feel of it. The bike's massive engine felt strong as he accelerated down the street.

"He couldn't have just disappeared into thin air," Shultz remarked to his driver, his head scanning right and left as they slowly rolled through the suburban streets. "There's no way he could have gotten out of this subdivision."

"There are 30 patrol cars searching this neighborhood," the driver responded, "In addition, we've got every exit closed down tight. We'll find him, sir."

Shultz reached for his cell phone. A few moments later, a voice answered the call. "I need a drone over our location... pronto."

Dusty took it easy, not wanting to be noticed, and trying to re-learn his limited skills on a motorbike. The community was massive, block after block of upper middleclass homes that seemed to stretch forever. Twice his hand reached for the rail gun's case, an approaching police cruiser causing fear to fill his stomach. But both times the cop had passed by, the officer trying to drive and search both sides of the street for the rental car.

He worked the motorcycle in generally the same direction, worried that someone would find or report the rental in the garage. He needed distance. He needed to get away from what certainly would be significant numbers of law enforcement converging on the neighborhood.

Stopping at an intersection, he noted what had to be a major roadway to the right. There was an exit.

But the flashing blue lights of three police cars blocked the road, the dark shapes of uniformed officers clear in the distance. There were a few cars waiting to merge into the thoroughfare traffic, and as Dusty watched, it was evident they were being searched.

"That makes sense," he whispered under the helmet's face shield. "I bet they've got the entire area sealed off."

He circled the block a few times, trying to figure a way out. He thought about trying to find a non-street route, thinking the bike could pass through a narrower area than any car. He might end up in a ditch or stuck or worse yet, let the bike fall and pin him underneath. *No*, he decided, *I'll stay on pavement*.

While he orbited the block, another cruiser passed by. Dusty nearly hit a nearby-parked car, not paying attention as he watched the cop hit the brakes in the rearview mirror. The policeman was turning around.

He gave his steed some gas, zooming ahead and executing through a couple of quick turns. *Time is running out*, he determined, trying to steer the unfamiliar machine and watch for the police. *The longer I stay in this subdivision, the more cops will show up.*

He came across another exit, this one blocked by two patrol cars with flashing blue lights. There weren't any residents trying to exit via this route.

Dusty glanced in the mirror again, the outline of yet another squad car visible several blocks behind him. "I've got to get out of here," he whispered.

He reached to the case behind him and removed the rail gun. The green LED was visible despite his darkened visor. A few moments later, he dropped the steel ball into the breach and then began rolling toward the roadblock.

His first thought was to blow away the two cruisers barricading the road, but as he ventured closer, he hesitated. The cross street beyond was full of cars, probably filled with rubberneckers gawking at the roadblock and speculating about what was going on. Businesses and homes filled the space beyond the obstruction.

The cop behind him was still evident in the motorcycle's rear-view mirror, moving closer and cutting off any retreat. He was committed. Two blocks away, a panic-induced idea popped into Dusty's mind.

He slowed the bike and stopped in the middle of the road. Raising the weapon to his shoulder, he centered the cross hairs on the pavement 15 feet in front of the two patrol cars and squeezed the trigger.

A surge of electrical current shot into the first magnet as it rotated around the steel projectile. It pushed the small metal ball forward. The computer-controlled sequence then directed the electrical charge at the second magnet. In less than a thousandth of a second, it pulled.

The sequence continued down the barrel, each magnet pushing and pulling, the steel bullet accelerating so quickly that heat friction turned it into a molten stream of slag before it ever exited the muzzle.

Despite the change of state from a solid to a liquid, the velocity continued to increase, approaching critical mass just a few feet beyond where Dusty sat on the bike. The universe couldn't allow any object to exceed the speed of light and reacted to protect itself.

A portal opened, creating a channel into a parallel plane of existence – an alternative reality where the speed of light was faster... where the rail gun's projectile wouldn't do any harm.

The portal was small, only a few inches wide. But where there had been the matter, gravity, mass and time of Dusty's reality, suddenly there was a new existence. Two objects couldn't occupy the same space at the same time, and an expansion occurred, the matter of this universe violently pushed aside. The displacement was more rapid and powerful than even a nuclear detonation.

The pavement in front of the two blocking patrol cars erupted skyward, the asphalt and earth below shoved out of the way by an irresistible force. The surrounding soil was compressed, making room for the portal as it absorbed Dusty's shot.

As quickly as it appeared, the pipeline into the alternative universe closed, leaving a vacuum in its wake. Just as rapidly as they had been pushed aside, matter and energy rushed to fill the void, and that reaction exponentially amplified the violence.

All along the path of Dusty's projectile, molecules slammed into each other at hypersonic speeds. The blast wave was devastating.

In the blink of an eye, the front halves of the two patrol cars were lifted into the air as if they were toys. By the time gravity recovered and sucked them back down, a ten-foot deep trench had been cut through the street. Both machines landed hard and then slid into the new ditch. The nearby officers were tossed aside, thrown over 30 feet through the air as if they were merely rag dolls.

The newly created canyon extended past the roadblock, vehicles passing in the street beyond, falling into what most drivers initially believed was a sinkhole.

With the rail gun folded and stashed between his legs, Dusty maneuvered the bike through the smoldering heaps of crumbled soil and pavement, barely squeezing through the instantly snarled gridlock of traffic before accelerating away.

"Dear God in heaven," he whispered as he passed through the destruction, "Please, please, please. I pray I didn't just take any more innocent life."

No one was sure what had happened. Some of the radio traffic indicated a gas main had erupted while others claimed a bomb had detonated. The FBI man knew exactly what it was; Weathers had shot his way out of the dragnet.

Ambulances were already on the scene by the time the FBI caravan arrived. The two dazed officers were being shuttled into the back of the emergency vehicles, paramedics bustling around the injured men.

Shultz flashed his ID and asked, "Can either of them talk?"

"They were both out cold when we arrived," answered the paramedic. "We've stabilized them, but neither is very responsive."

"I have to talk to them," Shultz insisted. "Can you do anything at all? A lot of lives are depending on it."

Another emergency responder appeared, "I'm not so sure that's a good idea, sir. I'm pretty sure both of them suffered severe blows to the head. Probably have concussions. I could barely get them to tell me their names before we loaded them on the backboards."

"I have to talk to them," he repeated. "It's *that* important."

The two-man ambulance crew exchanged puzzled glances, the senior shrugging his shoulders. "If you insist." He returned a moment later and broke a small tube under the patient's nose.

The patrolman's eyes fluttered, and he tried to pull away, the restraints and neck brace restricting his movements. "It's okay.... It's okay.... You're alright," soothed the paramedic.

"Officer Kendall, my name is Tom Shultz from the FBI. What happened?"

"Motorcycle," whispered the patrolman. "He was on a motorcycle... a rifle... and... and... I don't know after that."

Shultz nodded at the EMT, indicating that's all he needed. Before Officer Kendall was wheeled to the back of waiting rescue unit, the law enforcement networks were busy spreading the word that the suspect was now riding on a motorcycle.

Trying to keep his speed low and blend in, Dusty was having trouble focusing as he steered the bike through traffic. The helter-skelter pace and relentless stress were taking a toll, his brain slowly sinking into a fog of confusion.

Through it all, he could see Kemah Channel bridge in the distance, the high-rise structure a beacon of familiarity. Having no other place to go, he kept steering the motorcycle back toward the familiar landmark.

He finally arrived at the boardwalk, his destination unplanned. There just really wasn't anywhere else he could think of to go.

The place was bustling, thousands of people milling about, shopping, dining, and enjoying the now packed amusement park.

He pulled the motorcycle to the delivery area of one of the restaurants, identifying a narrow gap between a smelly dumpster and the back wall. He switched off the ignition, just sitting for a minute to gather his wits.

Movement at the edge of the parking lot drew his attention. He looked up to see three police cars rolling into the place and traveling at a high rate of speed.

"Shit!" he hissed, looking around for somewhere to run. There was water on three sides of his location, the only way out now filled with policemen.

Dusty started to panic, hopping off the seat, and stuffing the rail gun back in its bag. The sound of a nearby engine caused him to pause.

The sign on the side of the delivery truck read, "Rio Grande Valley Vegetables, Laredo, Texas."

It was a typical-looking farm truck, dual axle in the back with side rails surrounding the bed. Dusty could see what appeared to be crates of lettuce and carrots stacked in the back.

"He's delivering to the restaurants," he grasped. "There's my ride."

But the truck was already rolling, an elderly Latino man behind the wheel.

Dusty gazed about, trying to think of anything to stop that truck. He realized the motorcycle helmet was still on his head, and then it occurred to him.

Pulling loose the chinstrap, he yanked off his headgear, and then from behind the dumpster, he rolled it like a bowling ball directly at the truck.

The driver seemed quite surprised to see the odd looking, spherically-shaped object bouncing across the parking lot and heading straight for his front wheels. He slammed on the brakes and stopped just as the wayward helmet came to rest directly in his path.

The old farmer looked around as if he was waiting for someone to come and retrieve the missing property, but there wasn't anyone in the area. Shrugging, he finally took the truck out of gear and opened the cab door.

As he walked to the front and picked up the helmet, Dusty was sliding into the back of the bed, scrambling under a tarp and behind crates stacked with cabbage.

Seeing no one was going to claim the valuable piece of safety gear, the farmer again shrugged and carried his new prize back to the cab.

A few minutes later, they were rolling across the parking area.

The police manning the freshly formed roadblock didn't perform a thorough check of the vegetable truck, the newly arriving officers still chatting about the odd assignment and speculating on its true purpose. Dusty held his breath as he heard the quick conversation with the driver, who didn't speak English. In a few moments, they were waved through and on their way south.

Southeastern Texas rolled by as the old truck sped south. Dusty, noting the momentum and breeze, maneuvered to create a slight portal under the tarp which allowed him a nice vantage of the fleeting terrain. Flat, grassy and mundane, he'd spent little time in this part of his home state. "It's better than the accommodations at the local jail... or a coffin," he mused.

The journey seemed to pass quickly, his chauffeur making steady time toward the border city and presumably home. Dusty tucked the Glock into his boot, finding the weapon's presence gave him a sense of comfort.

A few miles outside Laredo, the driver let off the gas, a clear signal he was going to make a stop. Given his morning coffee and the long ride, Dusty hoped it was some place that had a restroom.

Soon enough, the turn signal began its rhythmic clicking, and then they were pulling into the nearly full parking lot of what was a combination convenience store and gas station. Dusty noted the congestion, but the fueling bays were mostly empty, the majority of the traffic centered just outside the retail unit. His limo evidently did need some gas, the appearance of a pump startling Dusty when he suddenly found himself staring at the dispensing handle right beside his peephole. Dusty hurriedly ducked back underneath the tarp and listened as the driver unhinged the hose. The distinctive odor of fuel soon filled the air.

The sound of footsteps indicated the driver was going inside. Dusty peeked out again and watched as the farmer entered the station. He quickly scampered out of the bed, his stiff body sluggish from riding in such cramped quarters for so long.

Trying to act as if he'd just hitchhiked in from the road, Dusty ambled into the convenience store and was surprised to find a long line of Latino men, most of whom were holding paper checks. His driver was one of them.

After using the restroom, he milled around, pretending to shop for snacks and drinks. In reality, he was watching the proceedings, fascinated by what appeared to be a significant banking operation. Why were all these guys cashing checks at a gas station?

He finally selected a cold bottle of water and a nutrition bar for substance. There was a separate line for those who weren't in need of financial services.

Dusty was waiting on the driver outside.

"Señor," he greeted, holding up a $20 bill, "could I catch a ride in the back of your truck to Laredo?"

The old farmer thought about it, looking Dusty up and down twice. Finally nodding, he pocketed the money and pointed toward the cab.

The two men were soon on the road again. Dusty waited a bit before asking, "Was that a bank back there? I saw a lot of men coming out and counting their money."

Misreading the curiosity, the older man said, "They cash my checks there, señor. This time of day there is always a line. That place charges me less than any of the others."

"Charges less?" Dusty mumbled, already having guessed the station owner took a cut. "Why don't you use a bank?"

The driver's brow wrinkled, "I can't go to a bank; I don't have a social security number. And the banks in Mexico, they charge more to cash a U.S. check than this place."

Dusty thought back to the line of landscapers, construction workers and other laborers waiting patiently. *There was a longer line here than at most banks*, he mused. *Talk about an underground economy.*

A few minutes later, Dusty was again curious, "I'm not trying to pry, but I receive the occasional check myself now and then. How much do they charge back there?"

"It depends on the check and if they know you. The ones I just cashed were from large corporations that own the restaurants in Kemah, and I frequently cash them at the station. They took 3%, which is much less than typical. For a new customer, they will skim five or even ten percent."

Amazing, Dusty thought. He'd never considered where the undocumented workers banked. He filed the information away. *That might become important for a man living on the dodge.*

Their route lead into an even denser cityscape, and before long the driver again slowed the truck. He pointed toward the motorcycle helmet resting on the floorboard. "I found this today. I think it has value. I'm going to see if this pawn broker will buy it from me."

They parked at the Frontier Pawn and Jewelry, the motorist wasting no time heading inside. Before following, Dusty took a moment and studied the nearby businesses, trying to memorize the landscape in case he had to make a hasty departure. There was a low-end hotel nearby. That's probably where he'd end up tonight. He also noted what stores and restaurants were close, as he would have to walk for food or any other supplies required. He didn't really know how long he'd be staying.

When he realized what he was doing, Dusty had to chuckle. "What interesting habits an outlaw develops," he whispered to the evening air. "I might actually get good at this living on the run."

He turned and entered the pawnshop, thinking a used laptop computer might help him become acclimated to his new surroundings a little quicker. "Gotta love the internet," he whispered.

The swarthy, muscular man behind the counter was still consuming his fast food drive-thru hamburger, casting the occasional semi-uninterested glance at the motorcycle helmet the farmer was holding up. Dusty closed the front door, noting the heavy iron bars that secured both the front windows and the doorframe. After glancing around for a few moments, Dusty wondered about the security arrangement.

The fortress-like exterior was an obvious attempt to protect the valuables stored within from burglars and nighttime thieves. The problem for Dusty was he couldn't figure out exactly why anyone would bother breaking into the place.

Row after row of what appeared to be yard-sale merchandise filled his vision. The assortment included power tools that were well past their prime, rusted wrenches and a shelf of televisions that looked like they had been manufactured in the 1960s. The early 1960s.

"Looking for something specific?" The counterman asked, obviously not that interested in the helmet – or at least trying not to act as if he were.

"I need a laptop computer," the gunsmith replied. "Nothing fancy, but it has to have wireless communication and a reasonable screen."

Without moving anything but his head, the man indicated Dusty should look along the south wall of the store. He then returned to examining the farmer's windfall merchandise.

Sure enough, there were several computers displayed in the far corner, some of them looking to be in reasonable condition.

He heard the pawnbroker offer $20 for the helmet. The old man seemed happy to accept. After receiving his money, the farmer approached Dusty and said, "I'm not going much further into town. I turn off soon. Do you want to stay or go on with me?"

Considering the nearby hotel and availability of food, Dusty extended his hand to the man, "I think I'll be good here. Thanks for the ride."

As Dusty returned to studying the computers, the door opened and admitted another customer. Dusty spied a middle-aged, very attractive woman who was carrying something wrapped in a kitchen dishtowel. Curious, he watched her march up to the counter and unwrap a stainless steel revolver.

"How much can I get for this pistol?" she asked, a hint of desperation in her voice.

"Do you want to pawn it or sell it?" The broker asked, almost like a spider who sensed a fly buzzing by his net.

"I want to sell it... I think. Can't I get more if I sell it?"

"Sometimes," came the answer.

"Then I want to sell it."

Dusty, being a man who earned a living working on firearms, was curious about the impending transaction. He'd caught just a glance of the wheel gun as the lady had unwrapped it, and wanted to get a closer look. He casually meandered toward a display case full of gold and silver, feigning interest in the shimmering baubles while casting side-glances at the weapon.

It was a .357 Colt Python, nickel finish with a snub 2.5-inch barrel. A classic! *It's the pawnbroker's lucky day,* Dusty thought.

After studying the computer screen for several moments, the man behind the counter peered over the top of the monitor and said, "It's not worth much. Everybody wants high capacity, plastic guns these days. I'll give you $200 for it."

It took all of Dusty's discipline not to shout out in protest. He wanted to find some way to signal the woman that she was being taken advantage of; he knew that weapon was easily worth $3800. This guy was trying to rip her off. He glanced up at the lady, hoping she would make eye contact with him. Her wrinkled brow made it clear she was trying to make a decision, but some inner voice was telling her it wasn't a good deal. *Look at me*, Dusty kept thinking. *Look me in the eye.*

Before she could respond, the jingle of a cell phone sounded in her purse. She reached in and checked the caller-ID being displayed, quickly glancing at the broker and mumbling, "Give me a minute." She then turned toward Dusty and answered the call.

"They're not supposed to turn off the electricity until five!" she hissed into the phone. "You go out there and tell that guy in the utility truck I have until 5:00 p.m. to pay the bill. They promised me when I called!"

She paused, listening to the speaker for a few moments before continuing. "I'm in Laredo selling one of papa's guns. As soon as I get the money, I'm going to pay the bill… okay… I will… love you too. We'll be okay sweetheart; I promise."

Dusty moved quickly as she fumbled to return the phone, trying his best to make his collision seem accidental. His slight bump into the harried gal gave him the excuse to reach out and grab her shoulder – a benign gesture to make she was steady. "I'm so sorry, ma'am," he said, "Are you okay?"

She waved him off, "Yes, I'm fine."

Dusty didn't let loose of her shoulder and leaned in closer. "That gun is worth $3,000. Don't take his offer."

For a moment, she didn't seem to understand what he was saying. She looked into his eyes for what seemed like a very long time before finally whispering, "Thank you."

Returning to the counter with new confidence, she reached for the pistol. "You're trying to screw me… probably just because you think I'm some dumb girl or something. That pistol is worth a lot more than 200 bucks. I'll take it over to the other pawnshop and see what they'll give me for it."

"Hold on," the man said, "Let me look at it one more time. So many of these look the same."

Dusty couldn't keep his mouth shut any longer. "Ma'am, would you mind if I took a look at that handgun?"

"Sure," she replied, nodding toward the beautiful piece of craftsmanship.

"A Colt Python .357 magnum," Dusty began, holding it up to inspect the serial number. "This one was manufactured in 1978 at the factory in Hartford. See that small stamp right there?" he pointed, "That means this specific pistol was issued to a law enforcement officer."

"Is it valuable?" she asked with an innocent tone.

"Oh, yes. Very. Many knowledgeable collectors believe this was the finest revolver ever made. This example, with its nickel finish and excellent condition, is worth a considerable sum."

She played it well. Placing her hands on her hips, she turned and stared hard at the pawnbroker. "Well?"

"I didn't notice any stamp," he grumbled, throwing Dusty a dirty look. "Let me see it again, please."

Again, he punched keys on the computer, pretending to research prices. Finally, "He's right. It is worth more than I offered. I'll give you $1200."

"Keep talking," she replied with a firm tone, "You're getting warmer."

"I've got to make a profit, too," he protested and then motioned around at the store. "I've got overhead costs, ya know."

Again, Dusty held his comment, watching as the shop owner considered his next offer. Apparently, he waited too long because the woman again reached for the pistol and began wrapping it in the dishcloth. "Okay... okay," the guy finally conceded. "I can go $2200, and that's my best offer. I will probably sell it for $2500 and make a small profit."

The woman glanced at Dusty, obviously wanting to take the money and pay her electric bill. He shook his head, indicating she should pass.

She tucked the gun under her arm and made for the door, saying "No thanks," over her shoulder. Dusty, realizing he probably wasn't welcome in the store any longer, followed her outside. "Ma'am, that firearm is worth about $3800 retail. I wouldn't take less than $3200 for it."

"I sure do hope you're right, Mister," she replied with frustration. "I'm running out of time. I've got two kids at home freaking out because they're about to turn off our electricity, and there isn't any milk in the fridge."

Dusty was a little taken aback by her hostility, and it must have shown on his face. "I'm sorry," she continued, this time softer. "Things haven't been going well as of late. I know you were just trying to help, and I appreciate that. I was ready to take his first offer out of desperation."

She held out her hand and said, "Penny Royce."

Dusty accepted the handshake and replied, "Andy Booker," using the name on his fake passport. He smiled and then added, "But people call me Dusty. Where are you going now?"

"There's another pawnshop. Armed with my new knowledge, I'm going to go there and see what I can get. I hope it's at least two grand, because I don't have time to shop around."

"Are there any gun stores in town? They should give you a fair price for a weapon like that."

"Yes. I went there yesterday, and they only sell used guns on consignment. They wouldn't tell me how much it was worth... acted like they were annoyed at the dumb woman bringing in the gun and asking questions."

Dusty scratched his chin for a moment. "I know you don't know me, but if you want me to go with you, I'll get you the best deal possible."

"What's your story?" she asked, "I've lived around here for quite a while and have never seen you before."

"I'm passing through, taking some time off. My wife recently divorced me, and her lawyers have bled me dry. Those vampires still think I have some cash stashed away and have hounded me for the last three months. I had enough of it and just headed out. There wasn't anything left back home anyway," he lied. "Besides, I'd hate to see you get ripped off. I know how it is to be tight on money."

She started to reject the offer outright, but then hesitated. She looked Dusty up and down and made her decision. "You did help me out in there," she said, nodding toward the pawnshop. "These guys see a woman coming in and think they can take advantage of her every time. I guess it would help to have a man along. I mean, what else could go wrong today? If you're an axe murderer, could you please make it quick?"

Dusty laughed, shaking his head. "Okay. Err... I mean, no, I'm not an axe murderer."

"That's what they all say. Hop in the back of the truck. It's really not that far."

Dusty walked to the tailgate of an old pickup and started to climb in. She watched him carefully and then changed her mind. "You might as well ride in the cab. I just wanted to see if you would really ride back there."

A minute later, they were pulling out of the lot, headed into downtown Laredo. The driver decided to confide in her passenger. "My husband and I own a small poultry farm not far from here. He was arrested last week and is still in jail. Something has been killing our birds, and he is convinced it's the new factory that's not far from our place. He confronted the management and got himself arrested."

Dusty grunted, a small sense of relief over not being the only criminal in the area. "Did he assault someone? Threaten to burn the plant down?"

She shook her head, "No, nothing like that. He threatened to call the EPA and local papers. The sheriff showed up and handcuffed him. They set the bail at $50,000 dollars, which might as well be a million to us. I've been trying to keep up with the farm, but it's more than I can handle by myself."

The old truck rambled into the parking lot of another seedy looking strip mall. "Thank you for coming along and successfully resisting the urge to cleaver chop me into tiny pieces. As you can see, this isn't the best part of town, and I wouldn't normally frequent such places."

"No problem," the Texan replied easily. "I really didn't have anything critical to do, and it's good to see the town."

They entered the pawnshop, finding a similar collection of items populating the shelves. Dusty presented the pistol, and immediately let the man behind the counter know he was fully aware of the gun's value.

In West Texas, horse-trading was considered an art, and this wasn't Dusty's first rodeo. On the other hand, the pawnbroker earned his keep via buying low and selling high. The negotiations ebbed and flowed, both men secretly enjoying the contest.

"These aren't as collectable as they were just a year ago. Your information is outdated," the buyer opened.

"My information is current, and if you had any idea of what you're looking at, you'd know that Colt didn't make very many of the snub versions in nickel. That makes this piece even more valuable. You could sell this item on the internet for at least $3800."

"Maybe," he replied. "I also might have to hang onto it for months before the right buyer comes along."

Back and forth they angled, each trying to convince the other of the item's value, greater or less. Twenty minutes later, Penny walked out of the shop with $3100 cash and a huge smile on her face. "I can pay the electric bill and buy groceries! I can even catch up our account at the feed store."

"Is your husband going to be upset that you sold his pistol?"

"It was my father's weapon, and no, Mike's not into guns so much." she answered. She glanced at her watch and announced, "I'll be happy to run you back to wherever, but I've got to stop at the utility company office first. I'm almost out of time."

"No problem," Dusty replied, "I'll just hang out and guard the truck until you're finished."

She chuckled, glancing over at the beat-up, rattletrap old Chevy. "It is a classic," she played along.

When she returned from the utility office, it was clear that a great burden had been removed from her shoulders. "Electricity is always a good thing," she said as she got behind the old truck's wheel. "Did you have to fight off any carjackers?"

"It *is* a classic," Dusty smiled, pretending he had contributed in some small way.

As she maneuvered through Laredo, she suddenly brightened. "Since you know so much about guns, why don't you come back out to the ranch with me and see if Papa had anything else of value? I know he used to work on older firearms in his shop. Maybe there's something there that would raise enough money to get my husband out of jail."

Dusty shrugged, intrigued at the prospect of actually doing something productive. "I don't have anything more pressing," he responded.

Day Three - Evening

The Royce place was just over 10 miles outside of town. "My father started this operation before I was born. Mike and I were high school sweethearts, and when daddy passed away, we just took over. About five years ago, free-range birds became all the rage, so we went that route. Now, our chickens aren't laying, and we're losing about 15 animals a day. The vet has no idea why... thinks it's some sort of virus. Mike's been convinced that something about that new factory is killing our poultry."

Dusty noted the small, but neat operation as they rolled up the driveway. A modest, ranch-style house surrounded by several outbuildings greeted them at the end of the lane. Two young girls sat on the front porch, both hopping up as the truck neared the house.

"What made your husband so sure it's the factory?" Dusty inquired.

"The timing of the whole thing. Our animals were just fine until the week after that damn place began operations. We started noticing egg production dropping rapidly. Then a few days later, he found five dead birds. The next day, the death toll was eight. According to the county co-op agent, we're the only ones having an issue right now."

Penny parked the truck, exiting the cab and immediately embracing her daughters. After hugs had been exchanged, she turned to Dusty and introduced both girls, "Mr. Booker, this are my daughters, Amy and Gina."

"Nice to meet both of you. Please, call me Dusty."

Content that their mother was home, both girls scampered away after being reminded of their chores. Penny turned to Dusty and suggested, "Come on; I'll show you papa's workshop."

She led the way to the largest building, a medium-sized barn that had once sported a dark red paint job. Grey, weathered wood now peeked through the faded pigment, evidence of the harsh Texas sun and a lack of maintenance. Pushing open one of the double doors, Penny motioned for Dusty to enter. Inside, he encountered a scene typical of most any agricultural storehouse, the interior filled with an assortment of farm equipment, pallets of feed and bales of straw. To the gunsmith from West Texas, it smelled like home.

One area of the barn was atypical, housing a workbench constructed of heavy planks. An interesting collection of tools adorned the pegboard backstop. Dusty smiled when his eye took in the Monarch lathe, the unit a slightly older model than the one he used at home. Leading the way to the bench, Penny pointed and reminisced, "Papa used to spend hours and hours out here in the evenings. Sometimes neighbors and friends would bring over their shotguns for him to work on, other times he would find a broken rifle for sale at the right price and fix it up. He loved spending time out here."

"I can understand," Dusty said, feeling a tug of homesickness pulling at his insides. "I have… had a similar setup at home. It's a good place for a man to spend his time."

"My father's guns are stored over here. Come on; I'll show you."

She walked behind an old Ford tractor, leading Dusty to the barn's second surprise. One corner had been finished off as a small apartment, complete with foldout couch, sink, microwave, and bathroom. Seeing her guest's eyebrows rise, she laughed and said, "Our house is pretty small, and Dad came from a big family. He built this spare room for his brothers, so they would be comfortable and have a little privacy when they visited. He even equipped this space with air conditioning."

"Nice," Dusty observed, thinking the smell of hay would be a wonderful greeting in the morning. He was sold the second he spotted the coffeemaker.

His hostess moved to a heavy, metal door and inserted a key. Rather than the expected closet, she opened the fireproof portal and revealed what was essentially a homemade gun safe. Inside were several long guns as well as a handful of pistols. Dusty's practiced eye swept the collection quickly, noting a few rifles of interest. "I'll have to inspect each one individually and judge its condition," he announced after a few moments. "Some of these might have value, but I don't know about enough to raise bail money."

She seemed disappointed. Sighing, she admitted, "I didn't think there was a winning lottery ticket in here... but you can't blame a girl for wishful thinking."

"Mom?" a young voice interrupted from the front of the barn. "Mom, are you out here?"

Penny yelled back at the same time making for the door, "We're back in the gun room, sweetheart. What's wrong?"

"Mr. Roberson just called and said some of our chickens were in his yard. He threatened to eat one of them if we didn't come get them."

"Damn it," Penny grumbled, her shoulders slumping. "Two of the fence posts on that side were getting pretty rotten. I guess they finally gave way. I've been meaning to get out there and mend that line, but just haven't had the time or energy."

The woman was clearly distraught, and it pained Dusty to see it. He followed her out of the apartment, having to step quickly to keep up. A minute later, they were in another of the farm's outbuildings, this one containing chicken-wire fencing and a small supply of posts.

"Why don't you take the girls and go shoo the birds back onto your land while I go fix the fence?" he offered.

She hesitated, not wanting to involve her guest any more than he already was, but yet needing his assistance badly. "I can't pay you anything," she admitted. "But I sure could use the help."

"That hotel is going to cost me $70 per night," Dusty countered. "I'll do some work around here and inventory the guns in exchange for room and board. How's that sound?"

Again, Penny was suspicious. She was also desperate. She finally went with her instincts. "Okay, but again, if you're that axe murderer, please make it quick."

Dusty laughed and then nodded toward the fencing supplies. "How do I get to the downed line?"

"Follow me," she said, briskly walking to another nearby shed. Inside was an ATV, complete with muddy tires and a small wagon attached to the back. "Mike bought this a few years ago. It runs pretty well. Should be full of gasoline."

She then pointed to the northeast and continued, "If you drive about half a mile straight that direction, you'll run into the weak section of the partition where I suspect the repairs are needed. I'll load up the girls and go chase birds."

"Got it," Dusty replied. "See you later."

And with that, he began loading tools and supplies into the small wagon, actually looking forward to the physical labor. As he drove the small vehicle across the bumpy south Texas turf, he thought signing up to work on the farm had been a very good idea. Aside from Penny's need for help, the remote property provided an excellent hiding place. He could save money, stay out of sight, and even work on some of those guns. It was a fugitive's paradise.

He crested a slight rise and immediately spotted the downed line. The birds, randomly roaming the pasture, were evidently familiar with the ATV and scattered to keep out of its path. He pulled up and realized Penny had been right – two of the posts appeared to have rotted and fallen apart. Pulling on a pair of work gloves and unloading the post-hole digger from the back, Dusty ventured closer to investigate.

Bending to examine the broken, exposed wood, he didn't see any rot at all. Looking closer, he spied an odd-looking indentation a several inches above what would have been ground level. "That's strange," he whispered to the re-gathering chickens. "What would have pushed these over?"

He scanned the area, seeing nothing but south Texas grassland interrupted by the occasion tree. Shrugging his shoulders, he began digging.

Fredrick closed the laptop's cover, shaking his head at the Dow Jones' closing numbers. It had been a volatile market all week, the varied assortment of funds he monitored again showing losses at the closing bell. *It wasn't Black Friday bad*, he mused, *but it wasn't good either.*

While the destruction of the Houston Medical Center hadn't been uplifting news for the markets, the event had raised a mere speed bump on the American financial highway. The destruction of a large swath of the Houston Ship Channel was a completely different story.

A significant percentage of the nation's petroleum was refined, stored, and distributed from the now-damaged port. Law enforcement wasn't commenting regarding the source of either incident, and that left a big, fat unknown in everyone's mind. Financial markets hated the unknown.

Pushing his chair away from the desk, he ambled to the window and gazed out at his BMW parked three stories below. The neighborhood wasn't terrible, at least not nearly as bad as the residential areas most of his clients called "Home." Still, he liked to keep an eye on the gleaming machine. *If there are many more days like today*, he thought, *it won't be car thieves I'll need to worry about. It'll be the bank coming to repossess my ride.*

He'd started his financial services business with a wholesome heart and noble intent. The south side of Houston was full of Latino families that had no idea how to leash the power of the stock market, mutual funds, and investment pools to grow their meager savings. While many were undocumented and struggling to stay under the radar, even the people here legally knew little about how the Anglos made money. He'd worked four years at a local bank while he put himself through college to earn a business degree. Eventually it came to him that he could kill two birds with one stone by opening a new, small business. He'd help his community while making good money himself.

Three months after signing a lease and opening his business, Fredrick realized he'd completely misjudged his friends and neighbors. Between a deeply seated distrust of the unknown and a general acceptance of the poverty cycle, the fledgling firm suffered from a lack of customers. Cooks, dishwashers, and yard crews didn't care about making 8% on the few hundred dollars they had stuffed inside their mattresses. They were worried about tomorrow or next week, not 20 years in the future. He could talk until he was blue in the face, and they would just politely nod, smile, and then do nothing. It was financially and morally devastating.

He had burned through his savings in less than three months and was updating his resume to seek his old job back. He was down to the final week in his office before eviction, when a middle-aged Latino man appeared in his modest reception area. The fellow was not extreme or flashy, but well dressed and extremely polite. He introduced himself as Mr. Vega.

Later, as Fredrick replayed the meeting in his mind, he realized Mr. Vega hadn't revealed anything about himself. Each well-rehearsed line of inquiry designed to give a sense of a client's net worth and seriousness had been deftly fended off. It had been the customer who had grilled and pumped the salesman.

Nothing happened for two days after the interview. Fredrick's pipe dream of landing a big, wealthy client and keeping his business open was beginning to evaporate. And then, without warning, Mr. Vega again appeared at the office.

"My business is a cash trade," the older man opened. "Any business generating large amounts of paper money draws an unwarranted scrutiny from the U.S. Federal government. And while my firm is prepared to pay a reasonable level of taxes, we wish to keep as much as possible of our enterprise under the radar. Can you help me manage, transfer, and conceal these funds from prying government eyes?"

Fredrick's initial reaction was revulsion. What did this man think he was? A common criminal? *The last thing I want to do is soil my good name by associating with some local drug dealer*, he thought, preparing to escort the fellow from the premises. But before he could act, Mr. Vega continued, "I know what you're thinking. You believe my firm is associated with some sort of illegal activity, but that is not the case. Any funds we invest with you will be earned by entirely legal businesses. We are really no different than any other corporation – we want to reduce our tax burden as much as legally possible."

"Why don't you want the IRS to know about the cash then?"

"Because they will report it to the countries where our investors are based. This will cause a secondary wave of taxation, in addition to the escalating level of bribery and other nefarious costs associated with local graft."

Still, Fredrick wasn't convinced. Out of curiosity, he asked, "How much are you talking about investing?"

Mr. Vega spread his hands, moving each up and down as if to simulate scales. "At first it will be modest sums... no more than five million dollars per month. If our relationship remains beneficial to both parties, that amount could increase dramatically."

Fredrick's mind screamed at the amount, his face immediately flushing pale. Mr. Vega didn't smirk outright at the reaction – that

83

would have been rude. But his eyes relayed the fact that he found humor in the response. "Of course," he said matter-of-factly, "if that amount is too high, we can start at a lower sum."

"No," Fredrick stammered, "No, that wasn't what I was thinking. I was trying to decide where I could invest such amounts without drawing attention to our activities," he lied. In reality, his thoughts had moved on to how much commission he would be earning.

"I, like any other client, would require the final approval where our funds are to be invested. I know that all such endeavors come with a certain amount of risk. Still, I would expect you to provide a creative, well thought-out list of alternatives from which I can choose."

The younger man leaned back, his mind whirling at the prospects of representing a man such as Mr. Vega. Before he could comment again, his potential windfall stood and announced, "I will give you some time to think over my proposal and to prepare a presentation on how you would manage my money. Would Friday be too soon for us to meet again?"

"No, that would be excellent. I look forward to seeing you in a few days, sir. I'll focus all of my efforts on this project."

Mr. Vega turned to leave, but then paused. His voice became so low Fredrick could barely hear his prospective customer. "I am a man who values his privacy. I assume everything we have talked about today will remain confidential."

"Oh, yes, of course it will, Mr. Vega. I'm a professional." Fredrick responded, trying to casually dismiss the concern.

The older man stepped closer to the broker, leaning just slightly forward, his eyes cold and cruel. For the first time, Fredrick felt a profoundly genuine fear of the man. "I'm very serious about this. Just so there is no misunderstanding, I wish to reiterate my feelings. I would appreciate it if you didn't mention this opportunity to your mother, or sister, or either of your two brothers. Not a word. Do we have an understanding?"

The young broker was so taken aback by his client's display, he didn't realize until much later that the man had rattled off an accurate inventory of his immediate family. *How did he know that? How connected was Mr. Vega? What was such a man capable of?*

By the time Friday rolled around, Fredrick was exhausted from a lack of sleep. While the countless hours of research had taken their toll, in reality it was his excitement that kept him from resting. The prospect of leveraging such amounts of money was more than he had ever dreamed. When he presented his options to Mr. Vega, the man had seemed pleased. After they had shaken hands, his new client exited briefly, only to return with two suitcases full of money. It had all happened that quickly.

As of last week, Mr. Vega had invested over 14 million dollars through Fredrick's firm, most of the money diverted to a varied assortment of mutual funds and safe offshore investments. The start-up business was no longer in any danger of failing, and the trust between the two men had grown with success.

Fredrick learned two very important lessons from his dealings with Mr. Vega. The first was not to ask questions of his client. The second was that having money beat the shit out of being poor. Watching the seemingly endless piles of cash pass through his establishment, the young man found himself wanting more and more. He quickly discovered an appetite for the finer things in life, including the BMW that was parked below. Lately, he'd begun thinking of previously unimaginable purchases, and it seemed like the time before his next commission check couldn't pass fast enough. *Greed*, he mused. He had always thought he was immune.

At least that was the situation until this past week. Now, he was wondering if he would earn any commission this month at all. The thought of returning to desperate poverty made his mind work overtime, trying to think of any way to escape the unacceptable situation. Vega was so successful - the only person he knew with serious money. Airplane money.

Mr. Vega always seemed one step ahead of the less-experienced man. When the client first noticed the new BMW, he had simply nodded and smiled. "I see you are developing a desire for luxury items, and this is good. It motivates people to work harder and become creative in their endeavors. I'm paying you for information, perspective, and research," Mr. Vega said. "Information is like any commodity, it has value. Our account is opening doors to you that wouldn't normally be accessible. I will pay extra commissions for valuable insight. Always keep that in mind. Our investors have an appetite to know the unknown, to hear the unspoken. They reward well."

"I wonder if he'd be interested in having an inside source next to Houston's highest ranking FBI agent?" Fredrick whispered to the empty office. "I wonder if that would pay enough to offset my soon-to-be zero commission check?"

Returning to his desk, he re-opened the laptop and signed into a VPN, or virtual private network server. Until Mr. Vega had shown him the technology, he had no idea such a thing existed.

From there, he loaded a special email client. The address he selected contained a two-digit code, which changed every Sunday night at midnight. It was the week of the year.

Despite all of the precautions, the message Fredrick typed looked identical to other marketing emails he sent monthly. Only one word in the last sentence was slightly different, a misspelling of the term "portfolio." That was a signal, a secret code for Mr. Vega to contact him. He'd never used it, and as he closed the laptop again, he hoped his client would be interested in purchasing the information he had for sale.

The new message in his secure inbox wasn't an unheard of event, but rarely was it good news. Sighing at the potential of having to solve yet another problem so late on Friday afternoon, Mr. Vega opened the message and scanned the contents.

The young investment banker wasn't so incompetent after all, he mused after reading the misspelled word. He glanced at his watch and judged the hour, deciding it was reasonable to believe "Freddie" would still be at the office.

Opening his briefcase, he pulled out one of many cell phones clipped to the calfskin interior and dialed the number.

"San Jacinto Investments," the familiar voice answered.

"You requested that I call?" Mr. Vega said calmly, guessing the nervous young broker wanted to tell him about the decline in their investment portfolio.

"Yes, Mr. Ve…. Err, Sir. I have some information that I thought might be vital to your investors. Actually, it is a potential source of information."

The older man thought about the statement, the odd phrasing and hesitation of the voice on the other end peaking his curiousity.

"Do you remember where we had lunch two weeks ago?"

After a brief pause, "Yes."

"Can you meet me there in 20 minutes?"

"Yes."

After disconnecting the call, Vega regretted the decision. He'd been managing the legitimate operations for the Gulf Cartel for three years without any hint of the authorities knowing his connections. Meeting naïve investment bankers, after hours, in public places, wasn't wise.

The organization had grown to such proportions that illegitimate proceeds had been funneled into legal businesses, ranging from venture capital funds to huge retail outlets and even car dealerships.

In the eyes of U.S. law enforcement, those operations were still tainted – the benefactors of ill-gotten gains. A complex game of financial cat and mouse became part of the U.S.'s war on drugs.

And then a few states legalized marijuana. Public opinion polls shifted, and talk began circulating in Washington – the discussions focusing on making recreational drug usage legal, and taxable. This was an unwelcome harbinger to the cartels. While pot was only a small portion of their income, it was their foundational, entry level offering. The trade in weed opened doors, recruited both future employees and the customers of more profitable product lines.

So the cartels had adapted, dumping their mountains of cash into layer upon layer of investments, hoping to create a web so complex that not even the largest government entities could unravel the money trail. Small enterprises, such as food trucks and payday loan operations now resided in their portfolios, as did entire regional banks.

The problem was managing such operations. Vega grunted, thinking about his job. The Gulf operation now had more accountants and investment managers than enforcers or collections experts. Tattooed street muscle and ex-Mexican Special Forces operators were now being replaced by Harvard MBAs and Ivy League managers. But recruiting was problematic, and that's why they used small, struggling investment firms like Fredrick's.

Still, they had to keep a low profile. Vega didn't fear the DEA or the FBI; he worried about the IRS and Department of State. Using a network of tiny, individually owned companies like San Jacinto was risky. It only took one mistake… a single misstep, and the authorities would descend in droves to seize assets and issue warrants. It was essential to keep a barrier between the illegal and legal assets of the organization.

Sighing, he deleted the email and then ran a small utility that would scramble his computer's hard drive beyond recovery by even the most sophisticated forensic software. He would meet Freddie, and if it turned out to be a wasted effort, he would wait two weeks, redirect the portfolio to another firm, and sever the relationship. They had to remain dynamic – it was their best defense.

Ten minutes later, he discovered the eager, young broker waiting in the restaurant's reception area. His hand was damp, a good sign to the savvy Mr. Vega. After they were seated in a remote corner and ordered appetizers and beverages, the cartel manager got down to business.

"This meeting is most unusual, Fredrick. I hope we are here to discuss more than the recent decline in the U.S. markets and our assets."

"Actually, sir, I was hoping to discuss anything but the performance of your funds," the kid replied with a nervous grin.

Good, thought Vega. He has a sense of humor despite being scared shitless. "Go on."

"My girlfriend lives with her sister, who happens to work at Houston General Hospital. A few days ago they admitted a new patient... a badly injured man who happens to be the FBI agent in charge of the entire Houston office."

Vega connected the dots instantly, but did his best to maintain a poker face. "Go on," he replied calmly.

"You had indicated that your investors were interested in hearing the unspoken. I believe this situation can provide an ongoing source of confidential information."

Why does he think I'm concerned about the FBI? Vega wondered. *I expected him to be suspicious of us, but to be so bold to come right out with such speculation is odd.*

"I'm sorry, Fredrick, but I fail to see the connection between the FBI and our relationship?" the older man replied. "As I've stated before, the proceeds you invest for me are all from legitimate enterprises."

Again, Fredrick surprised his host. Waving off the concern, he said, "Oh, I'm not talking about insider information of any criminal investigation. Did you read the *Houston Post's* article about 'God's Gun?'?"

"Yes... yes I did. I thought it was typical of over-hyped journalism designed to sell papers."

Freddie grunted, "So did I, but my source now informs me that the super-weapon is indeed real. It was directly involved in the ship channel incident, as well as the medical center explosions. And here's the best part – they believe the man who built the weapon might have escaped."

Patting his mouth with a napkin, Vega leaned back in his chair and smiled. Inside, he was preparing to change from the skeptic to the negotiator. What Freddie was offering was indeed of interest to his superiors, but he didn't want to give the man across the table even the slightest hint of any value.

"While that is interesting dinner conversation, I still fail to see why you think this would be valuable to my business associates?"

"Because of the energy potential and other uses of the technology," Fredrick explained. "I may be making incorrect assumptions, but I judge you a man of significant resources, both human and capital. If the owner of God's gun is desperate and on the run, it might allow the acquisition of that weapon, which could lead to all sorts of immensely profitable endeavors."

He knows who and what we are, but is playing coy, Vega thought. *Very smart.* The recent string of events around the Bayou City Houston hadn't escaped the cartel's attention. The Port of Houston was one of the key entry points for illicit cargo, and the repercussions of its closure were already being felt throughout the organization.

Beyond the mere economic impacts, the level of destruction at both locations was something that had raised more than one eyebrow within the organization. In-fighting among competing cartels in Mexico was a constant drain on resources, more and more profits being absorbed by the never-ending turf wars. Just to hold on to existing territories and markets required a small, very expensive army. And then there was the government itself.

Often appearing weak and unstable, the Mexican federal government was a juicy target. More than one of the big bosses had dreamed of one day taking over the entire country. Drugs, human smuggling, and prostitution were profitable, but nothing made as much money as government. The estimated amounts of bribes and graft in Mexico City alone made the Gulf Cartel's activity look puny by comparison. Throw in taxation, government-owned businesses, and the currency manipulation of central banks, and you had a recipe for a serious moneymaker.

The Post's article titled "God's Gun" had been picked up by numerous newspapers throughout Mexico and Latin America. No one quite believed it, but the mere concept was enough to make powerful men salivate with desire. If only such a weapon existed! Whoever possessed it could rule the entire planet.

"How reliable is this source?" Vega casually asked, trying to keep the excitement out of his voice.

"I believe what Juanita says. She is so stuffy and highbrow with her old-fashioned thinking and conservative Catholic values. She wouldn't lie."

The cartel man digested the statement for a bit and finally smiled slightly. He took a final sip from his glass, set his silverware in the center of his entrée, and glanced at his watch, his action disappointing the young banker. "I must be going. Thank you for making the effort to inform me of this situation. I'll be in touch soon."

Freddie stood with his client, his mouth trying to form a sentence of protest. "That's... that's it? You're not interested?"

Vega threw a scolding, disappointed look at the younger man. "I didn't say that. I will pass this information along and see if anyone has any interest in this resource. Until then, I suggest you have a relaxing weekend and think about how we can invest our money and not suffer the same decline of equity as this last week. Good evening."

Fredrick stood stunned for a moment, watching his benefactor weave among the crowded matrix of dining room tables and hustling wait-staff. He was just about to leave himself when their waiter appeared beside the table. "Here is your check, sir."

"Well, I'll be a son of a bitch," he mumbled. "He didn't even pick up the tab."

Vega's cell phone was in his hand before the valet had even pocketed the tip. As his plain, non-descript sedan pulled out of the lot, his boss picked up the call.

"You're working late tonight," the voice answered with a chuckle. "Or are you calling me at this hour trying to impress me with your dedication?"

"We should speak, sooner rather than later," Vega replied, his tone sounding with both urgency and respect at the same time.

"I'm in the south right now," the voice responded, indicating Panama City, or south of Mexico.

"This is a subject I would feel more comfortable addressing face to face," Vega answered, letting his superior know it was a matter of importance.

"Go to the airfield first thing in the morning. My plane will be there," came the instant response. And then the line went dead.

The Texas soil wasn't cooperating. Hard packed, clay-thick, and seemingly kiln fired, Dusty thought it would be easier to dig a hole in concrete. Even though, it felt good to use his muscles on an honest task.

Taking a break to wipe the sweat from his brow, he judged there was an hour's worth of daylight left. Despite the slow going, he would have enough time to finish the chore and make it back to the barn before the sun slipped below the horizon.

He was just reaching again for the digger when motion caught his eye. There was something stirring across the distant pasture, still too far away to identify with ease.

He continued to sink the post-hole, removing small amounts of dirt with each scissor-like action of the handles. Again, he glanced up, thinking he had heard the rumbling of a motor. He was right.

There, about 300 yards away, idled an ATV. The Texan's heart raced for a moment, as the two men standing next to the vehicle appeared to be wearing uniforms. *They've found me*, he thought, preparing to make a mad scramble for his own transport and wondering if he could outrun the law enforcement officials.

But they didn't approach. Dusty watched as one man lifted a pair of binoculars and gazed in the gunsmith's direction. *Maybe not*, he decided, and continued to dig with his back toward the onlookers.

The pistol was sitting in his ATV's seat, less than 20 feet away. When he heard their engine noise growing closer, he thought about making a dash for the weapon, but didn't. Again, his observers stopped – this time less than a football field away.

After a few moments, Dusty chanced a glance in their direction and found them still sitting in their ride. One man was again checking him out with the binoculars. There was an odd symbol on the side of the small off-road buggy, an emblem he recognized as the Tri-Materials logo. *Private security*, he realized, relaxing just a bit. *They're probably making their rounds and are so bored they've decided to watch a man do honest labor for a while.*

He was just setting the new post when he heard their motor again. This time they stopped less than twenty feet away.

Dusty looked up and nodded, mumbling a low "Good afternoon," as the two private cops dismounted. There was no reply. After waiting a few moments, he shrugged his shoulders and continued to work on the job at hand.

Without realizing it, Dusty stepped across the fence line, the position necessary to straighten the post. The dust hadn't even settled around his boot when a voice rang out. "That's private property! You're trespassing!"

Raising his head to first look at the guards and then scan down the fence line, Dusty threw them a look that clearly indicated he didn't see the problem. Both started walking closer, their pace aggressive and with purpose.

"Please stay off of the facility's grounds, sir, or I'll detain you for trespassing and call the authorities," spouted the older of the two.

Realizing immediately their intent was to intimidate him, Dusty ignored the remark and continued to work. They stopped a few feet away, their posture agitated and nervous.

"Threatening to have a man arrested for mending a fence isn't very neighborly," Dusty commented, never taking his eyes from his task. "I don't think I'm hurting anything by having one foot on your side of the property line."

He then looked up, scanning the two rent-a-cops with a critical eye. Both had pretty, crisp uniforms, complete with small patches and rank insignias. Both wore reflective sunglasses and baseball caps with logos that matched the emblem on the side of their ATV. Both wore shiny black patrolman's belts, complete with sidearm. Both looked nervous.

"It doesn't matter if it's an inch or a mile, sir. My instructions are to keep all non-authorized personnel off Tri-Mat's property. You are clearly on our side of the line."

Dusty grunted, sorely tempted to antagonize the over-zealous man. He stopped mid-thought, realizing that any action on his part might result in the county sheriff being called… a deputy who might recognize Dusty's face from a wanted poster.

Using a voice much more polite than what he was feeling, Dusty replied. "I think if you check the county ordinances, you'll find that adjoining properties are allowed an easement for repairs," he bluffed.

The statement obviously wasn't what the two men expected, and a hushed conversation ensued while Dusty continued to work on the hole. Eventually, the older guard returned to his ATV and picked up a small radio.

It was all Dusty could do to keep from laughing as he listened to the guard call his supervisor. The response that crackled over the airwaves was even funnier. "Hold on. I'll call the corporate attorney and see if that's true."

He unhooked the wagon and used the ATV to stretch the wire, all the while his audience monitoring his progress. With the final staple hammered into the new posts, Dusty set about policing up the worksite, picking up tools, and double-checking his work.

When he bent to retrieve the old posts, he noticed the odd indentations on the wood again. Glancing across at the guards' ATV, he noticed two scuffmarks on the unit's bumper. "No," he whispered. "They wouldn't go that far."

He eyed it again, deciding it was the right height. *Knocking down a neighbor's fence is akin to declaring war*, he thought. *Feuds have been started over less.*

Recalling the incident with Penny's husband, Dusty decided that might just be what he had walked into – a range war of sorts. The thought caused his temper to rise, any sense of self-preservation pushed to the back of his mind. He hefted the post and moved to the fence.

Both of the guards seemed shocked when Dusty started to climb through the wire carrying the broken post. "What are you doing?" the younger one asked, his hand moving to his sidearm.

Dusty ignored them, marching directly to their ATV. He held the post upright, matching the scarred wood exactly to the bumper on the front of the vehicle. "Well I'll be damned," he grumbled and then spun to face the two men, squaring his shoulders and spine.

"I'm not sure about down here in south Texas, but where I'm from, fouling another man's fence is a serious offense," Dusty said, his voice low and mean. "I don't know whose idea it was, or who did it, and I don't care. What I do want is to deliver a message. This is a dangerous game someone's started, and I'm *more* than willing to play. Mike and Penny Boyce are good, peaceable folks. *I'm not.*"

His little speech concluded, Dusty began to trek back to the Boyce property, intentionally sidestepping the two security men. The older one reached for his sidearm.

He was too slow… and too close. With one motion, the man from West Texas snapped the end of the post into the guard's lower arm, landing a numbing blow, and pinning the limb mid-draw. The pistol flopped to the ground. Before the antagonist could even think of reaching for the dropped weapon, the end of the post slammed into his midsection, a whoosh of air signaling it had hit its mark. The security man dropped to his knees as Dusty kicked the pistol away.

The second guard hesitated, stunned that the confrontation had spiraled into violence so quickly. Before he could react, the sharp, pointed end of the fence post was six inches from his eyes, Dusty's scowling face and weight-forward posture clearly prepared for a strike. "Go ahead, boy," Dusty growled. "Fill your hand with iron. I'll break your fucking neck before the muzzle clears leather."

The kid lifted his arms into the classic, "Don't shoot," position and backed away from the menacing post. "I didn't start any shit, Mister," he retorted with a voice a few octaves too high.

Dusty shook his head and spun, moving briskly back toward his home turf. He glanced over his shoulder twice, making sure no one was feeling frisky. He threw the post into the wagon with more force than necessary, the anger still surging through his veins.

He cast one last disgusted glance at his foes and then accelerated away from the scene. "What's this world coming to," he mumbled into the air rushing past. "That's about the most piss-poor security force I've ever seen."

Day Four

Vega kept a bug-out bag packed and ready for such events. In honesty, its primary justification was for a time when the authorities were gunning for him, but it had been used for regular business trips as well. Riding the elevator down to the garage from his 21st floor flat, he rehearsed his presentation to the cartel's top man.

"Uncle" or "Tio," as he was called in the Spanish-speaking world, was an internationally known figure. With an estimated personal worth in excess of 10 billion dollars, the head of the Gulf Cartel was ruthless, shrewd, and extremely aggressive. No one rose to the top of such a cutthroat enterprise without such qualities in abundance. Vega feared the man.

Notorious for punishing incompetence with slow, torturous death, legend had it that Tio often executed his victims personally. Vega had witnessed the results of his superior's management style, arriving at a prescheduled meeting only to find his boss eating dinner while seated on a stack of headless bodies. It was clear from the blood-splattered shirt that Tio had wielded the nearby machete with his own hand.

Now, Vega was on his way to meet with one of the most powerful men in the world. A man whose empire traversed into numerous countries and who possessed weighty influence on every continent. He wanted his presentation to be professional, fact-based, and to the point.

As he returned to his car, Vega tried to count the number of face-to-face meetings he'd had with Tio. In the 23 years he'd been employed by the cartel, there had been less than 20 meetings. Only a handful of those had been private, between just the two of them.

Accelerating the entrance ramp for I-10 east, he checked the time. He'd be early, the remote, private airstrip just over 90 minutes outside of Houston. Still, when Tio was involved, it was always better to err on the side of caution, allowing for the sort of unexpected delays so common in the nation's fourth largest city.

"God's gun," he whispered to himself. "With such a weapon, I could rule all the cartels myself. Hell, I could rule the entire world if it is as powerful as they say."

His mind raced with the possibilities, the adrenaline rush he experienced was as much of a surprise as his upcoming journey. *No wonder the U.S. authorities are keeping their mouths shut*, he pondered. If this weapon really was the cause of all of the recent destruction, they are wise to keep it under wraps. Who wouldn't want to possess such capabilities?

He shook his head as Houston sped by the windows, even the mere thought of treachery making him nervous. Tio was rumored to have a sixth sense when it came to disloyalty. It would be unpleasant if such tales were true. Still... to hold such power....

The ride from the Panama City airport to the Hacienda Polo & Country Club passed quickly, the stocky, scar-faced driver anything but talkative. Vega wasn't put off at all, such behavior common among the cartel's security staff, especially Tio's private guard.

The scenery outside the car's windows seemed more Mediterranean in flavor than Central American. The pastel colors, rounded architecture, and palm-lined boulevards tended to remind travelers of the south of France. There was luxury here, a mixture of plantation lifestyle and tropical charm that resonated through the more affluent communities. The passenger was well aware of desperate poverty in that locale as well, but the route to the polo grounds avoided such areas.

Panama was now considered neutral territory by the cartels. Ever since Operation Just Cause, the U.S. military invasion in 1989, the local government officials weren't bribable. During that mission, the

United States had sent in over 29,000 troops to depose the former dictator, Manuel Noriega, because of the dictator's corruption.

General Noriega had been a known associate of the Colombian cartels at the time. He woke up on December 20th of that year to find an entire Airborne regiment parachuting down on his head. Hundreds died in during the ensuing fight, with one entire neighborhood burning to the ground and leaving 20,000 citizens homeless.

Ever since that day, cartel activity was unwelcome and dealt with harshly. No elected official in his right mind wanted the 82nd Airborne Division to pay a visit, and they had proven it was a short flight from Fort Bragg.

In reality, the illegal behemoths could have circumvented even the most vigilant authorities and had done so in countless nations across the globe. Tiny Panama had been spared because the competing organizations had needed what most called the "Switzerland of Central America," a neutral territory where even the most acrimonious rivals could negotiate, relax, and even dine side by side without incident or fear of violence. It was the one covenant that all of them honored.

Still, everyone understood that the American DEA kept an eye on the comings and goings of area visitors. With their high-tech observation capabilities and practically unfettered access to Panamanian personnel, the drug lords kept a low profile while in country. *Leave it to the Americans to fuck up a good party*, Vega mused.

His driver entered the full parking lot of the Hacienda Country Club, circling to park inside one of the many stables that dotted the grounds. Before the vehicle had come to a complete stop, the rear passenger door opened, and Tio slipped in to take a seat beside Vega. The driver exited, leaving the Mercedes sedan running so the air conditioning could deal with the equatorial heat.

"I assume you had a pleasant journey," the boss opened.

"Yes, sir, I did. Your jet is a remarkable machine."

"Our time together is limited. My body-double is in the men's room, but even the burliest shit doesn't take so long. If I don't return soon, the DEA hawks will become suspect and send people to find where I've wandered off. Seeing us together wouldn't be good for your career in the United States."

Nodding, Vega got right to business, explaining quickly his recruitment of Freddie and the subsequent progression of the relationship. When he came to the part about the FBI agent and God's gun, Tio's gaze became intense, reminding his guest of a lion about to pounce on a herd of unaware antelope.

"So your source claims the weapon is real," the drug lord responded. "This correlates with other information I've received."

The boss then paused, clearly thinking about what he wanted to have happen next. "You've done well," he finally announced. "Take an extra 200K for yourself as a bonus. Use it to reward your resource if you wish. But now, you're through with this. You are not to associate with the type of activity that will be required from here on out. Right now, you're clean. I want you to stay that way."

"Yes, sir."

Tio reached across and patted Vega on the shoulder. "Enjoy your trip back to Texas." And then he was gone, a rush of hot, moist tropical air filling the void as he exited the vehicle.

Hank's pickup was waiting at the truck stop when the private tour bus arrived. The driver made an announcement that all of the passengers would have 90 minutes to eat, stretch, and use the facilities.

Grace had actually been quite surprised at how nice the trip from Houston had been. Most of the passengers were elderly, retirees who wanted to travel but didn't want the hassle or risk of driving or flying. The bus had been comfortable and quiet enough that she had actually fallen asleep.

She had used one of the no-contract cell phones to call her neighbor, Eva sounding a bit surprised to hear Grace's voice.

"Honey, are you okay? We heard about the incident at the Port of Houston and were concerned that Dusty and you might have been caught up in all that. We've been worried sick."

The attorney still didn't trust the FBI and didn't want to talk about anything over the phone. She decided to stick with her story. "I'm not sure what happened, Eva. I found myself wandering around Houston in a daze," she explained. "I had a little cash in my pocket and took a bus out here, but I need a ride home."

Eva seemed to catch on, the next question about Dusty never making it out of her throat. "I'll send Hank right away. He needs to get out of this house for a while anyway. He's not done much since his arrest."

And there he was, right where Eva said he would be.

Hank drove her straight home, the pair making only unrelated small talk about weather, the upcoming 4-H fair, and the price of grain during the ride. In a way, Grace was thankful for her driver's reserved demeanor.

Cooter was happy to see her, actually rising from his perch and affectionately wagging his tail. Grace had arranged for one of the neighbor boys to feed the old hound, and she was glad to find her pet's food and water dish brimming with substance.

Her first priority was to watch the news, actually hoping to hear nothing about Dusty or additional problems in Houston. The national cable channels carried little other than follow-on stories about the ship channel.

Next, she browsed the internet, just to be sure. A trifling blurb about a gas line exploding caught her attention, but she shrugged it off not recognizing the connection.

After browsing the stacked mail, her next task was a super-hot bubble bath. Then she was going to get to work on Dusty's behalf.

As she drew the water, a mental list of contacts was already forming in her head. Beyond the obvious senators and representatives, she recalled important, powerful people she had met in government and industry. Wasn't one of her law professors now clerking for a federal judge? Didn't one of her clients in Dallas now run a huge lobbying firm in Washington?

Grace smiled as she slid into the stress-melting water. She was happy to be back home, a strong feeling of wellness battling away what had been a hectic week. "Dusty needs to feel the same way," she whispered to the bubbles. "He needs to see his home again and enjoy familiar surroundings. I'm going to get him back here – one way or the other."

The hot liquid performed well, dissolving the stress and grime of travel. Grace leaned back, closing her eyes and letting her mind wander. Despite her desire to relax for just a few minutes, she couldn't help but worry about Dusty. The fact that the news reports didn't contain any specific information wasn't conclusive. *I hope you made it to wherever you're going*, she thought. *I pray you made a clean getaway.*

A squeak of a floorboard caused her eyes to snap open. She inhaled sharply when they focused. There, standing in her bathroom were three men. Clad completely in black, their chests bulged with pouches and body armor. Only their eyes were visible through narrow slits in their facemasks, evil-looking rifles aimed directly at her head.

"FBI," hissed the lead man. "Are you alone?"

It took Grace a moment to regain her composure, the intrusion so fast and overwhelming. Her first thought, after glancing at the narrow, claw foot tub, was sarcasm. The reply, "No, my security men are all in here with me," died before it left her throat.

When she finally began breathing again, one thought dominated her consciousness. *I guess this answers any question about Dusty making it out undetected.*

Mitch chanced a glance through the gap in the curtains, knowing the exercise was futile, yet unable to resist. He recognized both of the cars parked along the street, but knew the observation meant little. If the FBI were still watching him, he probably wouldn't be able to detect their presence.

News of the explosions and destruction in Houston had ripped at his soul. He knew instinctively his brother was somehow involved in the mayhem, the television news footage showing clear evidence of the rail gun's potential. The downing of the high capacity power lines had been the first sign that Dusty had managed to avoid the authorities after escaping College Station. Then the attack on the FBI headquarters had caused him to smile. He knew his brother's intolerance of bullying initiated aggression when the older Weathers felt cornered or wronged.

When the news stations had reported the number of causalities associated with the medical center event, he had been saddened by the entire affair. Deep down, he knew his brother was a gentle soul and would only have unleashed the power of the weapon if seriously provoked. Dusty wasn't a killer, and Mitch worried his brother would be scarred by the deaths. For some reason, his gut led him to believe Dusty had survived the encounter.

For a few days, everything had calmed down in Texas's largest city, Mitch secretly hoping his brother had escaped and was in hiding. When the airwaves had filled with the tragedy at the ship channel, he knew instantly that his sibling was involved. Again, there had been a significant loss of life, and the A&M professor would have given almost anything to be able to comfort his brother.

Since then, every time the phone rang with an unknown number, his heart had stopped. He couldn't help it, his mind always wondering if the caller was about to inform his of his brother's demise.

One of those calls had been from Dr. Witherspoon, head of the U.S. Department of Energy and a past associate. The conversation that had ensued had shaken Mitch to his core.

"I've spoken to the dean down there at A&M," his old mentor had begun. "We want you to initiate a project to recreate the rail gun's technology."

Mitch protested, "But, sir, why won't the president just grant my brother a pardon and set up a way to manage the technology for the good of all? Why waste the time and money to recreate a new device when we could have access to the original unit?"

"Your brother has inflicted too much damage for that, Mitch. The destruction down in Houston has turned Durham Weathers into political poison. No one in Washington would touch amnesty with a 10-foot pole."

Again, the A&M professor had objected, "He was framed from the beginning! I know my brother, and he wouldn't have harmed a soul unless he or his family was threatened. None of this would have happened if our leaders had listened to common sense."

"Look… Mitch… it was all I could do to get approval for you to be associated with this project. My argument only carried weight because you are one of the few people who have ever examined the device. Besides, it will keep you in the loop. It's the best I can do right now."

The statement had frustrated Mitch, to say the least. He wanted to scream at the other man through the phone, grab him by the shoulders, and shake some sense into him. Didn't Washington realize the technology represented by the rail gun was above politics or any single nation? Why couldn't those thickheaded elected officials understand the ramifications for mankind as a whole? Did party lines blur the fact that dimensional portals could provide free, clean, renewable electric power for the entire planet? The science behind it all could propel spacecraft, advance medical treatments, and revolutionize global travel. The possibilities were practically endless.

"You're flirting with disaster, Mr. Secretary," Mitch replied. "My brother understands the power of that device. He knows what he holds in his hands. If you put him in a corner, he'll come out fighting. He's already proven that. End this. Let me come and speak with the president. Let me address Congress. End this right now, I beg you."

For just a moment, Mitch thought he was getting through, but that hope was short-lived. "I'm sorry, Mitch, this is the most I can offer. Please don't throw away this opportunity."

Since the rail gun's discharge in the A&M lab, Mitch had been on administrative leave with pay. He realized Secretary Witherspoon was correct on at least one aspect – it would be good to get back to work. Besides, he was driving his wife crazy, moping, and wandering around the house in a permanent state of frustration.

Given there was little else he could do, Mitch rolled up his intellectual sleeves and dove headlong into the project. He didn't possess his brother's skills with a lathe or press, but that didn't slow him down. While Dusty could work miracles with steel and iron, the younger Weathers could manipulate computer based simulations and digital modeling with an equally deft hand.

At first, he was concerned he didn't have enough to go on. There was the film, video captured by both the cameras in the lab, and the little homemade movie Dusty had emailed from his shop. He had the test results from their test firing as well as what his brother had relayed verbally. That wasn't much, but at least he had enough to get started.

Then a file was delivered from the FBI investigation. The law enforcement agency had traced every purchase Dusty had made for the last two years. He found the model of Taser, cordless drill battery, and specific magnets used in the construction. The information helped.

His sophisticated computer software protested the design, basically claiming the unit wouldn't function at all, let alone at the levels he had witnessed. Dusty had overcome numerous barriers with his creation, most likely by trial and error. Mitch could see the external surfaces of the magnets, but had no idea of their internal dimensions. The binary code his brother had written to control the firing sequence was also a mystery.

Also in the file was the scientific analysis performed by the U.S. Air Force Space Command. They could detect the rail gun's discharge via its electromagnetic pulse, or EMP. Mitch found this particular bit of information interesting because there shouldn't be any such energy wave generated by the rail gun. Once he had entered the basic known parameters, he focused on this specific unknown.

This priority wasn't purely motivated by scientific research. If Dusty was still alive and fired the weapon again, they would pinpoint his location within seconds. Even an accidental discharge would allow him to be tracked. Given Washington's reaction to the whole affair, Mitch accepted that Dusty may be on the run for a while and might need to use his super-rifle. Being able to do so without giving up his whereabouts might make a difference. Besides, EMPs were a leakage of energy. Leaks were inefficient. Could he actually improve on his brother's discovery?

Day Five

The next morning, Dusty rolled out of the narrow, single bed and inhaled deeply, a smile crossing his face. "I knew the smell of that fresh hay would be a great way to start the morning." Physically and mentally, he was a bit sore from the previous day's work on the fence. The stiffness in his back and shoulders was actually comforting, muscles well exercised on a worthwhile endeavor. His anger, however, still simmered over the transgression against the Boyce's property.

His foul mood was enhanced by a less than restful evening. Sleep had been difficult, Dusty restless in his thoughts and hammered by nightmares. Grace and he had agreed upon a schedule that would minimize the risk of their communication being intercepted, yet allow each some peace of mind. He missed her already, and that was just the beginning of the troubling night. What he hadn't anticipated was a shootout with the police and then a confrontation with the local security thugs. Yesterday had been an eventful day.

He let the miniature shower's hot water soak his skin, a two-fold attempt to eliminate stress and wash the new-bed stiffness from his body. As he dried off, he realized his tension wasn't all about Grace and his escapades with law enforcement.

He knew his brother would be worried sick after the incident at the ship channel. *Hell*, thought Dusty, *Mitch might even be in mourning, believing I have suffered the ultimate injustice and an untimely demise.* Like most siblings, the thought of his loved ones suffering in any way didn't improve his mood. He would have to figure out a way to let Mitch know he was alive. The FBI probably continued surveillance on the A&M professor, so he would have to be creative.

His mental parade of self-pity continued, the next frame of concern being his son, Anthony. He had no idea what his sudden notoriety was doing to the boy's life or what his ex-wife was telling the lad. Just as he had avoided contact with Mitch, Grace, and Maria, he resisted the desire to communicate with his son, knowing the FBI would be watching the youngest Weathers like a hawk.

There was also a streak of self-pity running directly through the center of the daybreak's grumble. *He* was being displaced. *He* was suffering. *He* was the one having his liberty denied. While he missed his ranch and neighbors, what really bothered Dusty the most was the lack of a plan... the uncertainty of this very day, let alone his life.

Finishing the last of the so-so, microwave coffee, he decided to improve his outlook by doing a little investigation of the ranch. Already the walls surrounding him were producing waves of anxiety. He was a man accustomed to the outdoors and physical labor. Holding up inside of a prison cell-sized hideout just wasn't in the cards for the West Texas gunsmith. He would earn his keep on the ranch by more than just valuing the weapons. *Besides*, he mused, *I may be spending enough time in a jail. I should enjoy my freedom while I still can.*

As he closed the heavy wooden door to the outbuilding's apartment, the thought to acquire a computer flashed though his mind again. He made a mental note to ask Penny about it. He didn't need anything fancy or state of the art. Just something able to access the internet so he could look for work and keep an eye on the news. Besides, Grace and he were going to communicate via the web, and having access to the net from his room might make the tiny space seem more welcoming.

Penny's truck was sitting beside the barn, bed full of feedbags. His hostess appeared around the corner. "Good morning," he opened, and then nodded toward the full pickup. "I didn't know helping you acquire more pistol-money was going to cause me work," he teased.

She smiled, "No good deed goes unpunished. I was hoping my new ranch hand could help me unload all this. Did you sleep okay?"

"I was a little restless, but eventually got out. I kept thinking about what happened out by the fence. He paused as he hefted one bag on each shoulder, and then continued. "I don't mean to probe, but did your husband eventually call the EPA? Is that why they're so sore?"

"No. We called the Department of Agriculture first. When the birds started getting sick, we thought a virus or other disease was making its way through our stock. Our county agent, George, came out right away. He took one of the dead birds and made a few phone calls from his cell phone. He was supposed to get back with us within a week, but then he was in a car accident."

"He what? Was he hurt?"

Penny's face twisted into a scowl. "He was killed out on County Road 814 north of Laredo. They found his pickup where it had run off the road and struck a utility pole. The deputy told us they thought he had fallen asleep at the wheel."

"And the sample chicken carcass?"

She shook her head, frustrated, "I don't know what happened to it. It was all so upsetting at the time... I didn't think about it for a few days. A man who had helped a lot of the ranchers around here... a guy who we had all known for years was dead. By the time I thought to ask, no one knew what had happened to the sample bird."

"Did you call again?"

She nodded, "Yes, and they promised to send the replacement out as soon as someone was assigned. A few days later, some guy flashing credentials from the FDA showed up, looked around, and ordered us to quarantine our product. We weren't allowed to sell either meat or eggs. He took water samples and said he'd get back to us, but we never heard from him again."

Dusty's gaze focused on an empty point in space, mulling it all over in his mind. He was beginning to get a bad feeling about Tri-Materials, the timing of so many events unlikely to be coincidental or random. *You're being paranoid*, he thought. *Just because bad karma follows you around doesn't mean everyone else is cursed.*

Penny interrupted his thoughts. "Now it's my turn to play 50 questions," she began, setting down her bag of feed. "Why do you carry around that duffle bag everywhere you go? I noticed you never let it out of your sight."

Snorting, he replied, "Everything my wife's lawyers left me is in this bag. I've got some cash, a couple of weapons and some personal documents. When someone takes your life's work away from you, you tend to grasp onto whatever is left."

She seemed to accept the explanation, but Dusty made a note to be careful. She wasn't a stupid woman. Trusting, perhaps, but not naïve.

Glancing at the sound of a car coming down the road, a look of concern crossed her face. "We've got a cop headed our way."

Dusty turned and looked, his blood going cold at the thought of a confrontation with law enforcement. *Did those security guards call the police?* He cursed his rash behavior at the fence line.

The patrol car didn't turn into the driveway, instead coasting to a stop on a patch of grass on the highway's shoulder directly in front of the house. "What's he doing?"

"I don't know, but I don't like it. I thought you said you didn't hurt those two security thugs?"

"I didn't... well maybe I hurt their pride a little. I can't believe they would call the sheriff over that little incident. They didn't seem like the type that would enjoy explaining how a single, old rancher got the better of two strong, young bucks."

Penny snorted at her helper's description of himself. Glancing again at the now parked patrol car, she conjectured, "Maybe it has nothing to do with us. Maybe he's just setting up a speed trap or something."

"Could be," Dusty replied, his tone making it clear he didn't believe it. "Still, I would prefer to avoid the police knowing where I am. My wife's bloodhounds have connections, and a police report being entered into a computer would put them on my trail like a big, flashing neon sign."

Penny thought about his concern for a moment, "We can unload the feed later. Why don't you skedaddle on the ATV and stay out of sight for a bit... at least until we figure out what he's up to."

Dusty liked the idea. If law enforcement were onto his whereabouts, it would buy him some time. Besides, he wanted to get a closer look at the Tri-Mat facility. "Sounds good. I'll sneak back in a few hours."

The ATV started on the second kick and was soon rolling across the pasture. Dusty was careful to keep the big barn between him and the still-idling deputy.

After he was no longer visible from the road, he vectored in on the section of fence that he'd repaired the day before. He was relieved to find the barrier still intact, not sure of his reaction if the structure had been pushed down again.

Rolling slowly down the line, he noticed a few more dead birds in the pasture. The rest of the flock didn't seem healthy, their movements uncharacteristically lethargic. "Something is poisoning these animals," he mumbled.

The ranch's terrain gently sloped downward to a stream that bordered the north side of the property. Cypress trees, with their clutching web of exposed roots, clung to the banks of the waterway. It was a shady, tranquil oasis.

Dusty found a good parking spot under the low-hanging wisps and switched off the ATV. He dismounted his gas-powered steed and made for the bank, some part of the human consciousness drawing him toward the water.

The flow was steady, smoothly worn rocks and areas of sand lining the bottom and shore. He didn't see any evidence of industrial waste, pollution, or stagnation. "But then I probably wouldn't," he whispered to the flowing liquid.

Still, the scene before him was picturesque. There was a band of cattails a bit further upstream, healthy looking grass lining the creek's side a little further down.

He meandered along the stream, both enjoying and studying nature. The plant life looked healthy, and the darting shadow of a school of minnows seemed to indicate that the water was healthy enough to support fish life. Two crows were enjoying a morning bath and drink, further evidence of a non-toxic environment.

Then something caught his eye. Movement. On the opposite bank, 300 yards up the rise. He stopped mid-stride, and that decision saved his life.

The bullet's supersonic crack zipped past his chest so close he could feel the wake of air press into his ribs. The projectile slammed into a cypress trunk, the solid "thud" soon followed by the echo of a gunshot rolling across the prairie.

Dusty's body recoiled like a rattlesnake had suddenly appeared at his foot. His unthinking, natural reaction was to get his torso away from the deadly line of fire. He twisted and tried to back up at the same instant. The soft, sandy soil gave way, and he ended up flat on his back.

Some primitive instinct took charge, freezing his muscles, containing his body where it fell. He even found himself holding his breath. His mind began to clear a second later, quickly reaching the conclusion that perhaps lying still wasn't such a bad plan. Wouldn't the sniper think he was dead?

Several moments passed, Dusty trying to inhale at a slow, shallow pace. It then occurred to him that perhaps the assassin would come closer to inspect his target. What the hell was he going to do if the guy walked up? How long could he play possum? Would the shooter decide to put a second bullet into his carcass – just to be sure? This was maddening.

Less than a minute passed before he couldn't stand the suppositions his mind was conjuring any longer. Taking a deep breath, he rolled over and sprang for the ATV. Running half bent at the waist, his body was tense, expecting the hammer-like blow of a bullet any moment.

He slid like a baseball player stealing second base, coming to a stop behind the protective cover of the off-road vehicle. Or was it?

Almost in a panic, Dusty realized that the thin fiberglass body wasn't going to stop a high-powered rifle slug. Even the small gas motor and wheel probably wouldn't deter death by lead. The fear was almost paralyzing, at best causing him indecision.

In a matter of moments that began to change. Anger at the injustice of it all started filling his core, the rage building quickly. He hated the remoteness of the sniper's attack, the concept of a man not facing his enemy adding to his ire.

Chancing a brief exposure, Dusty reached into the ATV and grabbed the duffle bag. He yanked it to the ground and pulled out the rail gun.

The green LED illuminated instantly, its glow reassuring his shaking hands. He managed to drop the ball bearing into the breach.

"I will lay fucking-waste to that entire ridgeline," he growled as he shouldered the weapon. "I will evaporate that entire pasture and you with it, you son of a bitch."

He didn't care about exposing his head, bringing his eye to the mounted scope and focusing on the area where he'd spotted the movement.

Back and forth, he scanned, wanting desperately to identify a target. His wrath pushed aside any concerns over discovery, jail, or never seeing Grace again. He wanted to kill those who had just tried to end his life.

But the scope's magnification did not identify an objective for retaliation. Nothing but grass, scrub oak, and the occasional cactus filled the circular view through the optic.

"You cowardly piece of shit… you're hiding now, aren't ya. You know you're outgunned and outmanned. Come on out, and face the reaper you little piss ant," he hissed.

Still not identifying a target, Dusty's mood worsened. Burning, acidic fury filled his soul. He pulled the gun away from his shoulder and looked at the power level. His thumb pushed the control upwards, the red LED indicating 25… and then 35… and finally 100.

"To hell with all this," he grumbled, bringing the gun back to his shoulder. "I am so tired of all this shit. Mitch said I might crack the earth's crust. Let's see if he was right. Let's end all this right now."

His finger moved to the trigger as he centered the cross hairs on the distant ridge.

"Dusty? Dusty, you okay? I thought I heard a shot?" called a distant female voice.

For a moment, with the blood of revenge pounding in his ears, Dusty's brain registered the voice as Grace's. An image of the petite woman and her warm smile filled his mind. It was calming. It tugged at his heart.

He lowered the rifle, glancing over his shoulder to see Penny and one of her daughters approaching from across the pasture. *The sniper!*

He waved them down and shouted, "Stay back and get down! Someone just shot at me!"

Penny pulled the teenage girl close, and then the meaning of his words sunk in. She turned and began hustling back toward the house, casting worried glances over her shoulder.

Exhaling deeply, Dusty glanced at the weapon in his hands. He moved the power level back down to 02, and then returned to scouting the distant ridge. Nothing. Not a damned thing.

Finally deciding the shooter had scampered away, he ejected the ball bearing and returned it to the tube. He turned off the rail gun, watching the green LED fade to black. Still weary, he quickly mounted the ATV and sped off for the barn.

After negotiating the minefield that was her walk home from the bus stop, Juanita paused at the apartment door, something seemingly out of place. *It's quiet*, she thought. *Tessa is supposed to be home. Why is it so quiet?*

Shrugging her shoulders and anxious to get the hospital smell off her body, she inserted the key and pushed open the door. An extremely large hand appeared in the opening, clutching her arm with significant force and pulling her roughly inside. She never noticed the door slamming shut behind her.

Terrified, Juanita found herself facing three burly men spread around her living room. Tessa was there as well, sitting with a dishtowel full of ice held against the side of her head. Her sister's eye was already turning black, and it was clear the younger girl had been crying.

"Hello, Juanita," a deep male voice sounded. "My name is Victor, and I have a proposition for you."

Her first instinct was to help Tessa, but when she tried to move to her sibling's side, the man behind her grabbed her arms, holding her firm.

"Your sister will be just fine, Juanita," the smooth voice said. "She wasn't welcoming when we first arrived, and a minor accident ensured. We don't wish to harm anyone."

"Get out of my house," Juanita barked, rage rising in her chest.

"We'll be happy to leave, as soon as you've had a chance to hear me out," Victor calmly answered. "We know you work at Houston General Hospital," he continued. "One of the patients on your floor is of particular interest to my employers. We'd like your help obtaining information about the man."

The frightened woman glanced at each of the three invaders, knowing immediately who and what they were. "I don't help murderous, cartel slime. Get out of here."

Victor smiled, almost as if her reaction was anticipated. He took two steps to stand beside Tessa and reached for her chin. Tessa tried to recoil from his touch, but was held in place by the third goon.

Squeezing hard on the girl's mandible, Victor forced her to look up at him. "Juanita, do I see a family resemblance here? I beg you to reconsider," he said in a cold, vicious tone. "I would hate to see anything happen to the beautiful young woman."

Juanita tried again to go to her sister's aid, but the iron-like grip of the henchmen behind her impeded any movement. "Leave her alone," she hissed, struggling to free herself from thug.

Victor smiled warmly at the older sister, and then without any warning, clinched his fist and struck Tessa with a savage rabbit punch. The victim's head snapped backwards, her coal black hair flying in disarray. The other two men grunted.

"Noooo!" Juanita howled, doubling her futile efforts to escape.

Victor glanced at her and then grasped Tessa's blouse. With a single motion, he tore the thin material and ripped away the scraps. With her heaving, bare chest exposed, Tessa seemed to go into shock. Blood dripped from her nose onto the white flesh of her breasts.

"You animals!" Juanita screamed, "Help! Help us!"

In a flash, Victor was standing with his face inches away, his breath hot on her face. So menacing was his expression, Juanita abandoned her pleas for assistance.

"Stop this," he commanded, "Or I'll make your sister's pain unbearable and then kill you both. Assist us with your patient, and no one will be harmed. Refuse us, and I will turn my men loose on both of you. They will enjoy your company until content, and then dispose of the two of you. Do you want to see your sister violated in front of your very eyes? Believe me; my comrades are not so gentle. But you can stop this."

Juanita's eyes darted back and forth, moving from her sister to the man in front of her. Finally, she nodded and then whispered, "I'll do as you ask."

"Good," Victor replied, and turned to one of his men. "Take the younger one to the back and have her pack a suitcase. Watch her closely, but do not harm her."

He observed as they left and then returned his attention to Juanita. "We are going to take her with us, just so you don't change your mind. When our needs have been fulfilled, we will release her unharmed."

"But you said...," stumbled a confused Juanita, "but I said I would...."

Victor shook his head, grunted laughter escaping from this throat. "She won't be harmed; I'll treat her like my own sister. Now this is what I want you to do...."

Victor continued, outlining Juanita's duties. He never mentioned that he had killed his own sister.

Penny and the girls were waiting on him, staying close to the house and obviously concerned. After quick reassurances that he was uninjured, Dusty asked if he could borrow the truck.

"Where are you going?" she asked with a high level of suspicion.

"Someone shot at me from Tri-Materials, and I'm going to go confront them about it. Only three things can happen; one, they shoot me on sight. Two, they have me arrested. Three, we clear the air so you can get back to ranching. This standoff is ridiculous."

"You left out a forth option, they could just ignore you."

"I don't think so."

Penny clearly didn't think it was a good idea. "You could make things worse," she offered.

"How can things be worse? They had your husband arrested. They knocked over your fence and now they've shot at your hand. Short of burning down your house, I don't see how they could get much more aggressive."

"I'll give you a ride over there. Maybe they'll think twice if there are two of us."

Dusty shook his head, "No, that's not wise. If something happens to me, you're no worse off than before we met. Consider though, what would become of the girls if they had you arrested as well?"

She paused to contemplate that option, but then turned the argument against him. "Your ex is going to know exactly where you are if they call the sheriff while you're there. And don't forget, I saw what they did to my husband. His argument was almost word for word the same as yours... that is, before they led him away in handcuffs. The last thing I heard him say was, 'We can talk this through.' He's still rotting in a cell."

Dusty pulled off his hat and wiped his brow. *Maybe she is right*, he thought. *Maybe I need to cool my jets and think this through.*

Wanting to change the subject, he asked, "What happened to the deputy?"

"That's what we were coming out to tell you," Penny smiled. "He left about 10 minutes after you took off on the ATV. We were on our way to let you know."

Dusty tried to make sense of it all. Was the deputy somehow related to the sniper? Why would someone shoot at him? That seemed awful brash for a corporation.

"Do you have a computer? I'd like to do some research on Tri-Materials."

Relieved that he no longer seemed determined to rush into a confrontation, Penny smiled and nodded. "Sure do. Why don't we go into the kitchen? I'll pour you some iced tea, and the girls can help you get on the internet. I'm not as good with it as they are."

Ten minutes later, Dusty was reading the annual report for Tri-Materials Incorporated while he sipped his cool drink.

The company had been on the verge of bankruptcy just a few short years ago. Primarily serving the automotive industry, they specialized in making critical metal parts that required expensive coatings and exotic plating.

The next section Dusty read involved the miraculous turn-around initiated by a new Chief Executive Officer. The new head honcho was known as a hard-nosed, anti-labor, anti-regulation businessman who had held a variety of senior management positions in manufacturing.

The recently appointed CEO attributed the company's newfound profitability to the NAFTA trade agreement, the business friendly environment in the Lone Star State, and the explosive worldwide growth of technology.

"Our new plant in south Texas is manufacturing products for a third of the cost that was typical just a few years ago. We've added over

500 good-paying jobs to the community and integrated well with our existing facilities in Mexico. We hope to expand operations there next year," Dusty read aloud as Penny fussed around the kitchen.

"That's true," she commented. "Laredo was beginning to look like a ghost town during the recession. A lot of farms and businesses were failing. The new Tri-Mat factory was a godsend... or at least everyone thought so at the time."

"And now?"

"Pretty much everyone still believes that. They're now the largest employer in the area, and Laredo is building everything from new strip malls to a bigger, modern high school. Except for my chickens, the town seems to love them."

Dusty rubbed his chin, browsing the computer screen, but finding little else of interest. He sat back and then brightened. Turning to Penny, he announced, "I've got an idea. It might help us figure out what's going on. Do you have a digital camera and a cardboard box big enough to hold one of the dead birds?"

She had to think about it for a moment, but finally responded, "Yes... yes I do, but what are you thinking?"

"I have a friend who's a big shot up at Texas A&M. He loves a good mystery. If we send him one of the dead birds packed in dry ice, he might tell us what is happening to your flock. If they are being poisoned somehow, having reputable proof might give us leverage with Tri-Materials."

Penny seemed to like the idea. She produced the camera from a cabinet and a few minutes later, they were bouncing across the pasture in the ATV. It didn't take long to find a victim.

"I'm going to hold the bird so my friend can get a perspective. You snap a few pictures," Dusty said.

He bent and held the still-limp chicken, making sure his hand was positioned in a certain way while Penny snapped the photographs. "Take some of the surrounding pasture," he added.

They returned to the house, and while Penny printed off the photos and wrote a letter, Dusty packed the plastic-wrapped, sealed corpse into a box. They added a few printed images and the note, and then she set off to town to purchase dry ice and make a stop at the post office.

"Send it next day so it doesn't stink to high heaven when it gets there," Dusty advised as she pulled out of the driveway.

"Mitch is going to kill me," he chuckled as he watched her drive off.

Day Six

Agent Shultz didn't like the hospital's smell. Rather than elicit any impression of sterility, the aroma of disinfectant and floor wax seemed to heighten a foreboding sense in his consciousness.

It wasn't any surprise that he associated his surroundings with the most negative context possible. There hadn't been any chance to sleep for what seemed like days. The occasional fast food combo meal had kept his stomach from growling, but hadn't provided proper nourishment for the sleuth's body.

His new position as the lead investigator was proving more difficult than he'd ever imagined. It wasn't the workload, he surmised, but the constant second-guessing of decisions. *It truly is lonely at the top*, he mused.

As he exited the elevator and began the long walk down the corridor, he finally focused on what was really bothering him — delivering a truckload of bad news to his boss.

Arriving at the private room's threshold, he took a deep breath and braced for what was sure to be a bad encounter.

Special Agent Monroe was actually sitting up in bed, a paperback book being supported by one of his tube-laced arms. The injured man's greeting was sincere. "Tom! I'm so glad you stopped by," Monroe started, "I've been wondering what was going on."

After a quick round of polite small talk covering Monroe's state of healing and the recent heat wave, Shultz inhaled deeply and got down to business.

"Weathers is still alive, sir," he began, his tone evident of a drive to just air it out and get it over with. "He not only survived the incident at the ship channel, but also managed to elude us again down in Clear Lake."

Monroe's reaction wasn't at all what the junior agent expected. A look of concern crossed the older man's face and then, almost in a whisper, he asked, "Any casualties?"

"No, sir. We were lucky. He used the Olympus Device to blast his way past a roadblock, but no one was seriously hurt."

"Good. I'm glad to hear that we didn't lose any more men. We've had enough of that as of late. I had a feeling we hadn't seen the last of that man yet."

Shultz looked down at the floor, his tone reflective. "I made a call... a decision that now I'm questioning. Instead of throwing every resource available into capturing him, I ordered a low profile attempt to utilize the element of surprise. It didn't work, and now we have no idea where he's gone to ground."

Monroe actually smiled at his co-worker, his eyes showing genuine understanding and concern. "I wish I had a dime for every order I've second-guessed. While a certain level of introspection can lead to a healthy dose of wisdom, you can't dwell on bad calls. Everybody makes them."

For a moment, Shultz thought the fiery tempered man beside him was drugged. The calm, fatherly-like reaction the last thing he had expected. But Monroe's eyes were clear and bright.

"You seem surprised," the patient added.

Shultz grunted, "Let's just say I expected more of a passionate response."

Monroe smirked and shook his head, "Do you really think I made it to the top of one of the bureau's largest offices by pure hellfire and brimstone? I learned my leadership lessons the hard way, Tom. I have no doubt you did your absolute best given the circumstances, and that's all anyone can ask. We'll find him... we always do. What do we have to go on?"

The junior agent actually welcomed the chance to talk it through, surprising himself at how easily his thoughts started pouring out. "We know he purchased pre-paid debit cards and cell phones down at Clear Lake. We know he spent the night with Grace Kennedy at a hotel there. We've apprehended her at her property in Fort Davis, but she's not cooperating... claiming attorney-client privilege and a loss of memory."

Monroe smiled, "Figures. She's not stupid."

"I'm waiting on the Attorney General's office to make a decision on any charges concerning Miss Kennedy. But other than that, the trail has gone cold."

The two men continued to discuss details of the incident at Clear Lake, Shultz informing his boss that he thought Weathers was hesitant to kill. "He could have blown that roadblock to kingdom come, but he didn't. He fired it into the ground. He escaped via a stolen motorcycle, which we later found. He's also obtained possession of a helmet, which is smart as hell. None of our drones can see his face with it on."

"You'll get him, Tom. I'm sure of it. He'll turn up; they always do."

"Thank you, sir. I needed to hear that," Shultz said as he stood to leave.

Juanita saw the FBI man exit the patient's room, her nerves raw and flayed. She knew her sister was dead if she messed up, a part of her worried that it might be too late regardless of how well she followed her orders.

She reached into her pocket, pulling out what appeared to be a common ink pen. Grasping the device with sweaty fingers, she entered Monroe's room and found the patient sleeping. "Thank the Lord in Heaven above," she whispered silently and moved with measured steps toward a small table of flowers and cards in the corner.

There, behind a potted fern, rested an identical device. She made the exchange without Monroe waking, stuffing the voice-activated digital recorder back into her pocket.

It was only after she had exited the room that she took a breath, her heart racing as if she was being chased. Returning to the maintenance closet, she dialed a phone number from the cell phone Victor had provided. Only a slight shadow of guilt soiled her mind as she reported in. She would do anything to save Tessa.

Tio was listening to the recording for the third time. While his English was passable, he scanned a Spanish language manuscript while trying to visualize the meeting between the two FBI dogs. He wanted to detect every nuance of their conversation, dissect every inflection, and ensure his bi-lingual translation hadn't overlooked the relevance of any details.

When the recording ended, his initial reaction was a deep grunt, and then a sigh.

"So the weapon exists," he finally commented, looking up at Vega.

The cartel's financial manager was uncomfortable speaking of things that he hadn't seen with his own eyes. "It appears so."

Tio rose and stepped to the balcony, gazing absentmindedly at the beach below. The high-rise condo overlooked Tulum, Mexico, one of the cartel boss's favorite retreats.

The crystal blue waters and bright sand didn't seem to influence Tio's mood. Nor did the two topless girls sunbathing just on the other side of the thick, sliding glass doors. His mind was elsewhere, traveling down corridors that only he could fathom. Finally shoving his hands into the silk bathrobe's pockets, he turned abruptly and announced, "I must have this device."

Vega had been dreading such a response. During the drive to the resort and subsequent passage through the rings of security surrounding the condo, he'd been reasonably sure he could predict his boss's reaction.

It was rare that Tio ever changed his mind. The instructions he'd received at the last meeting with the cartel chief had been clear – he was to avoid any further participation in the matter. But then something had changed.

When the contents of the recorded hospital conversation had become known, the boss had thrown caution to the wind and ordered Vega to take charge of the project. The reversal, and associated risk of exposure, had been a surprise. It was a clear indication of the man's single minded intent to hold the rail gun in his hands. Such linear thinking was dangerous.

"All assets are to be utilized," Tio continued. "Pull out all the stops. I don't care what it costs or what the ramifications are – I want this weapon."

Vega was no stranger to superiors having impractical agendas. His six years in international finance before being recruited by the cartel had provided an eye-opening education into a lack of reality often shared by powerful men. Still, Tio was usually levelheaded. Brutal and aggressive, he had proven himself capable of ultimate violence while seeming callous, void of emotion.

Generally ruled by logic, he was most often realistic in his expectations. *The power represented by the rail gun is tempting,* Vega thought. *Even I would sacrifice much to hold it in my hands.*

"Our intelligence-gathering apparatus isn't nearly as sophisticated as what the Americans have at their disposal, sir. If they can't find this Durham Weathers using all of their available assets, I question our chances of success."

Tio spread his arms wide, "We have some capabilities that the Americans don't possess. Our network of businesses and people on the ground may provide information unavailable to the Yanks. They may have drones and sophisticated electronics, but we have people with eyes and ears. A lot of people. Utilize them, and find this man."

"Yes, sir."

As Vega rose to leave, Tio gestured with his head toward the women on the balcony. "Do you require female companionship? I'm bored with those two and plan on dismissing them later today. While they aren't unskilled, an hombre must vary his tastes or find himself stagnated. I'm sure they could provide you with an excellent experience."

Before Vega could respond, a sly grin appeared on his master's face. "It is especially entertaining to observe what they can do with each other," Tio added in a low voice.

Mitch eased his chair away from the computer keyboard and removed his glasses. Rubbing his eyes, he tried to erase the strain induced by countless hours spent staring at the simulation results. Sighing with frustration at the limits imposed by his frail, biological light receptors, he conceded there was no known treatment that offered instant improvement to his vision, opting instead to stand and stretch his chair-weary back. "My spine isn't doing much better than my eyes," he commented to the empty room.

Despite his physical condition, the professor's mind was still working overtime. He had abandoned trying to reproduce the effects generated by his brother's invention, instead deciding to focus on how to use the technology for positive, life affirming, non-destructive applications.

Without the physical rail gun to reverse-engineer, his super computers could only speculate on the shape of the magnetic field created by Dusty's revolving apparatus. Quickly realizing that was the key, he'd tried a few hundred different configurations without success. He could propel matter, but at no greater velocities than any of the common rail gun designs being developed by the military.

Mitch had then changed the point of attack. Instead of his sluggish, overworked human brain attempting to define the winning combination of shape, rotational speed, and configuration, he'd written code that would instruct the computer's much faster processor to calculate a finite number of possible solutions. After that, a process of elimination could be invoked.

It didn't work.

When the ultra-fast computer reached one billion different combinations, he'd terminated the program with a frustrated peck on the keyboard. It would take years to eliminate each possible variant.

Back to the drawing board.

But his heart wasn't in it. The irony of recreating Dusty's device at the behest of the government wasn't lost on the scientist. In fact, it flew in the face of all the sacrifice, risk, and suffering his brother was enduring. His frustrating encounters with the Department of Energy had proven, yet again, that Dusty was right. The technology would eventually find its way onto the battlefield, and that would ultimately result in doomsday.

With his vision partially recovered, Mitch rolled his chair back to the console. He paused for the hundredth time, wondering if he had done his brother a disservice by convincing him not to destroy the rail gun. Living on the run, seeing his face plastered all over the newscasts, and being target practice for virtually every law enforcement agency in the local, state and federal government couldn't possibly offer the quality of life Dusty had in mind for himself.

Mitch frowned, his intellect determined to prove his side of the debate as the correct position. Pushing all of those distracting concerns aside, he returned to the computer screen with a newfound vigor.

A broad smile creased the scientist's face a few minutes later.

"There you are," he mumbled to the monitor.

With deft fingers flying across the keyboard, Mitch began absorbing a series of numbers and graphs. Twice he inhaled sharply, the results displayed on the screen so astounding. Once he even whistled.

The capabilities predicted by the simulator were off the scale.

Human engineering had been producing usable mechanical energy from vacuums for over 100 years. Early locomotive engines used the expansion, and eventual contraction, of steam for a variety of applications. Modern day diesel motors still required a vacuum pump to function. There was nothing earthshattering about the concept of pressure differentials producing work.

But there were two unique characteristics about Dusty's invention. The first, and most important, was the fact that he used energy from the grid to produce a vacuum.

Mitch thought back to the small placard resting on his desk. "Energy can neither be created, nor destroyed," was the motto of anyone who understood modern thermodynamics. Perpetual motion, free energy and other such outlying concepts were often referred to as "howlers" by the scientific community, as learned men would often howl in laughter at some of the crazy concepts floated by the snake oil salesmen preying on the unaware public.

Accessing energy from the "grid," had been the latest buzzword used by the not so scrupulous, hawking everything from remarkable electricity generators to car motors that claimed to offer the efficient ability to drive hundreds of miles per gallon.

While grid energy was real, accessing it for usable work had been accomplished by only a handful of inventions since mankind had walked the earth. Gravity was a commonly known example, with mills from colonial times utilizing gravity's effect on water to turn their grindstones and produce usable work. Modern day hydro-electric dams operated on the same principle.

Sunlight was another example, used to generate electrical power from a star's radiation via solar panels.

But the list was short. Man's overwhelming utilization of fossil fuels was proof that large scale implementations were difficult, expensive, and thus rare. Dusty's invention changed all of that – and so much more.

Mitch was so astounded at the results generated by the simulation that it required several readings to overcome his disbelief. Using a primitive, unrefined design, he'd constructed a virtual power plant that would generate electricity via the rail gun's opening and closing of a portal.

A facility the size of a current-day bungalow could power the entire eastern seaboard of the United States. Five of the miniature plants would generate enough juice to satisfy North America. It would take less than 30 to bathe the entire planet in virtually free electrical current.

Billions of tons of air pollution would be eliminated. The cost per megawatt would be less than one penny each. Acid rain, ozone deterioration and other environmental concerns would almost disappear overnight.

But that was just the beginning. Drought stricken areas could employ desalination technology without the prohibitive electrical costs associated with current-day methods.

Mitch's attention wandered off the screen for a moment, speculating how much of the desert could be converted into green, productive farmland.

Affordable energy would be an equalizer like never seen before. Everyday life for much of the planet's population would improve. Third world countries with ready access to electricity would experience progress at exponential speed. Corporations wouldn't have to deal with the high cost of energy and could reinvest those savings into research and development, or hiring additional workers. Irrigation pumps could be powered by even the poorest of farmers. Transportation, medical care, manufacturing and agriculture would all benefit from clean, cheap energy.

How would the world's political landscape change if wars, disputes and distrust over energy were no longer a concern? If food production could be guaranteed and hunger were eliminated?

The professor stopped, realizing he could contemplate the possibilities indefinitely.

"This is how I clear Dusty's name," Mitch realized. "This is what people need to see and hear. This is the road to my brother's redemption."

Day Seven

The box resting on his desk wasn't unusual. Being a department head at a major university resulted in a large variety of correspondence - including free samples from vendors, wanna-be graduate candidates sending the results of their experiments, and the occasional thank-you gift.

The size and shape of this particular package was unusual. As had been the case since the incident with the rail gun, the box had been opened. He smirked at the concept of the FBI reading and searching all of his parcels and letters. "I should order some really, really kinky stuff off the internet just to mess with their heads," he whispered. "But on the other hand, they are saving wear and tear on my letter opener."

He pulled open the cardboard ears and looked inside, pulling out the neatly typed letter. "Why me?" he said as he read Penny's correspondence. "What would a physics professor have to do with dead chickens?"

Wrinkling his nose at the concept of what was inside the heavy plastic wrap, he almost dismissed the box entirely. Reaching to push it aside, something caught his eye. There was a photograph - a pair of hands holding a dead bird.

Mitch reached inside and snatched out the picture, tilting it toward the light to make sure of the details. His gaze focused on the hands holding the deceased animal, more specifically on the ring prominently displayed on the man's left hand. It was Dusty!

He couldn't believe it. This black and gold jewelry was unmistakable, their father's ring! It was a unique piece, designed by a goldsmith in El Paso and unusual in its design. They all had chipped in, buying the ornate extravagance, complete with a diamond encrusted "W" in the middle, for their father's 60th birthday.

Dad had pulled it off while lying on his deathbed, making Dusty promise to keep the bauble above ground. "I won't be needing it anymore," the dying man had whispered. "Make sure it always sees the light of day."

Dusty never took it off.

Mitch quickly dug through the box, hoping to find more proof. There wasn't anything else but the dead chicken and containers of dry ice. He then checked the return address and knew instantly where his brother was. It made sense that he would hole up down by the border. The relief flooding through his veins was enormous, a huge weight lifted from his shoulders.

Again, he almost dismissed the remaining contents as simply a cover for Dusty's message. Unable to settle down, he decided to double-check and make sure he hadn't missed anything; Mitch reread the letter hoping to find some encrypted meaning.

"My new ranch hand has informed me that you might be able to help us determine what is killing our birds," the letter said. "He assures me that you have access to the latest labs and equipment that may unravel this mystery."

Mitch's first thought was that the bird's corpse might have some embedded object or note, but quickly dismissed the notion. His brother had to know the FBI would be checking every package and letter.

He then reconsidered. Did Dusty really need his help? Did his sibling really want an analysis of the dead bird?

He wanted to see his brother. There was a strong need to look his sibling in the eye and make sure he was holding up. There were a thousand things that needed to be said and talked over. "The one way I can do that is to visit that chicken farm," he whispered. "Maybe that's what Dusty is trying to help me accomplish without the FBI becoming suspicious."

Mitch made up his mind. Reaching for the dial pad, he buzzed his assistant, "Get me Professor Middleton over at Agriculture, please. Tell him, 'It's urgent.'"

Mr. Vega looked away from the laptop, rubbing eyes that were burning with screen-fatigue. He stood and made for the apartment's kitchen. His action was more from a need to look at something, anything other than the computer's backlit display, than any need for nourishment.

Tio's slightest whim was law. Any member of the organization, regardless of his role, treated the man's requests as though they were biblical in nature and like the Ten Commandments themselves, carved in stone.

When the order had been issued to find one Mr. Durham Weathers, Mr. Vega had hesitated for only a moment. Tio wanted to know where the man was, and anyone who didn't take that command seriously was a fool. Soon to be a dead fool.

While Vega wasn't associated with the illegal enterprises of smuggling, narcotics manufacturing or human trafficking, that didn't mean he was without resources. The network of businesses under his control was significant and far-reaching. The problem was where to begin.

The first thing he did was order a file be created that contained all known images and information about the wanted man. The volume of data gathered in the effort had surprised Vega.

The car title loan businesses within his sphere possessed legitimate access to several state databases, including tax and banking information. In addition, the two law firms under his retainer added all of the recent activity available via the justice system search engines.

All of these sources were further supplemented by collecting what was publicly available on the internet. The *Houston Post* article, national news agency reports, and of course the numerous blogs and non-mainstream publications all contributed to a significant file.

Vega had been studying what was available, looking for any angle, unique circumstance or other key detail. Already, the man's image was being emailed to every regional member of the cartel's significant hierarchy. He just didn't believe that would be enough.

Searching the refrigerator for a snack, he pulled out a plate of freshly cleaned baby carrots and a tub of dip. Hesitating at the additional calories imbedded in the French onion creaminess, he shrugged and whispered, "What the hell. I've earned it."

Chewing on the fresh orange veggies, he realized his men needed another identifying parameter to narrow the search. It would probably be something small, unnoticed, or unimportant to law enforcement. If any major, glaring clue existed, the FBI would have already apprehended their suspect. No, this would be something appearing to be inconsequential.

Finding someone on the run wasn't exactly a new task for the cartel. In reality, the organization had pretty advanced capabilities, honed over the years to track down fugitives who absconded with money, turned informer, or were labeled traitor by joining a competing entity.

Hundreds of such cases had been pursued with a high rate of success. When huge sums of money were being passed around, criminals would act like... well... criminals. There was no honor amongst drug dealers.

Men carrying suitcases containing millions of dollars were susceptible to temptations. "I could disappear with this much money. I could live well in a foreign land, and no one would ever find me," wasn't an uncommon thought.

It was the assumption, "No one would ever find me," that the organization worked so hard to disprove. When the thieves were discovered, their demise was brutal, grotesque and very, very public. It sent a message. It established rules. It enforced loyalty.

But they had never pursued a man possessing a doomsday weapon. And what a weapon.

Dipping another carrot, Vega admitted he could understand Tio's unrelenting desire to control the device. It was obvious that the Americans understood its power and desperately wanted it for themselves… or at least to keep it out of anyone else's hands.

He chuckled at the thought of his boss possessing such power. All of the military and economic might of the United States would evaporate in a heartbeat. Their daunting Air Force, unbeatable land armies, and massive carrier battle groups would all become obsolete overnight.

Any city could be held hostage. Vega smiled, an image of Tio aiming the weapon at the New York Stock Exchange and demanding tribute. A similar mental image of Hoover Dam almost caused him to choke on his mouthful of food.

After a few sobering coughs, Vega again found himself hesitating to return to his search. Tio was already difficult to work with, the man's megalomania legendary. What would the world be like if he held ultimate power? Unchecked, unbridled and merciless? The horrific visions of a single, universal monarch, a tyrannical despot whose oppressive rule would immediately change the global political landscape. *God help us all,* Vega mused, wondering what end-of-the-world drama he had set in motion.

"It would be like… like… like the four horsemen had been loosed upon the earth," he whispered.

Then another image from his Catholic upbringing suddenly shot to the forefront of his consciousness.

"The Antichrist," he mumbled, now truly horrified and for once wishing he had paid more attention in Sister Mary Catherine's class on the New Testament rather than flirting with Angela Borino. Could the nun have been right? Is this how it happens? Is this the manifestation of John's Revelation that many Christians believe foretells the end of mankind? Will something like this rail gun provide the catalyst that allows Satan to rule the world?"

Vega's mind rebelled at playing any role that resulted in the unleashing of such apocalyptic forces upon the earth. He pushed away the carrots and dip, the nerves in his stomach no longer cooperating. Suddenly, the entire weight of the cartel seemed to find his shoulders. He couldn't let this happen.

Then a thought entered his mind. Tio was an animal, unsophisticated in his wielding of blunt force and managing by fear. What the world needed was a more refined hand to guide it. Someone who understood people, relationships, and commerce.

Vega suddenly felt better. He had an out. A plan. He would continue along, outwardly pretending to be the loyal employee, fulfilling his master's needs to the best of his ability. But if he did find out where this Durham Weathers was hiding, he'd step in at the last minute and secure the rail gun as his own. He could manage the world's affairs much better than Tio.

Walking back to continue his work on the laptop, he suddenly had an interesting thought. He would publically execute Tio, just to prove his own worthiness to rule.

"So you didn't think it was necessary to notify the authorities that the most wanted man in the world was alive, well and in your company?"

Grace looked at the lawyer from the Department of Justice and smirked. "I'm going to tell you again, he's my client. Even the most wanted man on earth has a right to representation. I have protection under the United States Constitution to meet and consult with my client. But even above and beyond that, I have a moral foundation – he's innocent."

The statement caused a genuine guffaw to roll out of the DOJ man's throat. "Sure he is, counselor. He's destroyed half of our nation's fourth largest city and killed dozens of law enforcement officers. He's as pure as the driven snow," he sarcastically taunted.

"Either arrest me or let me return home and stop this harassment. I'm not going to violate my client's rights or the privilege associated with them," she said calmly.

He ignored her statement, fiddling with his pen for a moment before looking up with a pained expression on his face. He reached into his jacket pocket and removed his identification, flopping the credentials onto the table between them. "This interrogation is temporarily suspended. We are now off the record, just two human beings having a chat. Why are you protecting him? I'm not speaking about legal bullshit or anything of the sort. Just as one citizen to another, I want to know why you are harboring such a dangerous person. He represents one of the most chilling threats to our nation... to our species... that may have ever existed. Why?"

Grace didn't answer immediately, her unblinking eyes staring hard. "He's not the dangerous actor in this play. You and your kind are. I know him. I know his values, morals, and heart. Our government... men like you... brought that violence on themselves. Shooting at Durham with jet fighters? Ambushing him with snipers? Attack helicopters and missiles? Really? If any person is going to hold the rail gun in his hands, I for one am glad it's a man of integrity like Dusty Weathers. God only knows what men of such high moral character, the men who run our country, would do with such power."

The DOJ attorney stiffened in his seat, "Our government has the right to protect itself. Yes, we have the occasional bad apple - any organization does. But we are *the people* too. Your neighbors, the person sitting next to you in church and the one cheering with you at the school basketball game; we're the government. There's no separate class or ruling caste. We are all the same."

Grace shook her head, "Oh really? So the IRS being used as a political tool – that's my neighbors? The NSA spying – those are folks that come and play bridge on Wednesday? How about police using Stingrays... those fake cell phone towers and never getting a proper warrant? That's the guy in the checkout line at the grocery store? You're full of shit, sir. Brimming with a fecal-thick belief that having authority makes you beyond reproach. Dusty didn't turn over the rail gun immediately because he doesn't trust our government with such power. I don't blame him. Your track record sucks."

His palm slammed the table, clearly indicating frustration and anger and... fear. Grace detected fear. His voice sounded with fright as well. "That's not fair! Your examples are tainted by your own bias and malignant with ignorance. We are fighting extremely capable and clever opposition. Do you think terrorist organizations don't utilize technology? Do you think organized crime hasn't heard of the internet? What about the enemies of the state? China, North Korea, Iran, Russia, and another half-dozen lesser players are all well-funded, technically savvy, and sworn to do us harm. We need every tool we can get to defend ourselves. I sleep better at night knowing my government is on guard, protecting our freedom."

Grace remained calm, her mind partially distracted, wondering why the all-mighty, all-powerful DOJ was so frightened. Finally deciding she wasn't going to solve that mystery, she responded. "I saw how your department cooked up a case against Hank Barns. I was arrested as well. I witnessed firsthand how you took innocent, unrelated events and stitched together a tale of fantasy against my client and me. So these tools you're so proud of... these supposed assets in the defense of democracy and freedom... they're being abused already. The more power our government possesses, the more totalitarian it becomes. You're not protecting anyone's freedom; you're restricting it."

Sighing, Grace's voice then became sad. "In law school, I was taught that there are so many laws and regulations, every American is unknowingly violating at least one of them every day. Any citizen can be ensnared in the complex web of federal, state, and local law. We are all criminals who only walk free because of the decisions of men like you. I now live in a country where freedom is granted at the benevolence of a select few who enforce those laws. No one elected you. Not one single person cast a ballot with your name on it. Well, no offense, sir – but that's not freedom. That's not liberty. That's not what America is all about. The chances of having my life ruined by men like you are greater than any terrorist threat. We've replaced one danger with something much, much worse."

The veins on her opponent's forehead emerged, his hands shaking with rage. Somehow, he managed to control his voice, keeping it low and threatening. "Durham Weathers is a terrorist. He is a murderer. He has destroyed millions and millions of dollars of property. He has affected tens of thousands of lives in a negative way. I can and will use any tool I have at my disposal to apprehend the man and see him executed for his crimes. If the stroke of my hammer misses the head of the nail on occasion, so be it. I will drive that nail home."

"Well, good," Grace smirked, somehow taking pleasure in the man's distress. "Now you understand my motivation in representing Durham Weathers. I'm just the tool to protect his freedom."

Agent Shultz glanced at the TV remote, eyeing the deli sandwich sitting beside it on the table with mouth-watering anticipation. Returning to the hotel suite, his temporary home, for the first time in days, he had been looking forward to a shower, shave, quick meal, and about 12 hours of sleep.

He almost decided against the television. Watching Hollywood's version of law enforcement was comical at best, boring at minimum. The real world just didn't work the way popular shows depicted and knowing the truth ruined any entertainment value.

Since he'd been immersed so deeply in the Weathers' case, he decided to watch some national news, maybe catch up on a few of his favorite teams. The shower and shave having been accomplished, it was now time to devour some food and then hit the hay. Despite almost 20 minutes under the hot water, he was still wound up pretty tight. He desperately needed to occupy his mind with anything but that damned rail gun.

Unwrapping the foot-long turkey and cheese, Shultz flipped channels between bites, hoping to find something that would distract him from what had been the sole focus of his existence for several days.

He skipped the celebrity dance show. The next image of a police car engaged in a high-speed chase was quickly bypassed as well. The foreign language soccer game held no interest.

He paused to chew and swallow while viewing a national cable news station, hoping to see some scores or a sports segment. Instead, the director of the FBI appeared after the commercial, sitting across the desk from the host of a nightly news show.

"Director, my sources are telling me that recent events in Houston are all related to an extremely powerful invention created by one man. A local paper in Houston even produced a story entitled, "God's Gun." In addition, I'm being told that this technology was offered to the United States government in exchange for some sort of guarantee that it wouldn't be weaponized. Is there any truth to that information?"

"I'm sorry, Bill, but I can't comment on an ongoing investigation," the boss replied, using law enforcement's equivalent of, "None of your fucking business."

"But sir," the commentator pressed, "the government's policies regarding this matter have little to do with the ongoing investigation. I'm being told this technology represents a tremendous advancement in physics and has the potential to generate clean, renewable energy on a massive scale. Why would our elected officials try and suppress such a discovery?"

"I can neither confirm, nor deny the existence of any such discovery, Bill. We are looking for a man suspected of terrorist activities... a man with known ties to foreign intelligence services. Anything beyond that is mere speculation."

The reporter wasn't going to let it go. "Something caused the massive destruction in Houston, Director. Law enforcement and your own bureau are being very tight lipped about the entire affair. My sources tell me that innocent citizens have been arrested and held in connection with case. There are even rumors that Mr. Durham Weathers offered to surrender, well before the last two incidents that took so many lives."

The head of the FBI remained stoic, "Again, I can't comment on an ongoing investigation. I'm not aware of the president offering any such pardon, nor would I make a recommendation for him to do so. We are dealing with a dangerous individual who may be supported by hostile foreign powers."

The host paused for a moment, the smirk on his face reminding Shultz of a predator who had just cornered his prey. It didn't take long for the newsman to drop his bomb. Shuffling a stack of papers on his desk, he began reading. "So you're saying that the Air Force Space Command's detection of at least seven events, described to me as 'miniature electromagnetic pulses,' has nothing to do with this investigation?"

"Where did he get that information?" Shultz said to the television. "How in the hell..."

The agent's boss, despite being ambushed on national television, didn't flinch. "I wouldn't be qualified to comment either on the U.S. Air Force's capabilities or on the subject of any such pulses."

"Aren't EMP events linked to the detonation of nuclear weapons, Mr. Director?"

"I believe so, sir, but I'm not a nuclear physicist."

The reporter continued, "I have the list of dates and times where these EMP events occurred, Director. It is interesting that they coincide exactly with some other spectacular news stories. For example, one such incident occurred at exactly the same moment as the high-tension power lines were downed in Houston a few weeks ago - an event authorities blamed on metal fatigue. Another pulse was recorded at the same moment that two Texas National Guard fighter jets went down. The NTSB reported the two planes had collided during maneuvers. A third EMP occurred at exactly the same moment that the police were attacked in downtown Houston – an explosion eventually blamed on a ruptured gas main. I could go on and on, sir. In every case, it appears as though our elected officials are covering something up."

The camera switched to a close up of the director's face. Shultz could plainly see the beads of sweat forming on the man's forehead. Still, the head of the FBI maintained his cool. "I'm sorry, Bill. Was there a question there?"

Now it was the reporter's turn to grow emotional. "I'll be blunt, sir. I'm seeing a trail of evidence that points to a cover up on a massive scale. And what's even more troubling is that I can't see any good reason why - unless there was a complete mishandling of the situation."

It was clear to Shultz that his boss didn't like the words "cover up," a deep scowl appearing on the FBI's head man's face. But he didn't say a word.

Frustrated, Bill turned to the camera and said, "In the next segment, we'll have the House minority leader here to discuss the new tax proposal being floated in Congress next week. We'll be right back."

Shultz switched off the television, partially disgusted by his lack of diversion, mostly troubled by the fact that the cat was out of the bag.

Despite 20 plus years as an FBI agent, he couldn't always walk the agency line. There were certain cases, narrow situations where he was forced to be nothing more than a simple man. A man who was forced to pay heed to his conscience and soul – not some law or a superior's wishes.

Deep inside, he knew the reporter on television was right. The entire case surrounding the Olympus Device had been mishandled from the start. Weathers had never been granted an ounce of "presumed innocence." The man had been judged a terrorist and enemy of the state based on circumstantial evidence, political innuendo, and...

Shultz stopped, suddenly realizing where this train of thought was taking him. It was fear that had driven Special Agent Monroe to react as he had. Fear of terrorists and another attack like 9-11.

He leaned back on the couch, staring at the blank screen across the room. The NSA spying, drone technology usage, and bypassing the warrant process were all symptoms of one thing. The agency's reaction to Weathers was a direct result of an underlying current that had swept through every federal agency since Bin Laden had ordered the planes into the towers.

The terrorists had won. If their objective had been to alter America, they had achieved their goal. Despite the loss of every major engagement on the battlefield. Regardless of the fact that most of the men who had ordered the attack on the United States were either dead or imprisoned – they had achieved their objective. More powerful than any elected official or political party, they had become policymakers. They had rendered permanent changes to every American's personal liberty in a single attack. No doubt about it, they had won.

When Shultz first joined the FBI, the act of gathering evidence via electronic eavesdropping was a major step, often requiring several levels of approval before a warrant was even sought. Now, electronic intelligence was harvested en masse, without question.

The use of military grade capabilities was never considered, not by even the Herbert Hoover. As far as Shultz knew, the agency hadn't even thought about using spy planes like the U2 or the Blackbird, despite that technology being available since the 1960s.

The Air Force had been launching sophisticated satellites for decades, concentrating those space-based eyes and ears on the evil empire of the Soviet Union. If anyone from the bureau had suggested using military birds for crime fighting in the 70s or 80s, they would have been laughed out of the organization.

Since the towers had come down, that was no longer the case. America had changed.

Shultz grunted, remembering the uproar over the leaked NSA papers and that agency's use of computer technology and the internet to gather intelligence. "If they only knew," he whispered to the empty hotel room.

After 9-11, America's ultra-powerful space-based technology was being employed within her own borders. The authorities were careful, utilizing small portions of the information being gathered here and there. Petty crimes, like murder, assault, and kidnapping rarely warranted access to the unbelievable amount of data available. It was a well-kept secret, even more so since the exposure of the NSA's capabilities and procedures.

Even a case as important as the Olympus Device required serious players at the very top of the government and military to clear the barriers. Other than rumors and the occasional miracle break in spoiling an anti-terror plot, Shultz had only heard whispers about the true capabilities.

Oh, there had been the rare mistake. A television reporter, monitoring the manhunt for the Boston Marathon bombers had accidently been shown images from one of the orbiting platforms. That video, depicting the heat signature of a body curled up in a small boat, had even been published as "infrared video shot from a law enforcement helicopter."

Shultz had used infrared devices – they couldn't see through glass, let alone the canvas cover of a boat. Some quick cleanup had been performed, state police logos added along with clever editing of actual helicopter footage. Few had noticed the security breech.

Was it right? Was it moral and just? Such questions were above his pay grade, but he couldn't help but wonder if the agency's actions hadn't catapulted a simple investigation into one man's war against his country's leadership. Would the Port of Houston be a smoldering ruin if they had just talked to Weathers? Would Schultz have over a dozen funerals on his calendar if they hadn't jumped to conclusions?

The interim FBI lead investigator knew what Monroe's response would be. He could just hear the senior agent's mental wheels turning, evidence of his intellect kicking into high gear. "We were not paying attention when Al Qaeda soldiers were taking flying lessons right under our noses. Over 3,000 Americans perished because of it. Every time we let down our guard, innocent people die. Someone didn't follow up on the Boston Marathon bombers, and we paid the price. Not on my watch. Not in my region."

Why didn't a man such as Durham Weathers trust his government? Shultz had spent a lot of time pondering that very question. Every indication was the West Texan was a common, law-abiding citizen. He was a political agnostic at worst, uninterested at best. Shouldn't Agent Monroe have investigated this citizen before unleashing the full force and vengeance of the United States upon the man?

There was now a pinprick hole in the government's dam of secrecy. Words like "cover up" had been broadcast on national television. It wouldn't be long before the term "conspiracy" would follow. More people would join the ranks of those who felt like Weathers, deeply distrusting their elected officials and perhaps even the entire system. How long before those ranks would swell to encompass the majority?

"The terrorist's victory grows more profoundly every single day," he mumbled. "Bin Laden wanted to ignite a revolution, and now a man from West Texas might just finish the job for him."

Agent Shultz wasn't the only person analyzing the FBI director's interview. In her living room, 600 miles away, Grace sat on her couch pondering what she had just watched.

Going to the press had always been the last straw. It was an irreversible act fraught with the potential of unintended consequences.

She fully understood the American political mind. No matter the subject, person or cause, one third of Americans would be on the positive side of the ledger, one-third on the negative. It was the uncommitted, middle-of-the road group that politicians, businesses, and marketers courted and cajoled.

Only rarely did these mathematical parameters vary. The list of exceptions included a very limited number of events where the population could be expected to behave outside this norm. Attacking U.S. citizens or American soil were sure ways to initiate public outcry by 90 percent of the general populace. Harming a child unified public opinion against the perpetrator at an even slightly higher percentage, but generally speaking, the country divided by the "one-third/one-third/one-third" paradigm.

Going public with Dusty's story wouldn't be one of the exceptions. She fully expected one-third to instantly demand his head on a pike, while the remainder of the population would fall somewhere between neutral and supportive.

The press had traditionally played the role of equalizer in the American story. Corruption, draconian policies, cover-ups, and graft had long been favorite objectives of the media. Of course, that news model had not been the norm for decades... not since the old days... when the broadcasts were about real journalism, more about searching for the truth and less about image surveys, target marketing, and ratings. She couldn't count on the press digging into the facts and using the truth to bolster Dusty's position.

"How would the average American view Dusty Weathers if I got on national TV and told his story?" she whispered in a hushed voice. "Would he become another terrorist like the men who bombed Oklahoma City? Or would he become a folk hero, swept into popularity like the lore of outlaws as recent as John Dillinger? Would he become a Paul Revere or a John Wilkes Booth?"

Switching off the television, she meandered to the kitchen and began heating water for tea. Given the turmoil in her world, a cup of the relaxing brew before turning in was now more important than ever.

As the burner's flames licked around the edges of the teapot, her mind wandered again to the topic that had dominated her thoughts for weeks – Durham Weathers.

Before tonight's broadcast, going public with their side of the story wasn't an option. The one article published to date, the piece in the *Houston Post*, had been dismissed by the national media as hyperbole and conjecture.

The fact that she would be going up against a very skilled and powerful propaganda machine wasn't to be sold short. Politicians, government officials, and law enforcement leaders were expert manipulators of public opinion. They routinely and deftly used the press as a promotional machine.

"The President of the United States versus Grace Kennedy, small town lawyer," she mumbled as the pot began to whistle. "What chance would I have?"

Dusty had caused the destruction of personal property and community assets as well as a mounting body count. His actions had directly influenced the lives of thousands of citizens, mostly in a negative context. The authorities would play that up, using the violence to rally public opinion against him. Before tonight, she wouldn't have stood a chance of being heard by open minds.

But now things had changed. The interview with the FBI director had cracked the government's façade. Perhaps only a tiny fracture, but an opening nonetheless.

Pouring the steaming water over the chamomile infusion blended with bits of peach and pineapple, she took a moment to savor the aroma. A half-teaspoon of raw honey resulted in a formula she often termed, "liquid happiness."

Carefully sipping the brew, she meandered back to her room to prepare for bed. "Do I have the skills to plead Dusty's case to the American people?" she questioned. "Can I overcome the spin-jobs, propaganda, and credibility of the DOJ and FBI?"

The answer, up until now, had always been a resounding "No." While there had been some examples of the government losing media backing, they were rare.

Cattle ranchers, a favorite American icon of independence and self-reliance, had managed to take on a myriad of agencies over the years to varying degrees of success. Native American uprisings were often viewed through a positive lens by the public as well. But those incidents were few and far between.

She placed her cup on the nightstand and pulled back the comforter and sheets. "I need the skills of a Madison Avenue publicist," she grinned. "I wish I could engage a personal image consultant to give Dusty Weathers a makeover."

Then another thought occurred. "If I do go public with this tale, every outlaw, tin pan dictator, and ne'er-do-well will want to get his hands on that rail gun. Plastering this story in front of an entire viewing audience might be the equivalent of signing a death sentence for Dusty, rendering all of his sacrifice and suffering for naught."

Taking one last sip of the calming brew, she reached a conclusion. "No, I'm going to work this in the background, out of the public eye. The stakes are too high."

Day Eight

Dusty poured the last of the feed into the dispenser, stepping back carefully to avoid hurting any of the gathering chickens. "I can go have breakfast now that you guys are fed," he said to the uncaring animals flocking around his feet.

He noticed Penny and one of the girls by the house and waved. They returned the greeting, and the older of the two motioned that he should join them.

"Good morning!" she greeted, obviously in a good mood.

"Fine day it is," Dusty replied with a smile.

"My husband's hearing is today," she announced. "I'm taking the girls with me to the courthouse. I hope to have my partner back this afternoon."

Dusty had mixed emotions about the news. He was just settling in and was unsure of what Mr. Boyce's return would mean to his room and board arrangement.

"I've finished the morning chores," he responded. "This is sure to be a stressful day for you - regardless of the outcome. Would you like for me to go with you?" Dusty offered, not really knowing what else to say.

Penny nodded and produced a slip of paper. "I've got a list of things we need from the co-op. If you wouldn't mind dropping us off and then doing a little shopping, it would save another trip into town."

Twenty minutes later, they were all loaded into the truck and heading into Laredo.

The Tri-Materials entrance was just under two miles down the road. As they passed, Penny couldn't help but glare at the facility, the massive building's silhouette projecting a foreboding image in the early grey light.

Beyond the guard shack and heavy gate, a winding blacktop drive lead to an impressive menagerie of pipes, valves, and storage tanks. The main plant, larger than a big-city high school, looked like some sort of evil baron's castle. The two skyward reaching smokestacks were the bastion's towers, each exhausting thin trails of some bluish vapor.

"Seems like an odd place for such a massive industrial plant. Not much else around here to help with the supply chain," Dusty commented.

"After the NAFTA treaty was signed, there was an explosion of growth along this area of the border. The oversized manufacturing companies found cheap land on both sides of the Rio Grande and a horde of small municipalities willing to provide tax incentives," Penny replied. "Most of the activity was closer to Brownsville. There are a few towns over that way that I remember as sleepy, quiet little farming communities. These days, the fields of corn, cotton and sugar cane have been replaced with acres of shipping containers and factories."

Dusty frowned, "I guess I don't know much about big business because I still can't make the connection. Why did the treaty change everything?"

Penny grunted, shaking her head. "They use cheap labor on the Mexican side and more skilled workers on our side. With the treaty, they can transport the goods back and forth without tariffs, inspections, or fees. If whatever your company makes requires both types of employees, this is the best place to do it – or so I am told."

Dusty nodded, the explanation making sense.

As they entered the outskirts of town, Penny fussed over the girls, straightening hair and inspecting clothing. "We're supposed to meet my husband's lawyer a little early. He wanted me to bring the girls to make a good impression on the judge. He said if we look like an all-American family, it might help lower the bail."

"Makes sense," Dusty replied, growing uneasy as they drove into the more densely populated area.

"Mr. Hastings is an old friend of my father's. He's been the one bright spot in this whole affair. He even came out of retirement to take the case," she added.

Dusty pulled the pickup to the curb and watched silently as Penny and her children climbed out of the cab. "I'll see you in a couple of hours," she smiled. "Wish me luck."

"It will be fine," he smiled, trying to quell the nervousness. "You guys look like you could have walked out of a Norman Rockwell painting, and that is sure to help the cause. Good luck!"

After watching the Boyce clan mount the courthouse steps, he put the truck into gear and pulled out into the light flow of small-town traffic. Penny had drawn a rough map for directions to the co-op, and he unfolded the paper as he rolled toward a four-way stop sign.

Figuring out the directions, he started to pull forward and almost hit two men who appeared out of nowhere, obviously in a hurry as they hustled across the street. Pushing hard on the brakes, Dusty managed to stop the front bumper just inches from the pedestrians.

One of the men, now upset, slapped his palm on the hood and bellowed, "Hey! Watch where the fuck you're going, buddy."

"Sorry, didn't see..." Dusty started, and then recognized the Tri-Materials security guard from the encounter at the fence.

The man knew instantly who Dusty was as well.

The two stared at each other across the old truck's hood for just a moment, and then the Tri-Mat security man continued across the street trying to catch up with his half-jogging partner. Dusty watched as the goon glanced over his shoulder, casting a nasty look in his direction. But he didn't stop. They continued on, quickly disappearing around the corner.

Dusty shook his head, whispering a half-felt joke about winning friends and influencing people in his new hometown. He started to cross the intersection again, when a sense of curiosity entered his mind.

"What are they doing at the courthouse?" he mumbled.

"That guy clearly wanted another shot at kicking my ass. Wonder where were they going that was important enough for him to bypass such a prime opportunity?"

Deciding he had plenty of time, Dusty turned at the next street, intent on circling the block to see where his antagonists might be going. He was halfway through the maneuver, slowly progressing down a side street while glancing right and left.

He almost missed seeing the pair of legs protruding from behind a nearby-parked car. Someone was lying on the sidewalk.

"Shit," he grunted, stopping in the middle of the street and throwing open the door.

He rushed around the back of the car and found an elderly man prone on the concrete. The old fellow was trying to rise up on one elbow at the same time as spitting blood from his mouth.

"You okay, sir?" Dusty asked, bending over to check on the injured man.

"I was robbed," the guy mumbled. "I think they damn near broke my jaw," he added, rubbing his face and chin.

Dusty helped the gent up, keeping close as the victim leaned against his car on wobbly legs.

"Did you see who did it?"

"No... no I didn't," came the mumbled response, the effort required to answer clearly causing the old-timer serious discomfort.

"Do you need a ride to the hospital? Should I call the police?"

Again rubbing his face, the man managed, "I was on my way to the courthouse to meet my client. Those two thugs took my briefcase. I'll fill a complaint there... always plenty of cops around."

"Is your name Mr. Hastings by any chance?" Dusty asked, now growing very suspicious at the circumstances.

"Why yes... yes, it is. Have we had the pleasure?"

"No, sir. No, we've never met," Dusty stumbled, not sure where to take the conversation.

After brushing off his suit pants and straightening his jacket, the lawyer glanced at his watch. "I've got to get going," he said. "The judge isn't going to be happy that I don't have my paperwork, but at least I can show up to stand with my client."

"Are you sure you're all right?"

"Yes... yes, I'm fine," came the reply. "I've not always been such an upstanding officer of the court, young man. This isn't the first time a fist has landed against my mandible. I'll be just fine."

Growing weary of the exposure and proximity to both a crime and the courthouse, Dusty decided to let it go without further ado. After patting the attorney on the shoulder, he returned to the pickup and drove away.

Two streets over, he almost experienced his second accident of the morning. A car sped past, completely ignoring a stop sign and almost t-boning Penny's truck. Dusty caught a glance of the passenger and knew instantly it was the two men who had just cold-cocked Mr. Hastings. He turned to follow.

The old truck wasn't a match for the sedan when it came to raw speed, but then again the streets of downtown Laredo weren't exactly a racecourse either. Dusty tried to keep back, but not too far back, as the dark green getaway car rushed through town.

It quickly became clear where the driver ahead of him was going. Almost retracing the exact route he and Penny had used to enter town, Dusty was amazed at the brazen attitude of the men he was chasing.

A short time later, he grunted as the two muggers signaled their turn into the Tri-Materials plant entrance.

He should have driven past, continued back toward the farm like an unaware traveler heading home. But he couldn't let it go.

He pulled into the factory's lane and stopped just as the gate was opening for the green 4-door ahead.

Dusty just sat there, 50 yards from the entrance, hoping the men in the car would notice his presence and realize there was a witness to their nefarious deeds. He watched as the muggers pulled through the gate and continued toward the distant facility. His voice of reason spoke up, telling the Texan that he should skedaddle out of there – make a clean escape from the enemy's home camp.

As the taillights of green car faded into the distant parking lot, Dusty noticed one of the security guards walking from the booth toward his idling truck. Throwing the shifter into reverse, he backed out onto the road and headed toward town.

He fumbled through the shopping list absentmindedly, picking up the supplies noted on Penny's note without really focusing on what he was doing.

The events of the morning had shed new light on the situation he had accidently bumbled into, the audacity of the Tri-Material's personnel both shocking and revealing at the same time.

Dusty struggled to plot a future course. On one hand, his survival instincts pushed him to flee. There was trouble here in south Texas, and it really wasn't his fight. Eventually, things were going to escalate, and that would inevitably draw unwanted attention to his whereabouts.

But there was a part of him that wanted to right the wrongs that were happening all around him. He had no idea what had put a burr under Tri-Material's saddle. There was no way of knowing whether it was because the factory wanted the Boyce land, or was polluting the area somehow, or wanted to send a message to the town making it clear who was the big dog on the block.

Whatever their reasoning, Dusty suspected they had the local city officials either in their pocket or cowed. The length of time it was taking to resolve Mike Boyce's minor offenses was a clear indication that the local employer held significant sway and influence.

He desperately wanted to talk to Grace about the entire affair, but knew the authorities would be watching her like hawks. The thought reminded him of their promise to keep in touch. "It's been a few days," he whispered. "I'd better let her know I'm okay."

He found the pawnshop where he'd sold the pistol without much trouble. A few minutes later, he walked out with a used laptop and charger.

The next stop was a local coffeehouse, entering the establishment reminding him of the last time he'd seen his brother in just such a place. With a Styrofoam cup of java in his hand, Dusty returned to the pickup with the password to access the internet. He powered up the new computer.

It took longer than he anticipated, but eventually he was connected to the internet via the free Wi-Fi offered by the coffee shop. Grace had made him repeat the address of a specific website over and over again, and now he was glad.

He entered the gardening site as a guest, quickly finding the link for the forum. Grace's post was a few days old, but he eventually found the last entry from GKinWTexas, a user ID for Grace Kennedy in West Texas.

"My lantanas are blooming a bright orange this year," the title of the post read. "Is anyone else seeing such a wonderful color?"

A few of her fellow gardeners had responded with various replies. Dusty had no idea what a lantana looked like, but started typing a response that included their secret word – Canadian.

"We are seeing similar colors here in Laredo," he started. "I'm giving credit to the cold Canadian air that swept through last winter. I was hoping for some red or yellow, but I'm just fine with the current bloom."

He wanted to say more, but couldn't risk the exposure. She would know where he was and that he was fine. Grace had told him that she frequented this and a couple of other forums on a regular basis. She didn't think the FBI would find anything unusual about the activity. He couldn't think of anything more to add that would read like an appropriate response from a fellow plant-lover and posted the message.

After finishing the secret correspondence, he began driving to the courthouse, hoping the attack on Mr. Hastings hadn't completely ruined the woman's day. He took his time, meandering through the side streets and avoiding traffic as much as possible.

"Why do you want to get involved in all this?" he kept asking himself. "You've got enough problems as it is. The entire United States government is looking for your sorry ass, and now you're contemplating getting involved in local dispute that's none of your business."

The pickup's cab didn't answer the question, so his conscience tried to fill in the gap.

Dusty realized he needed to do some good, to offer a sense of balance to the universe for the damage the rail gun had caused. The destruction in Houston... downing those jets and the loss of life were all weighing on his soul. "Death and mayhem aren't what I'm all about," he whispered to himself. He realized the answer, smirking at the simplicity of his mind.

Dusty wanted to help the Boyces because it would be an offset to the negative in his life. He wanted to partially right the wrong of his deeds.

"Run... run like the wind," his opposite voice chimed in. "You must survive. You must play out what the rail gun represents. You must make it back to Grace and Fort Davis. You have that right."

The internal debate raged until he parked nearby the courthouse. Penny had evidently been waiting and saw the truck pass by because she and the girls were approaching before he'd even finished backing into the spot. It was clear from the look on her face that things had not gone as expected.

After opening the passenger door and helping the girls inside, she gave Dusty a disgusted look and explained, "Someone mugged my lawyer before the hearing. The judge had to reschedule."

"Oh no," Dusty answered, playing ignorant. "It your attorney okay?"

"He took a punch to the face, and they stole his briefcase, but I think he'll be fine. He's a tough old bird." She paused for a moment and sniffed, her eyes growing moist. "Mike is still behind bars, and it's going to be another two days before the judge can hear our case."

Dusty shook his head, "I'm sorry to hear that. Any idea who robbed Mr. Hastings?"

Penny didn't answer at first, staring out the window as Dusty headed back to the farm. "I'm probably going to sound a little paranoid," she finally began. "I think it was probably those jerks at Tri-Mat. Hastings said his attackers bushwhacked him from behind, so I can't prove that."

Trying to play dumb and yet wanting to console the distraught wife, Dusty replied, "I don't think you sound paranoid at all."

"I can't blame every bit of bad luck or unfortunate incident on Tri-Mat," she said. "They aren't the root of all evil. Just because something bad happens doesn't mean they're behind it."

If you only knew, Dusty thought as they pulled into the farm. *If you only knew*.

The cartel always battled storing hefty amounts of cash on hand. Paper money was bulky, difficult to protect and always a challenge to process. For those reasons, they were always on the lookout for legitimate businesses that dealt primarily in hard currency. The crime empire would either partner with existing firms, or bankroll its own "company stores." Small businessmen were always seeking a source of cheap cash, and Tio's organization was often more than happy to provide it.

Food trucks, title loan companies, payday loan providers, gold and silver buyers and pawnshops were all prime candidates. While most of the firms providing such services were legitimate, family-run businesses, the cartels found those markets too tempting to avoid. Any business that exchanged goods or commitments for cash helped the syndicate transfer its ill-gotten gains into legitimate, bankable assets.

It was just such a "partner" that provided Mr. Vega with the first significant clue in the organization's search for Durham Weathers. A pawnshop, linked into the cartel's financial network, reported a motorcycle helmet being purchased on the same day as Weathers' shootout with the police.

Vega would have completely missed the obscure inventory item were it not for his searching for the keyword, "Motorcycle." The bulletins issued to Texas law enforcement agencies were easy to access, and it hadn't escaped the cartel's attention that the police were looking for a man who might be wearing such protective headgear.

The cartel acted as the pawnshop's financial partner, and it was an easy task to fax Mr. Weathers' picture to the manager. The answer was quick and positive – their target had been in Laredo just a few days ago.

In so many ways, Mr. Vega had dreaded locating the fugitive. He now had a decision to make, and it wasn't an easy call.

For the first time in his life, Vega was considering crossing the organization that had brought him so much wealth and reward. Such acts rarely succeeded, and when they failed, torture and horrendous death were sure to follow.

He couldn't keep the information from his boss. That was far too risky given that any number of people dealt with the pawnshop on a daily basis. Perhaps he could walk the narrow line between outright disloyalty and Tio gaining possession of the super-weapon.

He would downplay the lead... make it seem uncertain or questionable. If Tio wanted to send in an army, Vega would talk him out of it. He would use phrases like discretion, unwanted attention, and flushing the prey to bolster the argument. He, Vega, should travel alone to Laredo. He should investigate this lead solo. If it proved reliable, he'd call for support.

Repeatedly he played the conversation through in his mind. He tried to anticipate every question, move and counter-move Tio could execute. In the end, no matter how strong his logic, Vega knew it was risky. The cartel boss was unpredictable at times, and if the man insisted on sending in additional assets, there was absolutely nothing Vega could do about it.

With nervous fingers, he typed the message into the computer. A few moments later, a digital carrier pigeon was flying through the web, looking to deliver a message to Tio.

It was a very fast carrier pigeon.

Within a minute, Vega's phone rang.

"What do you propose," the unmistakable voice of Tio sounded.

"I suggest we keep a low profile and that I visit the region to verify the information," Vega offered.

"And?"

"If it is accurate, then I will notify you, and we can proceed from there."

The hiss of long distance communications was the only reply for several moments. Finally, "I don't know if I like this plan of yours."

"Let me remind you, El Jefe, that the Americans tried to apprehend our friend using force. It didn't work out so well. I believe a more measured approach might work to our advantage, but there is no way to be sure without additional information. This is why I believe it best to carefully scout the area."

"I don't care about methods or processes or measured approaches. I want that fucking weapon, and I don't care what it takes. Do it."

"I'll be in touch," Vega responded, trying to keep the relief out of his voice.

"Make it soon," came the threatening response, and then the line went dead.

He busied himself in the workshop, examining weapons and using his new laptop to reference information concerning some of the more eccentric models via the net. Working with what he considered fine instruments of craftsmanship, Dusty normally found his gunsmithing activities relaxing and therapeutic.

This afternoon, it wasn't working.

It was clear that Tri-Materials was a bully, flexing its influence that no doubt involved hefty contributions to the local tax base, various elected officials, and probably a little under the table gift-giving. They wouldn't be the first corporation to dole out a little cash in exchange for a favor here or there, and Tri-Mat probably wouldn't be the last.

Given his situation as an outlaw, none of that should matter. He didn't like it, wished it wasn't so, but in reality, it wasn't his problem. "You've got enough trouble in your life right now, cowboy," he mumbled to himself.

Still, it tasked him. He couldn't help but feel anger over men who hurt other people for the sake of profit. Dusty had zero issue with corporations making money. He didn't care how much chief executives took home. But when Mike Boyce was in jail while his wife and daughters suffered, that was just plain wrong. Shooting at your neighbors after knocking over their fence wasn't exactly model corporate behavior.

Then there was the death of the county agent, which Dusty now assumed was no accident. Clearly, the boys at Tri-Mat were playing a serious game, and murder didn't seem to be outside the rules. Even if that death was purely coincidental, anyone capable of beating up an old man in broad daylight wasn't to be taken lightly.

Wiping down the barrel of a WWII era bolt-action with an oily rag, his anger continued to simmer. Glancing over at the always-nearby rail gun, he grunted at the thought of simply leveling the neighboring plant. One shot on a modest power setting would eliminate the problem, at least until the company collected its insurance and rebuilt. He even went so far as to plot the facility's demise in the wee hours of the morning so there wouldn't be any workers inside.

But that would only provide a temporary solution and most likely bring the entire weight of the federal government down on his head.

Mike Boyce would still be in jail, and Tri-Materials' money and muscle would still be riding roughshod around Laredo and the surrounding county.

The fantasy of a smoldering heap of Tri-Mat ruins caused a dichotomy of swelling emotions to fill the gunsmith's chest. The mere thought of destroying more property and using violence to impart his sense of right and wrong went against his grain. The employees of the plant, probably innocent citizens of the surrounding community, would be the ones who suffered most. The resulting financial hardship of the unemployed workers would create a whole group of people like the Boyces.

Besides, the problem was really a broken system of justice and governance. Tri-Mat was just a small example of a flawed environment, the company's achievements merely symptoms of a deeper core of decay. Dusty was reminded of Winston Churchill's famous quote; *Democracy is the worst form of government except for all the others that have been tried.*

Again, Dusty glanced at the rail gun. "Perhaps I'm thinking on too small a level," he whispered. "Maybe I should pack up and head to Washington. Maybe my little invention can intimidate some sense into our elected officials."

As he cleaned the breach of a Remington 700 hunting rifle, Dusty let his mind fill with fantasy; daydreaming of a trip to the nation's capital. He would have to do something spectacular to get everyone's attention and enjoyed the mental process of selecting a target.

The White House? No, too much fine art and wonderful historical pieces were there. The same could be said of the Smithsonian and its endless halls of artifacts.

The capital building? A possibility.

The Pentagon? "Ah hah!" he declared, finally making a decision as he selected a revolver from the cabinet. "I'll call it in like a bomb scare and give them all 10 minutes to get out," he said to the empty barn. He'd give anything to see the faces of senators, members of Congress, and other politicians, as they gazed upon the smoldering ruins of the nation's premier icon of American military might.

"That would get their attention," he decided. "That would force them to listen."

A malfunctioning trigger interrupted his mental conquest of the world's only superpower, the complex device requiring his full attention. After ten minutes, he had the old Smith and Wesson revolver fixed and returned to his campaign to right the wrongs of his country.

"What would you say to them?" he wondered aloud. "What would you demand they change?"

He paused after a few moments, surprised that he couldn't think up any quick fixes or immediate cures. Every concept that entered his mind seemed questionable or easily circumvented by political spin.

Glancing again at the rail gun, he mumbled, "If power corrupts, you're not doing a very good job. I'm supposed to believe my slightest whim should be the law of the land. About now I should be thinking my ideas are irreproachable and damn near god-like."

The rail gun didn't respond to the criticism.

After returning the weapons to their safe-closet, Dusty picked up his invention and grunted, "Still, it might not do any harm to rattle Washington's cage."

The spell was broken by Penny's voice announcing that supper was ready. Dusty folded his invention's stock and stuffed it back inside the duffle before heading into the house.

Mr. Vega found the manager at the pawnshop very helpful. The broker remembered the guy who had cost him one sweet deal because of his big mouth and encyclopedic-like knowledge of the Colt pistols. *That would make sense for a gunsmith*, Vega thought.

The store's security cameras verified the target's identity beyond any doubt, with the parking lot footage providing the next clue. Weathers had gotten a ride with the woman trying to pawn the pistol.

"She lives on a poultry farm outside of town," explained the shop's manager. "That's about all I know."

Less than 30 minutes later, Vega had an address via the truck's license plate.

He drove past the Boyce homestead twice, taking his time while plotting the next move. He needed to find out where the woman had dropped off her passenger from a few days ago. *Follow the breadcrumbs*, he mused.

On the second pass, he decided a direct approach was best.

He pulled one the many business cards from the console, his role of managing investments for the cartel providing the benefit of numerous professional associations. Next, he pulled a picture of Weathers from the file and turned into the farm's drive.

Dusty and Penny reacted differently to the knock at the front door.

Wiping her face with a napkin from her lap, Penny glanced up and said, "Who could that be at this hour," and scooted her chair back to answer the call.

Dusty immediately reached for the ever-present duffle bag.

Penny glanced through the glass and saw a nicely dressed stranger holding a business card. The car in the driveway was a newer model import. "Who is it?" she called.

"My name is Carmine Vega," came the response. "I'm an insurance adjuster for Rio Grande Holdings Limited and would like to speak to you for just a moment, please."

Penny opened the door, the latched chain-lock providing just enough space to peek out. "Yes?"

Vega smiled broadly, holding up a picture of Durham Weathers. "Ma'am, my company is trying to locate this man. It has come to my attention that he was seen with you in Laredo just a few days ago, and it is very important that I speak with him."

For once, Dusty's cover story paid off. Penny's immediately thought was that Vega was one of the ex-wife's attorneys looking for the wayward husband. "Yes... yes I gave that man a ride a few days ago. I don't know anything about him though," she lied.

But Penny wasn't good at deception. Vega sensed her dishonesty, barely managing to keep his expression neutral. "Ma'am, could you tell me where you dropped him off? He is the beneficiary of a policy that could potentially pay a significant amount of money, and it my job to find him."

That's the oldest scam in the book, Penny thought, almost disappointed that the man on the other side of the threshold considered her so stupid. "I dropped him off in downtown Laredo... at the bus station."

He's here, Vega knew instantly. *She's protecting him for some reason.*

"Very well. Thank you for your time," he replied.

Penny watched the visitor walk off the porch and then shut the door. She double-checked the lock.

Dusty watched the stranger walk back to his car, returning the pistol to the unzipped duffle bag lying beside him on the ground. As soon as the visitor's taillights had disappeared in the distance, he stepped out of the bushes beside the front porch and returned to the dinner table.

"Did you hear all of that?" Penny asked calmly.

"Yes… and thank you," he responded. "I'm sorry my past is catching up with me."

"He wasn't a very good liar," she said. "I could see through that cockamamie story right away."

Dusty nodded with a grimace. "Clearly one of my ex-wife's lawyers, or at least one of their henchmen," he played along while his mind was screaming over the danger presented by the visitor. *Who was that guy? How did he find me? Was he FBI? A Tri-Materials goon?*

No longer possessing an appetite, Dusty toyed with his plate for a few minutes and then rose to excuse himself. "Thank you for the fine meal, Penny," he announced calmly. "I'm going to turn in early. Nite."

In reality, he was expecting law enforcement SWAT teams to descend on the ranch at any moment. Heading back to the barn, he couldn't help but scan left and right, looking for men in uniform or worse, yet, the muzzle flash of a sniper rifle.

The rough plank walls of the apartment provided some relief, especially after he verified the structure unoccupied. His mind raced with possibilities and paranoia.

He had hurt the authorities badly during their last two attempts to arrest him. Were they finally wising up and being cautious? As his mind replayed the recent visit by their "guest," he didn't sense that the man on the front porch was law enforcement.

He had to be someone from Tri-Materials scouting for information, Dusty decided. "The FBI would know better than to give me warning," he whispered to the rail gun, now unfolded, powered up, and resting on his lap.

Vega managed the outskirts of Laredo and found a hotel.

After checking in, he absentmindedly washed his face and hands, trying to plot the chess moves that would dictate the path of his future. If he didn't play a masterful game, Tio would insure that his life came to a premature, excruciating checkmate.

He had to inform the boss of his discovery, at least the confirmation that Weathers had been in Laredo. Vega didn't normally work on such projects and had no idea how in-depth Tio's contacts penetrated the organization. For all Vega knew, the pawnshop manager was Tio's cousin and on the phone with the cartel leader even now.

Setting up his laptop, Vega entered the appropriate codes and passwords. A few minutes later, an innocent-looking message was on its way across the internet. Encrypted in the text was a phone number.

It was 20 minutes later that his clean cell phone rang. He didn't need to guess who it was.

"Good evening, sir," Vega answered, trying to keep his tone calm and neutral.

There was music playing in the background, the sound of a crowd making it difficult to hear Tio clearly. "What have you got for me?"

Clearing his throat, Vega answered, "The target was indeed in Laredo. I have managed to account for his whereabouts as of two days ago. I'm still following up on some possibilities."

"Good. Do you need help?"

Vega had anticipated the question. If he weren't planning to abscond with the device, he would have normally welcomed the help. He had to play the role of the dutiful employee for a while longer.

"Yes, sir. I would like two or three good heads who will follow instructions. I don't need any vaqueros... but men who will do only as I ask. I feel like we should continue to pursue this man while maintaining a low profile."

For the few moments it took Tio to respond, Vega thought he'd made some mistake. "I'm not so sure I like this approach," the cartel boss began. "It seems like you are being very shy about finding that man."

I'm not planning any subterfuge, Vega repeated in his mind. *I'm not doing anything underhanded. How would I react to Tio's statement?* Finally, he offered, "I'm open to suggestions, sir. Would you prefer I take a different course?"

That seemed to cause the boss additional pause. His eventual answer was a relief. "No... no I suppose not. I will have three men drive down from Houston and join you. Their faces shouldn't be known to anyone in Laredo."

Vega thanked his boss after providing the hotel's name and address. Disconnecting the call, he noticed that his hands were shaking. "If I'm that scared of Tio before he controls the rail gun, what will it be like after the man wields that sort of power?"

The whole world will be shaking, he realized.

Tio handed the phone to the closest security man, a scowl painted on his face. "Is everything okay, boss?" the burly guard asked.

"I'm not sure," came the response. "My intuition warns that something is wrong in Texas."

His gaze moved across the orchestra of lights and sounds emitting from the swank nightclub. Despite the early hour, the place was already half full of well-dressed people out for a good time. Scantily clad waitresses moved briskly here and there, trays of libations poised above their shoulders while the high-tech sound system thumped the latest dance music.

But Tio really wasn't looking at the crowd or the club. His mind was currently in Laredo, the place that was now to blame for his sudden change of mood.

"I'm not up for partying tonight," the cartel boss informed his security man. "Let's head back to the condo. I've got some work to do."

With only a nod, the big man raised his wrist and spoke into a microphone. "We're leaving," he informed the rest of his team.

The broadcast initiated several immediate responses. At four other locations scattered around the club, Tio's significant security force began heading toward the door. A block down the street, two up-armored SUVs revved their engines. A third vehicle would follow soon after gathering the outer ring of protection scattered about the neighborhood. When Tio moved, he was shielded by a team that rivaled any head of state in numbers, quality, and technology.

But the world wasn't the drug lord's oyster, and it troubled him deeply.

He would have loved to use the luxury transport's cell phone during the drive back to the condo, but he couldn't. He knew American satellites and drones were always overhead. These robotic foes were equipped with digitalized voice recordings that would match his voiceprint just as assuredly as a computer could match a fingerprint.

Every communication, transmission, and spoken sentence required extreme diligence and caution. Today, he was riding in the comfort of his personal vehicles, but that was only possible when traveling in his hometown. Rentals, borrowed cars, and sometimes even stolen units were required when he was on the road.

"I can't enjoy the fruits of my labor," Tio complained to his bodyguard. "The Americans are crafty and have unlimited budgets. They hide under every rock and behind every bush, and it sickens me. If this next endeavor pays off, I'm going to turn the tables on them. They'll pay… and pay dearly."

The security man nodded, but didn't comment. While he'd heard Tio express his discontent about the American authorities a hundred times before, there was a new vigor in the man's bitching. Clearly, the boss was excited about something, but that wasn't any of his business.

"Look at you, my friend," the cartel lord continued, gazing out at the passing scenery. "As long as you keep me alive, your family is well taken care of, and you want for little in life. But can you enjoy it? Can you truly relish in your success? No. You've never sold an ounce of cocaine. You've never smuggled a single person across the border, and yet to the Yankees, you are a criminal. They would throw your ass into a prison to rot just the same as they would me."

Again, the only response was a nod.

Tio grunted, his anger growing deeper by the minute. "I'm sick of it," he hissed. "I tire of the constant restrictions, fear, and paranoia. Pull out your cell phone… pull it out right now."

Confused, but conditioned to following orders, the bodyguard reached inside his jacket and did as he was told.

Tio pointed at what appeared to be a small package wrapped in common aluminum foil. A harsh, barking laugh filled the SUV's cabin. "Is that your cell phone or leftovers from dinner?" he teased.

"But sir," the embarrassed man responded, "you know we must keep our phones wrapped in tin foil. It's the only way of making sure they can't be tampered with or tracked."

174

The boss nodded and then spread his hands wide. "Don't you see how absurd it all is? You are employed by one of the world's wealthiest men, my friend. If our organization were a company, we would be listed in the Dow Jones industrial average based simply on our profits. Yet, our key employees must wrap their cell phones in common kitchen tin foil like yesterday's sandwich. I remember the day we discovered that little trick. We were all so happy! We could defeat the Americans and their multi-billion dollar eavesdropping equipment with a peso's worth of kitchen wrap. But now I'm sick of it. I want to pull out my phone and make a call without worrying about black helicopters appearing overhead."

After the bodyguard made sure his boss was finished, he stuffed the phone back into his pocket. Tio had a point. He usually did.

As their driver turned into the high-rise condo, Tio made a decision. He wasn't going to lose a moment's sleep over the true motivations of his man in Laredo, or whether Vega ultimately succeeded or failed. He was going to do things his way, and that meant force. A lot of blunt force.

He had a plan. It had begun as a work of pure self-indulgent fantasy, a mental equalizer to offset the extreme pressure of running one of the world's most powerful illegal organizations. Just the exercise alone provided Tio a level of comfort.

As time passed, he reworked and refined various scenarios, always with the same basic motivation – to give the Americans payback. He wanted to hurt his foes. Make them suffer. Shake their all-confident, highbrow demeanor to its very foundation.

Eventually, he'd exposed his musings to some of the professional military men in the employ of the cartel. They had gladly participated in what they termed "sandbox maneuvers," helping Tio understand that logistics, organization, and proper intelligence were just as important to military operations as they were to the business conducted by the cartel.

As the head of his security team opened the door, Tio looked up and demanded, "I want my captains here… tonight. I don't care what it takes, but I want them all here."

"Yes, sir," the man responded.

After Tio had been escorted to the private elevator, the team leader turned to one of his men. "Better send someone after coffee. It's going to be a long, long night."

Colonel Maximillian Zeta set down the cell phone, his gaze fixed on the electronic device. Hatred resonated from the man's eyes, a fountain of anger spewing from deep inside his core. "The day has finally arrived," he whispered to the empty office. "And I am ready."

With extreme effort, the Mexican Army officer held his emotions in check, professionalism grappling with his rage to an eventual point of control. Slowly, his eyes moved to a framed picture that resided on the corner of his desk. Consuela.

He reached across the surface and gently lifted the photograph as if it were a newborn infant. He brought it close, studying the details of his sister's smiling face. She had been lost less than a month after the print had been made.

A passing tourist had snapped the image. A young Lieutenant Zeta, fresh, shiny, and proud in his newly earned uniform. Consuela had ridden a rickety, old bus to Mexico City to share his first leave after graduation from the academy. They had been sitting in a park eating ice cream, smiling and full of the future. Now, today, almost 18 years later, Zeta could still hear the musical tone of her laughter.

"She was so proud of me," he said, staring with affection at the young woman's image. "She kept telling me over and over again." He would never forget those three days. Not only were they wonderful, they were the last he would share with his sibling.

Zeta had grown up poor. He mused at the phrase "dirt poor," thinking it was a cruel oxymoron. They had plenty of dirt, but that was about it.

Their mother had died giving birth to the younger child, an event that their hardworking, peasant father never fully recovered from.

Still, he worked the fields, scratching out a meager living and raising the two children with help from the local villagers. Working the family's small patch of leased land was backbreaking labor. When they were old enough to walk, both of the young ones joined their father in the never-ending toil to put food on the table.

It wasn't an occupation that enabled long life spans. Señor Zeta died at the age of 38, leaving his two children behind to fend for themselves.

And they did.

The Catholic Church helped some. Distant relatives contributed what they could. Often their empty stomachs were filled by the random kindness of strangers.

Zeta managed to get a basic education. After working 10 grueling hours in the fields each day, he reported to the parish priest to study the alphabet and basic mathematics. The secret, he soon discovered, was learning to read. With that capability, he could find books that would open doors to all other knowledge.

Candlelit nights were spent in their shack, scouring the armloads of books borrowed from any source he could find. Consuela learned too, but her pre-teen mind wasn't as sharp or hungry for understanding.

One day, a stranger wearing a uniform arrived in the village. He was there to gather the conscripts – young men who had reached the age of 17.

The army initially didn't see much value in young Zeta. Most of the draftees were given menial tasks, the organization more resembling a nationalized version of the Boy Scouts of America than a military training machine. In reality, the men running the operation were watching and testing – always on the lookout for young men with potential. Maximillian, like his namesake emperor, was soon moved to the head of the class.

A year later, he was enrolled in his country's military academy. While this was a rare opportunity for the son of a peasant farmer, Consuela suffered in his absence. She was shipped off to an aunt who didn't want or need another mouth to feed.

"She paid a high price for my success," Zeta explained to the photograph. "She sacrificed as much as I did for these ribbons and rank – maybe more."

The years passed quickly for the aspiring soldier. Classes, schools, and field maneuvers filled his days. He sent half of his modest paychecks home, fully aware that the vile aunt was probably taking advantage of his sister's stipends.

Then, seemingly in a blink, it was graduation time. Consuela's letter announcing her trip to the big city had pleased him to no end. They had celebrated, dined, toured, and shared for those three remarkable days.

"I have something I need to tell you, big brother," she said on their last day together. "I'm going north into the United States. My best friend's brother owns a café in Phoenix, and I can get work there."

"No, Consuela, please don't. There is great danger in crossing the border," he had protested. But it was to no avail.

"I have a life too, my handsome, strong brother. I can do well for myself in the States. There is nothing for me at home. In America, I can enroll in school and earn a decent wage. There is no dream for me here in Mexico… no future. I don't want to spend the rest of my days harvesting food and babies. I've been saving the money you have so generously sent and have already paid for a guide."

Despite his best effort, her mind was set in stone. His baby sister had become a strong-minded, stubborn woman, and he couldn't talk her out of her plan. There was also a streak of guilt that restrained his effort. He had left her behind, single-minded in a quest to better himself. Who was he to deny her a chance at a better life?

On their way to the bus station, the siblings had passed a small sidewalk stand selling handmade silver trinkets and jewelry. Zeta had stopped and pointed, saying, "If you are determined to set out on this journey, let me give you something to comfort you during your travels."

He'd purchased a cheap St. Christopher's necklace, splurging to have it engraved as they watched the artisan carve Zeta's message of love and luck.

Sitting in his office now, the colonel's fondest memory of those days was his sister's reaction to that tiny hunk of silver dangling from the serpentine chain. She had glowed with joy, cradling the prize and kissing him relentlessly on the cheeks. At the time, he'd assumed it was his gift that initiated her warm response. He had replayed that event so many times in his mind, the years of wisdom and afterthought finally revealing the true reason for Consuela's warm reception. While meaningful, the religious symbol formed into a metal disk did not prompt her reaction. Rather, the colonel's gift-giving gesture acknowledged his sister's sacrifice for him, and that had made Consuela feel so valued.

For days, he'd waited on news of her safe arrival. Every mail call was a disappointment, every phone message read with anxious eyes. After a week, he knew something was wrong. At ten days, he requested an emergency leave to go and find his beloved Consuela.

It took three days to track down the coyote that had lead his sister's group of hopeful men and women across the Arizona border. The young man was in the hospital, suffering from dehydration.

"The U.S. border agents caught us just on the other side," the young man had claimed. "They started shooting at us, and we scattered into the desert night. It was chaos, everyone running in all directions. They found me three days later, almost dead, and deported me back here."

"And my sister? Consuela? What became of her?"

"The gringos told me they had found several bodies that day. That is all I know, señor."

Zeta lost control of his temper. He sprang at the bedridden man, clutching his throat with an iron grip. "You lie! You are a criminal and a villain! Tell me! Tell me the truth!"

Something in the coyote's eyes saved his life that day. Zeta remembered the man didn't struggle or fight, but merely stared back into his attacker's face.

"I'm telling you the truth, señor. You can kill me if you wish. I don't care. The ghosts of those lost souls will haunt me for the rest of my days. It would be a relief to stop seeing their faces when I close my eyes."

For some reason, Zeta believed the man and spared his life.

Zeta had used his position to gain a visitor's visa into Arizona. He'd driven a rented car to the main Border Patrol facility in the area indicated by the coyote.

"We find bodies in the desert all the time, slick," the gruff, uncaring American had responded. "You'll have to be a little more specific."

Zeta suppressed the urge to strike the man, barely holding his temper in check. He provided the date, general area, and description of his sister.

After several clicks on the computer keyboard, the agent finally responded. "Yes, we recovered a body matching that description in that area."

"Her remains?"

"Our policy is to wait five days for the deceased to be claimed. After that, the corpuses are buried by the state. I have photographs of the body if you would like to attempt an identification."

Zeta's world became suddenly small and meaningless as he stared at the photographs. It was Consuela, her skin red and purple in death. He didn't see the blistered, cracked lips or sunburned skin – only the vision of her vibrant eyes and wonderful smelling hair filled his senses.

"And the cause of death?" the Mexican hissed.

"Gunshot wound."

"Who? Who would shoot an innocent, unarmed woman?"

The American behind the counter frowned as he read the computer screen. "There was no autopsy or forensics performed. Our agents don't normally fire on illegal immigrants unless they're fired upon. Was she smuggling dope? Was she a mule being escorted by armed men?"

The exasperation and anger in Zeta's voice was obvious, "She wanted to be a waitress, sir, nothing more. She had never even held a firearm. Where is she buried?"

The border agent provided the address. As Zeta turned to leave, the man had called out. "Sir, there were also some personal effects recovered from the victim. If you'll hold on just one minute, I can retrieve them."

A few minutes later, the man returned carrying a small plastic bag of clothing and the St. Christopher's medal. Zeta pulled out his sister's bloody blouse and found two bullet holes in the back of the stained garment. Rage pounded in his head as he gripped the cloth with white knuckles.

Somehow, he managed to steer the rental to the gravesite. There were no markers or stones, just an open field with numbered wooden posts sticking up from the ground. He found #462, the site where the American had said his sister was laid to rest. In the distance was a landfill, a place where garbage was buried.

It all overwhelmed the young Zeta. His sister had been nothing but trash to the Americans. They didn't see a young girl, hopeful and full of life. They only saw a trespasser who was trying to circumvent their law. The injustice of it all raked his soul with claws that left deep scars that would never heal.

The pain overwhelmed him, causing him to drop to his knees and sob over her grave. So intense was the agony... so deep the remorse, he thought for a moment he would surely go insane with grief.

But then a pinpoint of light shone in his conscious. It wasn't much to begin with, but it grew. Zeta's sanity was salvaged by that small shimmer of relief. Revenge. As he wept in that open, Arizona field, the shimmer of vengeance grew into resolve, pushing aside the remorse and agony. It anchored in a corner of his mind, stabilizing him with a platform of reason.

"One day I will revenge your death," he had promised his sister's ghost. "One day the Americans will pay."

Zeta, now a respected senior officer and the commander of men, leaned back in his chair and sighed. "Today is the day."

Professor Middleton pushed his spectacles up his nose, and then nervously scratched his chin. "This is most concerning, Dr. Weathers. I've never seen a concentration of this specific compound before. Where did you say the sample originated?"

Mitch pretended absentmindedness, "It was mailed to me, Doctor. I can't recall the address, but I have it on file."

The older man nodded in understanding – he had trouble remembering where he had left his checkbook. "Regardless, this needs to be investigated. I would also recommend you notify the CDC and the EPA."

"What could the possible causes be?"

The older man returned his eye to the microscope before answering. "If this was the 1960s, I would say it was industrial pollution… probably airborne. Given this animal was clearly born after that decade, it most likely is an unknown waste site. Perhaps even a landfill that is leaking into the water supply. Whatever the source, this is dangerous."

Mitch wanted to be clear before he chose a plan of action. "So you're saying this compound doesn't occur anywhere in nature?"

"Absolutely not," replied the professor, slightly annoyed at his colleague's lack of knowledge. "Hydrogen cyanide, oxycyanide, and borocyanide were once used in the plating of metals, such as anticorrosive galvanization. They were cheap, extremely effective, and accomplished several steps for preparation in one nasty-ass chemical bath - the only problem being that they were also practically impossible to dispose of. Most communities don't want cyanide in their water supplies or landfills."

Peering up from his instrument, Middleton continued, "Like so many things in commercial manufacturing, the cheapest method is often the most dangerous. Our automobiles cost more because of the banning of substances like this, but in my opinion, it's well worth it."

Mitch thanked the man and exited the Agricultural Administration building. "Damn it, Dusty. How do you keep bumbling into shit like this? Cyanide? Wow!" he whispered.

Still, there was a bright side. He couldn't justify the risk of visiting his brother based simply on his emotional needs. This would provide a good excuse.

Returning to his own office, Mitch found one of his undergraduate students working at the reception area. "Danny, do you know where that file of conference invitations is?"

Scanning around for a moment, the young student pointed to a nearby filing cabinet. "I believe you'll find it in the top drawer, Professor."

Mitch pulled the thick folder, thanking his aide and then shutting the office door behind him. He had to be careful because he assumed the FBI was always watching and listening.

He quickly thumbed through the file's contents. Being a department head at A&M, the younger Weathers was always in demand to speak, contribute, partake or attend various conferences, reviews and trade shows. He ignored 99% of the invitations, always busy with ongoing university business or family events.

As he thumbed through the myriad of correspondence, he found a single-page letter inviting him to attend the Fourth International Conference on Photonic and Optoelectronics. His eyebrows shot up when he saw the meeting was at the Corpus International Convention Center... and had started today.

He spun quickly to his PC, pulling up a page of search results. Already, his colleagues were posting pictures of the event on social media. It looked like a pretty good size show, with several dozen exhibitors on the convention floor.

Wanting to minimize any risk, Mitch then pulled up a list of tomorrow's sessions and speakers. There were a few that he would be mildly interested in and could justify attending if questioned.

So if I drive down there, how do I shake my FBI shadow... if they bother to follow me? he questioned.

Leaning back in his chair, Mitch thought it through. Like a meticulous physics experiment, his trained mind processed every step, forward and backward.

184

He hadn't seen a single indication of continued FBI surveillance, but that didn't mean it wasn't there. He operated daily under the assumption that they were reading every email, listening to every phone call and probably had his office bugged, perhaps even with video capabilities.

A short time later, he sat at the Java Barn nursing a cup of the best coffee on campus. The table of paper in front of him was already filled with two pages of notes.

I can do this, he thought. *I can see Dusty, and they'll never know.*

Day Nine - Morning

The undergraduate was absolutely thrilled Dr. Weathers had selected him to attend a professional conference. Part of the exhilaration was replaced with puzzlement when the department head asked if the student could drive his own personal car. The elation completely disappeared when the professor announced they had to leave at 4 a.m. In the morning. Tomorrow morning.

Still, it would be good to get out of College Station for a few days, and the university was paying mileage and meals. It was agreed.

The predawn adventure began with both the passenger and the driver keyed up, but for completely different reasons. The student was anxious to impress the man who would control his grade and potentially his career. The teacher was charged with energy because he going rogue and risking imprisonment.

"I reserved us a spot in one of the lab demonstrations," Weathers announced as the Texas countryside passed by. "Dr. Cummings from Texas Tech is conducting a workshop on the restrictive principles of sub-element velocities."

After a deep yawn, the driver nodded vigorously. "I've read about that. He's trying to develop a desktop version of a particle accelerator."

"Yes, you're correct. Personally, I'm a bit worried about the direction the project is headed. He's using the vibrations from gamma radiation as a substitute for miles and miles of magnetic fields. While I applaud the concept, any usage of radioactive materials in the lab is a concern."

The kid decided not to comment on that, the science more interesting than any political or social fallout concerning terrorism, bomb-building materials, or community exposure.

The two continued driving south, managing to bypass the outskirts of Houston before the gridlock of morning traffic. Corpus was still another three hours away, but Mitch felt comfortable with his schedule.

Dusty hadn't slept. Throughout the night, every little creak and rattle had sent him peering into the darkness with a white knuckled grip on his weapons. Twice he'd been tempted to just start walking to somewhere... anywhere. But there wasn't any place to go.

The fiery-red sun cresting in the east provided him with some relief. Deciding there wasn't anything he could do at the moment, he prepared to refill the birdfeeders. If evil found its way to the ranch, then he'd do the best he could to survive, and that was that.

Given his newfound resolve, he stopped and took a moment to admire that fresh-day smell and note the heavy dew that sparkled on every surface.

The new day was a relief for his troubled mind. He'd never quite understood why watching the sun come up filled him with warmth and calm, but it seemed like it always did. "Maybe it's some engrained primordial instinct," he whispered to the new Sol. "Maybe after a 100,000 years, we're programmed to celebrate surviving the night."

Whatever it was, he enjoyed it every time, and some days, like this morning, it was powerful therapy. *This is the one good thing I've discovered about being an outlaw,* he mused. *I really do appreciate the little things that I might not experience tomorrow.*

Penny's voice interrupted his thoughts, "Good morning!"

"Ma'am," he replied, tipping his hat.

"Mr. Hastings called last night and said I should be at the courthouse tomorrow and to make sure and bring bail money. I've used up most of what we got for that pistol and was wondering if you've found any of Papa's other guns that were worth selling."

Dusty thought for a moment before replying, "Yes, there are a couple that might bring in some serious money if we can find the right buyer. I'm not sure Laredo is the best place to shop them though. I was going to talk to you about maybe listing them online after I finished cleaning them up."

"What about Corpus Christi? That's a much bigger city."

He shrugged, "Couldn't hurt to try, I suppose. I'm not familiar with that town – never been there."

Penny smiled, "I was thinking of taking the girls and driving over that way this morning. It's not that far really, and I have a sister who lives there. I was going to hit her up for a loan just in case the guns were worthless. If you want, we can load them up, and you can ride over with us. While I'm visiting Sissy, you can take the truck and visit a few gun shops."

The thought of exposing himself to more people didn't initially sit well with Dusty, and his concern must have shown on his face.

"We can have some fun while we're at it," Penny said, bolstering the idea. "I suspect we would all benefit from the fresh sea air. And since you've never been there, we can visit a few of the tourist attractions. I think the girls could use a little fun in their lives right now anyway."

Her enthusiasm was difficult to debate. "Okay," Dusty finally agreed, "I'll get a few of the guns ready just as soon as I finish feeding the poultry."

"Good!" she replied. "I'll roust the girls, and we can get going right after breakfast."

They arrived at the conference later than Weathers had anticipated - the drive-thru breakfast, need for gasoline, and one additional restroom stop delaying his timetable. Still, they could just make it if they hurried.

After obtaining their ID badges and welcome packets, the two men found the ballroom housing the workshop. It was all that Mitch had hoped it would be.

Texas Tech was trying to elevate the reputation of its physics program and had clearly spared no expense. After being distributed a pamphlet reiterating the necessary safety precautions, Mitch and his charge found themselves in a line of academics, waiting to enter the main conference room.

They inched forward slowly, patiently progressing through the cue until they were issued disposable safety suits, complete with hood and radiation badges. "These are provided in the unlikely event of the worst case scenario," a post-grad announced as she circulated through the crowd helping attendees don the coverings.

A small booth had been erected, the function being identical to a nightclub's coat check. Mitch watched his partner remove his A&M jacket and handed it over to the smiling attendant. "Better leave your cell phone and keys," Mitch advised. "I hear there are some serious magnetic fields involved in the lab."

"Of course," the embarrassed student responded. "I should know better." A sly grin formed at the corners of Mitch's mouth as he watched the kid empty his pockets.

When the girl handed over the two numbered tickets, Mitch casually reached out and pocketed both. His student didn't notice.

After the coat check, the two men began pulling on their white, astronaut-like costumes. Mitch leaned close to his charge and whispered, "This is bullshit - nothing but a bunch of hype. We ran similar experiments two years ago, and there's not enough radioactive materials involved to blow your nose, let alone require safety suits. What a publicity stunt."

The kid nodded his agreement and said, "Still, it's good marketing. You have to admit that. All these eggheads can take selfies and show the folks back home how serious the conference was."

"The only serious work being done here is at the hotel bar," Mitch responded.

Once they had slid the plastic clothing over their street clothes, the duo was then escorted into a makeshift lab that had been created within the huge convention center.

Dozens of people were attending, the throng milling about. "Looks like a convention of Pillsbury Dough Boys," Mitch observed as they joined the multitude of white-suited academics.

"Either that, or we're on a filming location for a bad 1980s music video," came the response.

"Hey!" Mitch protested in jest. "I'm a child of the 80s. Be careful now."

Soon enough, the meeting was called to order. The gathered attendees formed a semi-circle around the centerpiece of the lab, a large table adorned with complex-looking lab equipment. The man in charge, Dr. Cummings, was introduced and stepped to the center of the display.

"Ladies and gentlemen, thank you for attending our workshop. Today we are going..." and so it started.

Mitch waited impatiently for the boring introductions and preamble to pass. When their host actually reached the interesting part, the professor put his hand on his stomach while leaning in closer to his student.

"That egg sandwich I had this morning isn't settling well," Mitch announced. "I feel like I might toss my cookies. I'm going to go back to the hotel and rest for a bit."

The kid seemed concerned and turned to go with his professor. Mitch put out a hand and said, "No, you stay here and attend the rest of the meetings and labs. We have to justify this trip to my boss, so at least one of us has to see what's going on. Besides, I'll probably be back in an hour or so. I'll catch up with you then."

"I hope you get to feeling better, Professor."

"Thanks. Oh, and you'll probably need this once you're done in here," Mitch remembered, handing the kid the wrong coat check ticket.

Faking his stomachache, Mitch pulled off the lab suit, replacing the protective cover with his student's jacket. On the way to the side exit, he passed by the booth of a lab equipment manufacturer and provided his email address in exchange for a free baseball hat. The aviator sunglasses from the undergrad's coat rounded out his disguise.

Gradually making his way to the restrooms, he recalled the convention's layout from the schematic published online. Instead of turning right for the men's room, he double-checked no one was watching and then cut left.

Bright sunshine assaulted his eyes for a moment as he exited the side door. He glanced around, almost expecting a hoard of FBI agents ready to pounce. The area was empty, and that fact help settle his nerves - somewhat.

As he turned for the parking lot, he prayed his assessment of the bureau's capabilities was accurate. They probably had his cell phone tagged, perhaps his clothing, and most certainly his automobile. There was even an outside chance an undercover agent had followed them into the convention center.

As he dug out the car keys, he checked again to see if he was being followed. No one was there. A few minutes later, Mitch was headed west toward Laredo, his eyes constantly checking the rearview mirror.

The technician leaned back in his chair, pulling another sip from the oversized coffee mug that always seemed to be present. The large computer monitor residing on his desk displayed a blur of characters scrolling downward as the automated system cycled through its processes.

At that moment, the FBI's Houston office was monitoring 1631 mobile devices, tracking locations, phone calls, and internet browsing activities. There were 122 that were "hot listed," meaning any call, movement or loss of signal was to be analyzed by human eyes.

Not that turning off their cell phones would do any good. Even removing the battery was a wasted effort, as the FBI had full access to the NSA's sophisticated monitoring systems.

Each modern mobile device sold in the United States contained two batteries. The largest and most commonly known could be removed by the user. The second was tiny, powering the memory of the phone even if the primary power cell was removed. That secondary power source also enabled the phone's radio frequency identifier to transmit an intermittent signal.

From his desktop, the technician could do some amazing things with the typical smart phone. With the click of a key, he could turn on the device's cameras and watch live, streaming video. The owner would never know.

He could also turn on the microphone, access the GPS location history, read every text message and even program the phone to record every call. Those recordings could be transmitted during the night and then automatically erased. If programmed to do so, he could sit and view every photograph.

But that was all child's play. The really sophisticated capabilities had been brought online just a few months ago.

He could now scan any fingerprint left by accidently brushing over the camera lenses. The magnetometer in the newer models was so accurate, the system could often detect if the owner were carrying a gun.

Pulse rate, body temperature and other biofeedback data could be captured as well.

But the really serious money had been dedicated to the automated analysis systems. There were over a billion cell phones on the planet, and even the U.S. government didn't have the manpower to watch, listen, and monitor every single one.

Black budgets had been appropriated to write the most complex software ever devised by mankind. Huge banks of supercomputers occupied underground centers in Utah, Fort Meade and other clandestine locations – all with the dedicated purpose of tracking, scrutinizing and storing the daily habits of cell phone users. It was as if the various government agencies had a law enforcement officer in every American's purse or pocket.

Earlier that morning, the system had flagged one Dr. Mitch Weathers as having executed movements outside of his normal travel zone – essentially College Station, Texas and the A&M campus.

The third shift tech had immediately notified the surveillance team assigned to Dr. Weathers, who didn't appreciate receiving the pre-dawn call. Despite the grumbling, they quickly verified that the good doctor was attending a scientific conference in Corpus Christi. It all appeared to be on the up and up.

The FBI computer expert returned the cup to the desktop coaster and smiled at the monitor. There was no flagged activity, which meant he could visit the cafeteria at the regular time – a rare occurrence as of late.

"All the little rabbits are right where they should be," he mumbled to himself, wondering if the tuna salad was any good today.

An hour later, Dusty piloted the old pickup out the driveway, both of the young girls giddy with excitement and looking forward to the unexpected trip. As they rolled east, Penny got caught up her daughters' enthusiasm, recounting stories of previous excursions to the big city.

Dusty drove on, mostly silent and only showing the occasional polite smile. He had agreed to the trip because he didn't intend on coming back. He planned to make up some excuse in Corpus and send Penny and the girls back to the ranch alone. It had been a great gig while it had lasted. Despite his best intentions, he couldn't help but have a sense of foreboding about the journey.

Vega watched his quarry speed away. Lowering the binoculars, he turned to Victor and instructed, "Follow them. Stay back, but follow them. They may be trying to run."

"Why don't we just ram that truck into a ditch and get this over with?" responded the cartel enforcer. "It's only one man and three females. I think we can handle them."

Vega started to scold the man, but caught the harsh words before they left his throat. Both of the muscular fellows in the back seat worked for Vince. It was rude to scold a manager in front of his charges, and besides, he didn't want to give any of them a hint regarding what he had planned.

"He is well-armed and skilled," Vega finally explained. "Our Uncle's instructions were very clear – we are to take down this target without drawing a lot of attention. Having a shootout along the road isn't a low key activity."

Victor seemed unconvinced, but the cartel boss had ordered him and two trusted compadres to follow Vega's instructions. He would do so, no matter how silly things seemed.

Less than an hour later, it became apparent that their prey was heading to Corpus Christi. As they approached the metropolitan area, Vega spoke again. "Move closer. The last thing I want to report to our uncle is that we lost them in traffic."

Penny pulled a brochure from her purse and began showing the girls pictures of their sightseeing options. It was soon agreed that everyone wanted to tour the aircraft carrier USS Lexington, which was now a docked museum and one of Corpus's most popular tourist attractions.

It wasn't difficult to find the big ship, her outline visible from quite some distance away. "Okay, everyone… we have two hours before we have to be at my sister's house for lunch. Let's get this show on the road!" Penny declared.

Even in his foul mood, Dusty had to admit that the huge vessel was a sight to see. The museum's parking lot was right next to the permanent mooring, and the size of the "Blue Ghost" was daunting.

As they exited the truck, he couldn't help but share the girls' excitement as everyone approached the gangway to buy tickets and begin the outing.

Dusty picked up a pamphlet at the ticket booth and began to learn a little about the history of the great ship. The USS Lexington was a veteran of WWII, having entered service in 1943. Decommissioned in 1991, she had earned her spooky nickname via to the wartime Japanese Navy, who believed they had sunk Lexington no less than three times, and took to calling her a ghost ship.

"They've got a theatre, gift shop, and restaurant on this boat," Penny noted as the group entered the main hangar deck. "It's like a floating city."

And it was.

For an hour, the foursome climbed through narrow passageways, marveled at the scope of the flight deck and stared out the windows, taking in the magnificent view of the bay offered from the high-rise bridge. The girls were wide-eyed and excited.

They had just finished touring the machinery spaces when Dusty caught a glimpse of a face that looked familiar. He paused for a moment, searching the tourists scattered in the various rooms and compartments. Penny and the girls continued, stepping through a watertight hatch into another section of the ship.

He couldn't spot anyone he knew and was just about to dismiss the whole episode when a scream rang out from up ahead.

Through the steel bulkhead doorway, Dusty could see Penny holding up her arms in the classic "Don't shoot" position. She was pale white and clearly shocked.

The big Texan moved quickly, reaching in his belt for the .45 caliber Glock tucked inside. "Please... Mister... please let her go," Penny was pleading.

Sidestepping for an angle, Dusty spied a man's arm holding a pistol against the older girl's head. Another voice responded to the mother's desperate plea. "We want to speak to Weathers. Come out Mr. Weathers, I know you're back there."

"What do you want?" Dusty called, remaining out of sight.

"We want what you have in that duffle bag, Mr. Weathers. Hand it over, and no one will be harmed," came the reply.

Dusty was confused. His mind had immediately concluded that the Tri-Materials thugs followed them from Laredo, but they didn't know about the rail gun. *Or did they?*

He knew it wasn't the FBI, as they wouldn't take a hostage. *Or would they?*

A dozen thoughts surged through his head, the blood pounding in his ears making it difficult to react. Unable to reach a decision, he couldn't come up with anything other than to stall.

"You want the money? Is that it?" he called through the doorway, knowing that wasn't the case at all.

A throaty laugh was the initial response, quickly followed by, "No, Mr. Weathers. You know exactly what I want. Now please show yourself or we will begin executing these females."

Dusty could see Penny, her eyes wide and darting around the room in sheer terror. She had managed to pull the other girl around behind her, shielding the frightened child with her body. The voice had said "we," which meant there was more than one goon on the other side of the doorway. *But how many?*

"You've miscalculated," Dusty answered. "Those women mean nothing to me," he stated flatly, as he slowly began unzipping the duffle.

There wasn't an immediate response. After a few moments, again the voice sounded from beyond. "I don't believe you Mr. Weathers, and time is of the essence. Like you, I don't want an encounter with the authorities, so stop trying my patience and hand over the bag."

Dusty pulled the rail gun from the duffle.

The voice from the other side was Latino. In south Texas, that didn't mean anything specific, but it gave Dusty his next response. "Who are you?"

The green LED glowed bright.

Again the laugh, "Mr. Weathers, you're stalling, and I'm growing tired of our conversation. My identity isn't important. What matters is that the men with me are more than willing to execute these women. Hand over the weapon immediately, or I'll prove than I'm not bluffing."

Gently, quietly, Dusty inserted a ball bearing into the breech and checked the power setting. "Okay, I'm coming through."

Tucking the pistol back in his belt, Dusty raised the duffle as if it were a shield, the rail gun in his free hand. He was a little surprised at how shaky his legs felt.

He stepped over the bottom of the bulkhead door and into a large room lined with display cases and other exhibits. There were four men inside.

"What are you doing, Mr. Weathers?" the head-goon asked when he noticed the rail gun was in Dusty's hands. "We both know that if you discharge that device inside these enclosed spaces, everyone here will die."

"Exactly," responded the Texan in a low voice. "And I'm thinking that might be the best outcome for all of us. You're not walking out of here with this weapon."

Vega seemed puzzled by the response, his forehead wrinkling in a frown. "You're bluffing. I don't judge you as a man intent on murder or suicide."

Before Dusty could answer, a new voice rang out. "What's going on in here?" called an older man in a watchman's uniform from a doorway at the back of the room.

Every eye turned to see one of the museum's security guards standing in the opening. It was the distraction Dusty needed.

Surprised by the new arrival, the man holding Penny's daughter turned just slightly as Dusty reached for the Glock. The kidnapper was well over six feet in height, towering above the teenage girl by almost a full twelve inches. Plenty of margin for a shot of less than five feet.

Dusty aligned the sights on the thug's temple and forced himself to squeeze the trigger. The roar of the big caliber round inside the close, metal walls was deafening. A second shot was on the way as the gunman's head snapped back from the impact, a cloud of red and purple mist appearing as the 230-grain bullets exited the back of his skull.

Before the dead man began to fall, Dusty was reaching for the paralyzed hostage while moving his aim toward the next-closest kidnapper. Absolute bedlam erupted inside the room.

One of the assailants was carrying a MAC-10 machine pistol, an automatic weapon capable of spraying over a dozen deadly lead pills per second. Surprised, stunned, and unsure of what was happening, the man's finger pulled on the trigger before he could bring the weapon to bear. A stream of 9mm bullets began ricocheting off the steel walls at the same time that Dusty fired his third shot.

The Texan managed to grab the former hostage's arm, literally throwing the girl back through the portal and out of the line of fire. With the pistol pointing and barking where his mind thought targets should be, Dusty started shouting at Penny and the girls, "Get out! Get out!"

The human brain struggled to reconcile the combination of smoke, earsplitting noise, surprise, and movement. Bullets screamed, sparked and thudded throughout the enclosed space as Dusty was shooting and pushing Penny and the remaining child thought the entrance way. Glass exploded from the display cases as random bullets tore through the air. The fluorescent lights above showered more shrapnel and added strobe-like effects to the bedlam.

"Go! Run! Go!" Dusty heard himself screaming at Penny as he backed out of the chaos. He fired two more shots into the opening and then the Glock locked back empty.

A glance showed the girls were indeed moving, scrambling toward the entrance to another of the seemingly endless passageways.

And then they were through, scurrying down an elongated hall with cool air rushing past, adrenaline-fueled legs pumping faster than they ever had before.

Their desperate flight was motivated even more as a shot ripped off the wall, a clear indicator that the kidnappers were in pursuit. "Through there! Through there!" Dusty shouted as they approached a doorway. Another bullet whizzed by, adding emphasis to his command.

Up a stairway they clamored, both of the girls fighting tears and terror. Penny had somewhat recovered, pushing her children to move faster… faster than they had ever moved before.

The sound of footfalls behind them echoed throughout the enclosed space, and Dusty realized that the grown men chasing them were faster, quickly closing the gap. The thud, whack, and ping of a bullet fired from below confirmed his suspicions.

Then they were darting through another door and dashing again down a corridor, the bland navy-grey walls rushing past.

Penny stopped so suddenly that Dusty almost knocked her over. Before he could even challenge her abrupt halt, he realized the problem. The maze of passageways had hit a dead end.

"Shit!" he hissed, turning to see how closely they were being followed.

"I can't open this hatch," Penny wailed, trying desperately to turn the wheel-like mechanism. "It's stuck."

Dusty glanced again over his shoulder and then moved her out of the way. He put everything he had into turning the crank. It wouldn't budge.

Another bullet slammed into the wall beside them, evidence that their foes had caught up. Dusty had stowed another magazine for his pistol in the duffle, but there wasn't time. Even if he could manage a reload, it probably wouldn't do any good. They were pinned in a confined area and would eventually go down in a hail of lead.

"Lie flat, close your eyes, and cover your ears," he snapped at the girls. "Whatever you do, don't look up."

He waited until all of the Boyces were on the deck and then took a knee, bringing the rail gun up to his shoulder.

Behind him, down the corridor, he recognized the pursuers' heads popping out to chance a glimpse. "They're no doubt trying to figure out how to take me down," he whispered. "Come on out, boys. Do I have a surprise for you?"

A hand appeared, clutching the machine pistol. Yellow and red flame sprouted from the weapon's muzzle, and then Dusty detected human shapes filling the passageway.

He squeezed the rail gun's trigger.

The computer control sequence of voltage surged through the rotating magnets, each pushing and pulling the ball bearing. The black pipeline to another dimension appeared in the lead man's chest, and the cartel shooter simply disintegrated.

A sphere of molecules was pushed outward, traveling at near the speed of light. The energy expanded in the narrow, steel-lined enclosure. Armored bulkheads folded like cardboard as air condensed to the consistency of iron slammed against them at several thousand meters per second.

The tourists waiting outside to board the great ship instinctively ducked as the outer hull exploded over the bay, ripping a massive hole in the stern of the vessel. Geysers spread across the water below as fragments of steel plate and machinery fell into the bay.

Then as suddenly as it had opened, the portal closed. Gravity, light, and matter rushed to fill the vacuum, the effect unleashing even more violence on the already tortured universe.

Dusty was bowled over by the reverberating shockwave of noise and atmosphere. He experienced a sense of weightlessness and then landed on top of Penny, pinned against the bulkhead.

The first thing Dusty noticed was the absolute silence. A warm trickle running down his neck forced him to move an arm just as Penny surged beneath him. Rolling off the struggling woman, Dusty blinked several times, worried for a moment that he was blind and deaf.

Now free of his weight, Penny moved to check the girls, relieved that both of them seemed to be unharmed.

The smoke was the next thing they all noticed.

Dusty heard his own voice say, "Fire! We've got to get out of here," as he attempted to rise on unsteady legs. A minute later, they had all managed to stand, and then they were stumbling down the corridor toward a dim light shining in the distance.

Black smoke began to boil into the space as they reached the first entrance. Again, they were climbing stairs, some aspect of survival prompting them to climb rather than descend. Alarms were clanging all over the ship.

The fire suppression system engaged next, showering the foursome with cold, stinging water as they exited the stairwell. Dusty pointed toward the red, glowing letters of an exit sign, and then they were in the open spaces of the main hangar deck.

Sightseers were scrambling for the gangway, uniformed museum employees funneling the frightened crowd toward the outside air and safety.

Dusty managed to shove the rail gun into the duffle, and then they hustled toward the growing line of disembarking passengers.

The bright sunshine was a welcome sensation after being in the confined bowels of the ship. Penny and the girls followed the orderly evacuation down the ramp, eventually reaching the parking lot.

"We have to go... and go right now," Dusty heard himself shouting. "I can't stay here."

Mrs. Boyce didn't argue the point and began herding the girls toward the pickup. They exited the lot just as the first police cars and fire trucks came speeding onto the wharf.

Corpus was in their rearview mirror before anyone inside the truck spoke. Dusty fully expected Penny to be furious, but she wasn't. "We need to talk as soon as we get back to the ranch," were her only words.

Dusty was thankful for the respite. He would use the long drive home to calm down and gather his wits.

Day Nine - Afternoon

Vega awoke on a stretcher, a fire department EMT hovering over his head. "I've got multiple trauma wounds, a severely damaged right leg, and internal bleeding," the man was reporting into a radio.

A wall of pain racked the cartel man's brain, seemingly every nerve in his body screaming in protest. Struggling to remain conscious, he heard a desperate voice call out, "Did anyone find his left leg?"

His vision was dark around the edges, as if he were peering through some sort of stained lead crystal. Still, he could see well enough to note he was alone in the back of the ambulance.

He was dying. He thought of his mother and sister, their humble flat in southern Mexico. He worried about what would happen to them without the financial support of his regular monthly checks.

Anger began to fill his soul. What little blood was left in his body simmered with the rage and injustice of his demise. He was too young. Healthy. Vibrant. The man with the rail gun was just as evil as Tio. Weathers was a butcher, no better than the man who ran the cartel.

Whispering a prayer, Vega managed to reach inside his jacket pocket and withdraw a cell phone. He dialed a number from touch alone, his vision too blurry to read the keypad.

There were two rings, and then voice mail answered, just as he expected. "We are all dead. The rail gun killed us all. You will find it at the Boyce Poultry Farm outside Laredo, Texas."

Somehow, knowing Tio would achieve his goal didn't make death any easier. Revenge didn't satisfy in death as it had in life. The visions of Tio killing Weathers put a foul taste in his throat.

Vega's arm dropped to his side, the phone rattling onto the metal floor as his chest exhaled a final breath.

The helicopter landed in an area of the Lexington parking lot that had been roped off by the Corpus police. Agent Shultz was met by the man in charge of the regional office.

As soon as they were far enough away from the whining turbine engine, Shultz began a staccato round of questions. "How many bodies have you recovered so far?"

"Just two dead. There are two more with life threatening injuries and another dozen or so that had minor bruises and lacerations. We've got people watching at the hospitals, keeping an eye on the wounded."

Shultz nodded, "And the roadblocks?"

"They were in place 45 minutes after we received your call. It's just not possible to shut down a city the size of Corpus any faster than that."

The two agents paced toward the now-crippled carrier, Shultz gazing at the torn metal and gaping hole in the stern. The local man took advantage of the pause to ask his own question. "Any idea what kind of explosive we're dealing with? My people have never seen anything like this."

"What do you mean?"

"We've got six-inch steel plate that now crumbles in your hands like chalk. Mr. Burns, one of the museum's curators, served aboard the Lexington during World War II. He claims to have seen the damage first hand from a Japanese torpedo strike – damage that wasn't nearly as extensive as what we have now."

Shultz stopped mid-stride and looked the junior man squarely in the eye. "You don't want to know. You have to trust me on this... you really don't want to know. Now what about the surveillance tapes?"

"You can see them over here," came the reply.

The two men approached a nearby van that was surrounded by a dozen men in windbreakers, each sporting gold-embodied initials from several government agencies, including ATF, FBI, and CCPD. Shultz was led to the back where a small, flat screen monitor was made available.

He began watching grainy video of what appeared to be the typical tourist crowd meandering up the gangplank leading to the ship. In less than two minutes, he pointed to the screen and snapped, "Stop."

The image frozen on the screen was of a woman herding two girls along the ramp, closely followed by a man with a duffle bag strapped onto his back. The low-tilted western hat blocked much of his face, but Shultz could see enough to identify Durham Weathers. "That's our man," he whispered. "But who was he using as a target?"

Then, almost as a second thought, Shultz instructed, "Pull copies of the pictures of that family, and pass them around. I want to know if anyone noticed them, what they were doing, or who they might be. Did they pay with a credit card? Did anyone see them leave the parking lot?"

Shultz then studied the woman closely, sure he had never seen her before. "Okay, let it play," he instructed the technician.

The monitor showed a break in the foot traffic, the early weekday crowd sparse. Ten minutes of video-time later, Shultz again asked that the playback be paused.

This time he was looking at four men who somehow seemed out of place. Turning to his local co-worker, Shultz inquired, "Do you know any of these men?"

"No, sir."

"Circulate these as well. My gut says these are the shooters."

"We've recovered dozens of 9mm casings and another handful of .45 empties. They were scattered over two decks and one stairwell. We recovered a MAC-10 off one of the bodies, but so far there's no sign of the weapon that discharged the bigger rounds."

Shultz thought about the statement for a moment before responding. He glanced at the huge vessel and thought, *Who were you fighting, Weathers... and why?*

It took Penny a while to settle the girls down, the young ones worried that bad men were going to visit their house.

Dusty washed up and changed clothes quickly, then dawdled with his hat in hand by the back porch. The look on his hostess's face made it clear that a serious conversation was about to ensue.

"I know who you are... now," she opened. "I don't watch the news much, especially concerning matters in the big cities like Houston. But now I know."

Dusty sighed, scuffing some dirt with his boots. "I'm sorry I lied to you, Penny. I only ask that you give me a few hours head start before you call the police."

"Pfffffft," she exhaled, waving her hand through the air. "I'm not sure who's worse these days... a man who blows up ships and cities or the local cops."

Dusty had to laugh at the statement. He glanced around the ranch, a little unsure that they had left all of the trouble behind. "I didn't mean to bring anything down on you or your family. I'm just trying to buy my friends some time so we can get this whole mess straightened out."

"So tell me your story, Durham Weathers. Make me understand why a man I've grown to trust is the most wanted fugitive in the world."

"I built a device in my workshop. Purely by accident… only via circumstance… I mixed the right components together and created a monster," Dusty began. He stopped for a bit, nodding toward the duffle bag with his head. "Man, can I bake a cake."

Penny chuckled and then tilted her head, "Go on."

"I took it to my brother who is some sort of physics genius at A&M. Even he couldn't explain the 'why,' but he had a pretty good idea as to the 'how.' It became real clear, real quick, that I had opened the Pandora's box to practically unlimited power and energy. Suddenly, I went from a redneck West Texas gunsmith to a guy who could relate to why Albert Einstein was so worried about splitting the atom and creating a horrible weapon."

"So why didn't you just destroy it and go back to West Texas?"

Dusty grunted, a hurt expression crossing his face. "I wanted to. I've started to destroy the blasted thing a dozen times… but my brother convinced me that it could be the single greatest step forward for our species… our greatest advancement of all time. He believes it can create free energy and perhaps even save the human race. So we made a pact. I would hide the gun from those who would use it as a weapon while he worked with the authorities to set up some way… some method that would ensure only the peaceful benefits would see the light of day. It was a noble plan, but things just spiraled out of control."

Penny shook her head, a grin appearing at the corners of her mouth. "I think I liked you better when I thought you might be an axe murderer," she teased.

Dusty exhaled, a deep sigh of regret summing up his feelings. "I don't know who those men were today or how they found out about the rail gun. Really, it doesn't matter. You can't be associating with a known criminal, or you'll be in hot water too. So I'll be on my way just as soon as I can pack up my things."

Penny nodded, a look of sadness crossing her face. "You did right by the girls and me. I'll be sorry to see you go. I hope it all works out for you."

Dusty turned to walk toward the barn when a voice sounded from the corner of the house.

"Well I'll be damned," Mitch said. "They'll let anyone hang out around these parts."

Furious would have been an understatement. Tio paced the worn concrete floor of the warehouse, the energy of anger obvious in every step and motion.

None of the 50 odd cartel soldiers standing idly around wanted to be noticed by the boss in his current state of mind. They pretended to be busy, checking weapons, whispering hushed remarks about the weather, the local cantina, or a señorita who had caught their eye.

Each of them fully understood the ramifications of the boss's temper boiling over. Such volcanic eruptions weren't common, but all of them had heard the sordid stories of such events. None wanted to suffer the consequences of the Uncle's furor.

The rumbling of a diesel engine signaled yet another truck was arriving. All heads, including Tio's, glanced toward the loading dock bay, many hopeful that the newest arrival might explain why they had all been urgently summoned from the far reaches of the cartel's territory. This was an unprecedented gathering.

A few moments later, a large, open bed truck bearing the military logo of the Mexican Army rolled to a stop and began disgorging the platoon of what were obviously troops, but dressed in civilian garb. For a moment, everyone except Tio tensed. The army could be friend or foe, and no one was quite sure what was going on.

The tension quickly dissipated when a senior officer approached the cartel boss and extended his hand and a warm smile. Friend. But what the hell was going on?

In fact, there were nine trucks in a convoy, each dispatching its soldiers in an orderly fashion. The huge warehouse soon became crowded.

Someone handed Tio a bullhorn, and the low rumblings of the crowd silenced as the boss climbed onto a desk, his dark gaze sweeping the throng.

"For years we have been forced to endure the arrest, detention and death of our comrades," Tio began, his voice slightly distorted by the electronic device. "Our livelihood has been assaulted by authorities, corrupt officials and competing organizations. We have all lost friends and family members, felt the sting of money being withdrawn from our worthy pockets, and stood by helpless as the Yankee DEA has locked away our associates."

Tio paused for a moment, scanning the crowd as if to judge their collective reaction before continuing. "But our fight has been more than a battle of right versus wrong. The American policies that deny our brothers and sisters at the border... deny them a chance at a better life... this is wrong. They claim to embrace free enterprise and market driven commerce, yet they declare our product illegal and seize our hard-won gains. I could go on and on about how the Americans play with two faces, but you all already know the facts. And I, for one, have long harbored a desire to fight them... to set things straight... to right the injustice they impose upon our people and our land."

Again he paused, noticing several heads nodding in agreement. "Today is a great day. Today an opportunity has presented itself... an opportunity to throw off the smothering veil of American imperialism and repression. Today we have a chance to change the course of our people's lives. Today we have the chance to come out of the shadows and correct the stigma of evil that corrupt men hang over our heads. If we are successful, we'll no longer be lurking criminals trying to eke out a living under the repressive boots of men who are truly holding down our people. Today we can become true heroes and set our family and friends free."

Tio lowered the megaphone, giving his words time to sink in and judge the reaction of the men surrounding him. Most appeared simply curious, while a few others showed surprise.

"We are going to invade the United States of America," he declared, a broad smile filling his face as murmurs of disbelief rolled across the gathering. "Now before you think your uncle has gone completely loco, let me explain. Just on the other side of the border, in the town of Laredo, a new technology is within our grasp. A device has been created that will change our world forever… a device that I intend to control with my own hand. We must take and hold only that one small slice of U.S. territory for a few hours and capture this invention. Once it is in my possession, the Americans will have no choice but to surrender."

Like a jolt of electricity, shock circulated through the gathered men. Despite all of them being hardened veterans of extreme violence and urban combat, they believed that taking on the United States was suicide. Tio had truly gone mad.

But the cartel boss had expected just such a reaction. With a simple nod of his head, Tio was joined on the platform by a Mexican Army colonel. The man's uniform bore a significant number of ribbons and awards, a clear indication of authority and experience.

After Tio handed over the bullhorn, it was the officer's turn to address the small army. "My name is Colonel Zeta. Many of you know me to be an honorable man. I say to you with 100% confidence that Tio is neither lying, nor crazy," he began, getting right to the point. "I am aware of this device of which he speaks, and

I agree with his analysis of the situation. If we can fight hard and hold Laredo until this super-weapon is in our possession, then the battle will be won. We can conquer the world's most powerful military by just that one single action – a victory that will forever change our world. It is within our grasp."

For many in the crowd, the army officer's words carried significant weight. The colonel was known as a professional soldier and respected by men from both groups. His further explanation of the situation sealed the deal.

"The opportunity that lies before us supersedes each of our own meager lives. Regardless of which side of the law you live, there is now a chance to make a difference for Mexico and her people. We can invoke a transformation... improve the world for everyone who strives for a better life. We only have to suppress our fear and doubt and execute to the best of our abilities. The rewards will far exceed anything any of you has ever imagined."

Then it was Tio's turn to address the crowd. "We are going to invade the United States with over 2,000 comrades. When I leave this place, I'm going to another location where a similar number of men are gathered. And then another... and then another. We will overwhelm the American authorities, capture this device, and then withdraw before they can mobilize any military response. By then, it will be too late. I only ask that you fight well... that revenge fills your hearts and minds – vendetta for your brothers and sisters who have suffered under the yoke of American dominance."

A handful of the listeners was truly inspired and shouted their enthusiasm. In a few moments, the reaction spread throughout as Tio exited the building surrounded by his security force.

Without pause or delay, another officer climbed on the desk and began issuing instructions for the distribution of ammunition, weapons, and supplies.

There were four motor vehicle bridges crossing the Rio Grande River between Mexico and Laredo, Texas. A fifth carried rail traffic.

Since the signing of the NAFTA Treaty, cross-border traffic had become so congested that a sixth span was in the works. Daily, hundreds and thousands of trucks plied the bridges, carrying goods, sub-assemblies, and components back and forth between the heavily industrialized areas lining both sides of the great river.

To the massive presence of the U.S. Border Patrol, a gridlock of semi-trucks crossing into Texas was a common sight. So voluminous was the traffic, that the largest bridge was restricted to commercial vehicles only. Eight lanes of trucks, trailers, tankers, and delivery vans carried their cargo back and forth between the two North American neighbors.

It was due to this congestion that the 40 over-the-road semis hauling Tio's private army approached the crossings unnoticed. When the lead units of the cartel's convoy were next in line at the border control station, all of that suddenly changed.

The back doors of the first five trucks sprang open, armed men in balaclava masks pouring out of the trailers. All of the disembarking hoard wore load vests bulging with pouches, spare magazines, and hand grenades. Battle rifles with folding stocks, holographic optics, and stout slings swept in all directions.

Two-man teams began boiling out of the trailers, deploying heavier weapons equipped with bi-pods and belt-fed strings of ammunition that dangled from their breeches. They formed up quickly and then began hustling toward the small booths that signaled the U.S. border.

Each of the small glass and plywood enclosures was manned by a single, lightly armed agent. The outcome was inevitable.

Automatic weapons' fire shattered the otherwise uneventful afternoon, short bursts by the cartel's lead units overwhelming the stunned border agents in a matter of moments. More armed men appeared at the bridge, their mission to direct traffic and clear the way for the rest of the cartel's invasion force.

Frantic 911 calls soon flooded the Laredo Police Department's system, the initial reports claiming active shooters were robbing trucks on the bridges.

Laredo was the 10th largest city in Texas with a population numbering over 200,000 residents. The border city boasted a well-trained and equipped city police department as well as county, state, and federal lawmen. Within minutes, over 100 patrol vehicles and two SWAT units were responding to the disturbance at the span over the Rio Grande. Before they arrived, the situation got worse – a lot worse.

Pleas for help began coming in from all of the bridges. Reports flooded the emergency lines, frantic voices describing dozens of armed men firing automatic weapons and storming the Border Patrol facilities. Other calls claimed the US Customs facilities were under attack. The responding patrolmen were confused, the dispatchers unsure of exactly where to send them. The bedlam didn't last long. Less than three minutes into the assault, the 911 system was overwhelmed and ceased to function.

The first officers to arrive were met with a hailstorm of bullets from both AK47 and G-3 battle rifles. Completely surprised, most fell before they could even exit their shredded cruisers. The handful that managed to broadcast a warning to their fellow officers merely added to the confusion.

The few patrolmen who did achieve defensive positions were quickly overwhelmed. Department-issued sidearms, shotguns, and the occasional M4 patrol rifle were no match for RPG rockets and belt-fed weapons.

Tio's invasion force wasn't entirely dismounted infantry. A second wave of invaders was soon pouring across the border, a hastily gathered assortment of pickup trucks and busses allowing the cartel's forces to quickly press its advantage and expand the riverside beachhead.

There was a list of primary objectives assigned to the various teams from Mexico. The city police station, courthouse, television, and radio stations were high on the Uncle's military inspired agenda of targets.

Three lead elements of the cartel's army headed directly for the Laredo International Airport, their mission to deny any counter-attacking force the long concrete runways. Trucks full of armed men burst through the chain link fence surrounding the facility and sped across the tarmacs. As hundreds of horrified passengers watched, masked men brandishing military weapons commandeered every available fuel truck, forcing the stunned airport employees to drive their mobile bombs onto the runways.

Air traffic controllers, seeing their landing strips blocked by thousands of gallons of jet fuel, began diverting all incoming flights. The tower supervisor, thinking the facility was under attack from terrorists, managed to get off a brief warning before heavy combat boots kicked in the door, and the main control room filled with shouting, masked invaders. Laredo International Airport was closed.

A few of Laredo's finest managed to barricade themselves inside the police headquarters, keeping the attackers at bay with concentrated small arms fire from the cover of the brick and mortar building. For a brief time, their pocket of resistance slowed the wave of conquest spreading rapidly throughout the south Texas berg.

Colonel Zeta, surrounded by a company of his most trusted troopers, was monitoring radio traffic a short distance away. "We have twenty to thirty enemy fighters holding out at objective number three," sounded the report. "I have four men down."

Zeta didn't recognize the voice, but knew that the target had been assigned to one of the cartel's units. The colonel quickly rallied his troops and began running toward what he knew was the county's main law enforcement complex.

He arrived to find two clusters of Tio's men occupying the parking lot. Numerous police vehicles dotted the area, most showing battle damage. Smoke poured from several windows, piles of glass and shredded metal evidence of the ongoing firefight.

The colonel's arrival drew a hail of bullets from the barricaded defenders, the incoming fire forcing Zeta's reinforcements to scramble for refuge. "Give me covering fire!" he ordered.

The Mexican officer watched as two of his men rose and began spraying the complex with controlled bursts of automatic fire. Small puffs of mortar and stone erupted from the building's façade as his men began walking suppressive lead into the structure. A moment later, another, deep baritone voice joined the chorus as the squad's machine gun came on-line, the heavy weapon slamming rivers of high velocity death into the foe.

With the enemy hopefully ducking for cover, the colonel sprang forward, zigzagging across the lot as random, hastily aimed shots cracked through the air past his head.

He found Tio's lieutenant huddled behind a small rise, the harried looking leader surrounded by several of his team.

"What the fuck are you doing?" Zeta shouted. "Use your grenades and blow the hell out of this place. We don't have time for a protracted fight."

The cartel man seemed momentarily confused by the order. "We can't use the RPGs... I think my brother is in that jail. He was arrested three days ago, and I think they're holding him..."

216

Zeta slapped the man across the face. "I don't give a fuck if your mother is inside!" He screamed. "We are losing men and momentum. Now take this objective, or I'll relieve you of command."

Stunned by the response, the team leader hesitated, shaking his head. "I won't... I can't," the man stammered.

Zeta moved like a striking snake, pulling his pistol and shooting the man in the face. "You're relieved," he growled and then turned to the shocked onlookers. "Who's second in command here?"

One of the nearby assaulters raised his hand, "I am, sir."

"I want you to rally anyone on your team with an RPG on this spot. Go! Do it now!"

Zeta watched as the cartel thug hustled off. After satisfying himself that his orders were being executed, he pulled his radio and thumbed the button. "I want our grenadiers to form on me."

"Yes, Colonel," came the instant response.

A few moments later, the colonel was surrounded by four men equipped with rocket launchers, each accompanied by a teammate carrying reloads of the heavy missiles.

"On my command, I want a simultaneous barrage," Zeta shouted to the new arrivals. "Two there and two there," he ordered, pointing at different sections of the building.

"Fire!"

Four trails of white smoke followed the sizzling, rocket-powered warheads into the police headquarters, balls of red and fire flame erupting as the projectiles impacted. Clouds of slicing, screaming shrapnel tore through the ranks of the defenders inside, lacerating flesh and crushing bone.

"Reload! Reload!" Zeta commanded.

Twenty seconds later, a second barrage of missiles impacted the facility, their detonations decimating the numbers of those still fighting.

Before the rumble of the explosions had rolled across the grounds, Zeta was up and waving his men forward. "Go! Go! GO!" he screamed, frantically motioning for his men to enter what remained of the building.

When the distant explosions first rumbled through his cell, Mike Boyce thought it was an odd time of day for a baseball game.

The stadium hosting Laredo's minor league team would shoot off fireworks to celebrate the occasional home run, but most games were at night. It soon became clear to all of the prisoners that the ever-increasing drone of thunder wasn't due to any baseball game.

There wasn't any question about the gunfire.

When the shootout at the jail first erupted, the prisoners were as bewildered as the rest of the city. Rows of incarcerated men began nervously pacing back and forth in their cells, each explosion and volley of gunfire agitating the population to a higher level of panic.

Mike and his cellmates were as frightened as anyone. Detained for a DUI, the oldest of the three inmates remained at the cell door, his eyes nervously darting up and down the corridor beyond. As the muffled sounds of violence escalated, shouts and cries sounded throughout the floor, scared men trying to make sense of what had clearly become a major battle.

The walls literally shook when the Mexican RPGs had slammed the building. That event, closely followed by the cracking sound of the random bullet zipping through the area, sent most of the prisoners to the floor. Grown, toughened criminals could be heard crying and whimpering.

Without warning, the door to Mike's cell flew open. The farmer gasped when he looked up to see a bloody, disheveled deputy standing in the opening.

Streams of crimson flowed down the jailer's face, his uniform torn and caked with dirt and dried blood. Holding a 12-guage shotgun across his chest, Deputy Turner motioned for the occupants to get out. "You three, get the fuck out of here... right now... come on... I don't have much time."

Despite weeks of yearning for his freedom, Mike was confused by the opportunity. "What's going on?" he mumbled, unsure by all the commotion.

"The jail's under attack. We don't know by who, but we can't hold out much longer. Now get the fuck out of here."

A loud string of gunfire accented the jailer's statement, the deputy bringing the shotgun to his shoulder and pointing it toward the main offices. "Get the hell out of here!" he repeated.

The inmates didn't have to be told again, the need for their departure accented by another burst sounding even closer than the last.

As Mike went to squeeze past Deputy Turner, the lawman reached out and put a hand in his chest. "I want you to know I'm letting you go because I never felt right about your being in here to begin with. I knew your daddy, and he was a good man. Now you lay low until this all blows over and then walk home. Go take care of your wife and those girls. Now get going!"

Mike managed a smile and nod before being startled by another round of shots. The fighting was clearly getting close. Glancing over his shoulder as he ran toward the emergency exit, he saw Turner take a knee and raise his weapon.

Bullets came screaming down the corridor, pinging ricochets sparking off the steel door and bars. Mike ran as if he were being chased by hell's hounds, the roar of combat ringing through his head. More lead struck the wall, geysers of plaster and wood rising from the surface and blinding the fleeing men.

Some deep, primitive survival instinct overrode Mike's legs, forcing him to dive to the floor. He covered the last ten feet before the exit with a mad, scrambling crawl. As he rolled out of the building, he glanced back to see Turner working the pump shotgun as fast as his arms could move.

Just before clearing the opening, Mike saw Turner go down, his rescuer's body vibrating as several bullets tore through his torso.

Boyce found himself at the back of the jail. He somehow commanded his legs to move and soon was running like the wind down the nearby alley.

He could hear the shouts of voices behind him, but didn't dare look to see if he was being pursued. He cut a corner, made another left across a parking lot and then spied what he hoped would be a good hiding spot.

The green dumpster somehow looked appealing to the fleeing man. Without hesitation, he pulled himself up and over the edge, landing in a heap on top of several cardboard boxes and bags of office trash.

He scurried out of the light and into a dim corner, covering himself with the nearest bag and box.

Boots sounded outside the metal container, harsh voices shouting in Spanish. Mike's heart stopped when a long string of automatic fire sounded, his mind placing the shooter right outside of his hiding spot.

Then the turmoil seemed to move away, the running men and shooting slowly fading into the distance.

Mike didn't move. With his heart still racing, he was determined to stay put no matter how bad the inside of the dumpster smelled.

Some citizens, quickly realizing that their community was under attack, tried to fight back with personal weapons. Like the police, they were completely outmatched. Brave individuals took down the occasional invader, but were quickly overwhelmed by the massed firepower of the organized cartel troops. Many residents perished alongside their vehicles, others at the thresholds of their homes and businesses.

Bedlam and complete chaos erupted throughout the small municipality. No one knew what was happening, who was shooting, or why the quiet border town had suddenly turned into a combat zone.

For the first time since the War of 1812, an American city fell to a foreign invader.

Tio had recruited the rogue army units with promises of bounty and national pride. Within an hour of the first shot, every bank, jewelry store and business cash register was being looted by the victorious invaders. The residents of the now-burning town were herded into schools, parks, and shopping mall parking lots while gangs of men roamed the streets taking what they wanted and putting down any pocket of resistance.

With 250 handpicked men riding in 18-wheel trucks, Tio headed east to the Boyce Poultry Farm and what he knew was the ultimate prize of the day.

As Laredo fell, another significant force was speeding across south Texas. It had taken a few hours, but eventually Shultz and his FBI technicians had figured out where their fugitive was hiding.

A surveillance camera at a nearby bank had provided the clues. A man driving a pickup in a hat that matched the one worn by Durham Weathers. A woman riding in the passenger seat with two children in between. The truck speeding by four minutes after the explosion. A license plate number.

A quick computer cross-check with the Texas Department of Motor vehicles confirmed the identity of Mrs. Penny Boyce, the Lexington's video image matching her driver's license picture and leaving no doubt.

Interviews with eyewitnesses put Weathers with the woman and her children. It was good enough for Shultz.

The elite FBI Hostage Rescue Unit was already on the way to Corpus. Shultz rallied every available law enforcement officer at his disposal. Within two hours, a sizable force was on its way to Laredo, Texas – more specifically the Boyce Poultry Farm residing a few miles east of town.

When the confused radio reports first started drifting in from Laredo, Shultz initially thought Weathers had gone completely insane and had started blowing the hell out of the border city.

As bits and drabs of information came in, he realized that he and his men were approaching something else.

Less than an hour away from their objective, Shultz received a cell phone call from the bureau's Corpus field office. They had identified the fingerprints off one of the casualties, one Mr. Victor Bustios, a known Gulf Cartel enforcer with several outstanding warrants.

Pieces of the puzzle began to fall into place. As the miles sped by, Shultz realized that the cartel had somehow found out about the rail gun and Weathers' location. That knowledge had prompted the shootout aboard the Lexington – an effort that had obviously failed. Now the crime syndicate was making another attempt.

While he didn't know all of the facts, it didn't take genius-level deductive reasoning to associate the violence in Laredo with Weathers. The cartel was making a serious play to possess the rail gun, and he couldn't let that happen.

The Latin American drug lords were ruthless men who had little regard for human life. Shultz physically shuddered at the concept of such individuals controlling the power of Weathers' device. So far, Durham had been reserved and low-key, no doubt hoping Washington would come to its senses and strike a deal. The men who ran the world's largest criminal empires wouldn't operate with that same restraint.

It took another 15 minutes before he finally reached the director. Already confused by the limited, contradicting reports coming out of Texas, the top FBI man sounded as if he were surrounded by a storm of pandemonium.

"We are already mobilizing everything we can," the harried man responded. "But it takes time. I'm being informed that we'll have air assets en route within the hour, ground assets on the way by this evening. We're sending everything we've got to Laredo to repel the invasion."

"Sir, Laredo is a decoy... a diversion. The real target is Weathers and the Olympus Device."

"What? What are you talking about?"

"I'm certain, sir. There's no reason for the cartel to take such a huge gamble. They have to know we'll hunt every single one of them down. The only logical explanation is the rail gun," Shultz explained.

The director was skeptical, "Let me consult with the president on this. What you're saying makes sense, but I need to brief the Commander in Chief before we divert any forces."

Shultz was desperate, "Sir, that's not going to work. This will all be over in the next hour. I've got just over 50 men with me, but I fear that's not going to be enough. We're a little more than 30 minutes out, and I'm worried we'll be too late. Sir, we must have military forces mobilized and moving toward Laredo. Please, sir, I beg of you... call the governor, call the president... call the Pentagon," Shultz pleaded. "I don't need to tell you what the consequences would be if those desperadoes get their hands on that weapon."

There was a long pause before the director responded. "Every Texas highway patrolman is on the way to south Texas, as well as deputies from surrounding counties. Give me a rally point, and I'll see to it that they are ordered to join your task force."

Shultz had already pulled up a map of the Boyce farm on his smart phone. He quickly scanned the area, recognizing every second was critical. There was only one significant landmark nearby – Tri-Materials.

He quickly provided the director the name and address.

"I'll have every available resource meet you there. Good luck... and God bless."

The two men embraced several times, Dusty still reeling from the shock of his younger sibling's unannounced and unexpected arrival. Mitch was all smiles, absolutely thrilled and gushing with relief after finding his older brother in one piece.

Penny stood by, marveling at the emotional current clearly shared by both men. Dusty had been so stoic and reserved in her presence, and it was interesting to see this side of the man.

"Okay, so now that we've got all the mushy stuff out of the way, tell me what the hell you're doing here, little brother? And how can you be so sure the FBI doesn't know where you are right now?"

"I borrowed a colleague's car, and the feds think I'm attending a convention in Corpus. There are about 3,000 eggheads at the event, and I slipped out a back door and made triple sure no one was following me."

Dusty grunted, both a thousand questions and reprimands flooding his mind. He wanted to scold his sibling for taking the risk while at the same time was thankful for his presence.

Mitch answered the next question before Dusty could ask. "The sample chicken you sent me – that was very clever, Dusty. I had the tissue analyzed and know what's killing those birds. Besides seeing you, I wanted to locate the source of the poison that is causing the carnage."

"Poisoning?" Penny sounded from the porch.

Mitch turned and nodded, "Yes, ma'am, your birds are being poisoned. It is an industrial compound... a complex molecule that basically includes cyanide. This particular variant has been banned in the U.S. for decades. It was used primarily in the process of coating metals."

The new information distracted Dusty for a moment, taking his mind off the desperate need to flee. Maybe he could make up for this morning's disaster at the Lexington – at least indirectly. He looked at Penny and said, "So your husband was right. It is Tri-Mat that is killing your birds."

Mitch interrupted, "We don't know that for sure. It could be an old industrial waste site or any number of sources. Before I use the university's weight and bring down the EPA on anyone, I would like to get a look at the facility. It would take some very special storage tanks to hold this chemical, and I think I could identify them from a distance."

"I kind of need to get out of here, Mitch. There are some very bad men who are probably on their way here right now."

Scratching his chin, Mitch said, "I tried to see the plant from the road, but couldn't get a good angle. Can we just take a few minutes and see if I can get a better view from Mrs. Boyce's property?"

"You can take the ATV," Penny offered, no doubt hoping to help her husband's cause.

Dusty glanced around the quiet scenery of the farm and then up and down the empty road. "Okay," he conceded, "But let's make it quick. I have a bad feeling that a ton of trouble is getting ready to fall on my head."

Tio rose from behind the disabled police car and fired a short burst from his AK, quickly dropping back down behind the minimal cover provided by the rear axle. Bullets zipped past where his head had just been exposed, a few of the stray rounds shattering what little remained of the cruiser's rear glass.

"This is taking too long," he shouted to one of his nearby lieutenants. "Take five men and flank them to the south. Do it! Now!"

Knowing better than to show himself in the same location twice, the cartel leader cowered low to the ground and duck-walked to the rear fender. A moment later, he loosed another burst from his weapon, hoping to give his men a little covering fire.

The U.S. lawmen had learned quickly - a little too quickly for Tio's liking. Several of the Laredo police had formed up with other responding officers and began a loosely organized fighting retreat.

Tio's convoy had encountered the first such resistance just outside of the city limits as they headed east to capture the rail gun. Rather than try to hold their ground, the policemen had ambushed the convoy, an effort clearly designed to slow the intruders' advance. The officers had jumped in their cars and scampered away before Tio's forces could dismount and form up to finish them off.

Again, a mile outside of town, they had attempted another delaying tactic, spraying random, haphazard fire at the lead truck and then speeding away before the cartel's men could engage.

A few miles later, they had used several vehicles to form a roadblock and were making a desperate stand.

There were seven police cars and two government SUVs blocking the two-lane road. Having had one of his precious transports already shot out from underneath him, Tio had ordered the convoy to stop and disembark the troops at a safe distance.

What had ensued was nothing short of a pitched battle.

But the 14 defenders couldn't hold off the superior numbers of invading shooters. In a few minutes, Tio's men had begun pushing back the stubborn resistance, eventually flushing the Yankees away from their cover and onto open ground. The pavement was now littered with smoldering, shattered law enforcement vehicles, the destruction littered with lifeless bodies from both sides.

Still, the survivors didn't run or break contact.

Tio watched as two squads of his men scurried across the open prairie bordering the road. One of the men went down as the Americans spotted the maneuver and responded with a barrage of lead. Still, the invaders from the south maintained the pressure.

"Let's go!" Tio turned and shouted at another group of his forces. Rising up, he waved his arm for them to follow and moved off to envelop the Americans. *This will all be over in a minute*, he thought as he scrambled up and down the ditch and into knee-high grass.

Before they had moved 100 yards, the sound of an engine reverberated over the next rise. Tio and his followers stopped, watching as a single black SUV raced off, bouncing as it sped away across the field.

"Run, you son-of-a-bitches! Run away, you cowardly fucks!" he shouted at the retreating truck.

Bringing two fingers to his mouth, he issued a loud whistle and began waving his men back. "We've got to get to that poultry farm... and we've got to get there right-fucking-now!" he cursed.

Watching his men hustle back to the trucks, he noticed the road sign for the first time. "Plant Entrance - 2 miles ahead. Beware of slow moving trucks."

"I'm fully aware of slow moving trucks," he whispered to the sign.

There weren't any binoculars at the farm, so Dusty grabbed a couple of hunting rifles from the gun room, hoping their scopes would provide adequate magnification. With the ever-present duffle, Mitch and Dusty were soon in the ATV and scattering the chickens as they bounded across the farm.

"There's high ground on the back side of this property," Dusty informed his brother. "I bet we can get a good view of that plant from there."

The two men sprang out of the ATV and soon found themselves at the crest of a small rise. The huge smokestacks of the Tri-Materials facilities towered in the distance.

Mitch began scanning with the rifle, slowly sweeping the factory's grounds with the magnified optic. Dusty was busy as well, keeping an eye out for any security guards that might be patrolling the area. A few moments later, a line of flashing blue and red lights drew his attention.

"Are you sure you were not followed?" he asked Mitch, nodding toward the long line of police vehicles speeding along the plant's drive.

"Wow," Mitch replied, changing his focus to the parade of cops. "What the hell is going on?"

They scrutinized the scene as the convoy of law enforcement officials began pouring out of their transports, all of them dashing toward the road rather than the buildings that comprised the plant. "What the hell are they doing?" Dusty asked, not really expecting Mitch to know.

Before his brother could speculate, the thumping sound of a helicopter sounded behind them. Believing the authorities had discovered him, Dusty's heart began to race. He reached for the duffle and pulled out the rail gun.

The blinking lights of the aircraft soon became visible, vectoring in on the Tri-Materials complex from the north. Dusty found the bird in his riflescope and could make out enough detail to see the emblem of a badge painted on the fuselage.

The gunsmith lowered the rifle and reached for the rail gun when a streak of smoke and sparkling flame rose up from the earth beyond, its course vectoring as if it were seeking the helicopter.

A brilliant ball of white flame erupted around the incoming copter, a boiling cloud of red and orange appearing in the sky where there had been a flying machine just a moment before. "Holy shit!" Mitch barked as the rumbling roar of the explosion rolled across the Texas landscape.

"Somebody just shot down that helo with a missile," Dusty announced, somehow needing to verify what both men had just seen. "Somebody just knocked a police helicopter out of the sky!"

Before either man could comment, a wave of gunfire erupted below. The two bothers snapped up their long-range optics and began desperately scanning, trying to figure out what was happening.

Dusty spotted several men in FBI jackets, some of the feds running while others took a knee and began firing AR15 rifles. He watched as two of the agents fell, one man writhing on the ground in agony. He could make out muzzle flashes in the distance as the sound of more and more firepower joined the firefight.

"Mother of God," Mitch announced, unable to tear his eye away from the scope. "I just saw a guy wearing an ATF jacket practically cut in half. Who are they fighting, Dusty?"

The older Weathers was just about to conjecture when a newly arriving police cruiser exploded in a massive ball of flame. Sweeping the vicinity, he managed to catch a glimpse of a man rising up from the ditch with a huge weapon on his shoulder. Dusty watched in horror as the RPG left its launcher. He followed the smoke trail as the missile slammed into another highway patrol car and detonated.

Like a slow-motion replay, the Texan inhaled sharply as he watched the vehicle lift off the ground by the blast. He could discern doors, the hood, and bits of metal flying in all directions. A moment later, there was nothing left but a burning pile of scrap metal and a wounded man thrashing on the ground nearby.

"That's a damn war down there, Mitch. Someone is fighting the cops... and they're winning."

"What's this?" Mitch said, pointing toward the Tri-Materials building.

Dusty changed his angle and quickly found what his brother was watching. Men were scrambling around the main structure. A few moments later, four ATVs were racing across the lot, each carrying two security guards.

"Looks like the Tri-Materials guys are joining the fray," Dusty commented. "They've got more balls then I thought."

He followed the progress of the private force as they raced down the drive. Movement in the field beyond drew Dusty's attention where he spotted a small group of men setting up a bi-pod mounted weapon. A second later, flashes of white began spitting from the position, the strobe-like cadence signaling someone had begun firing a machine gun.

The ground around the Tri-Mat ATVs erupted in geysers of dirt and turf as the belt-fed weapon poured rounds into the guard's procession. Dusty shook his head, recognizing the rent-a-cop group was grossly outmatched, wondering if a single security man had survived.

The noise boiling up from the conflict below would ebb to an occasional popping and then build to a crescendo of mayhem. Several of the police vehicles were burning down by the road – there were corpses scattered in every corner of the West Texas landscape. Mitch's next comment caused Dusty's stomach to tighten. "The lawmen are losing, brother. They're getting their asses kicked."

Before the elder Weathers could reply, the sound of an engine caused both men to turn. The Boyce pickup approached, bouncing across the uneven sod of the main pasture.

"Now what?" Dusty grunted as he turned to see why Penny had joined them on the battlefield.

The farm's owner was pale and out of breath. Both of the girls were lying on the floorboard, their eyes wide with fear. "When I heard all the explosions and gunfire, I turned on the news. Texas is being invaded from Mexico! Most of the channels are reporting that it's a private army that's coming from Mexico proper. The attackers have captured Laredo and killed a bunch of cops. A few of the commentators believe a drug cartel is behind the whole attack. Nobody can figure out what their angle is."

Dusty's gaze turned toward the sound of the distant battle, an enlightening bolt of clarity flashing through his already overwhelmed mind. "It's because of me and this... this invention," he mumbled.

"What are you talking about?" Penny questioned. "What do you mean it's because of you?"

Dusty began shaking his head as the pieces of the puzzle fell into place. "The man at the door... during supper the other night. The kidnappers on the Lexington. Somehow, our friends south of the border caught wind of the rail gun. They want it. That's why so many of them are over that rise, fighting with the cops."

The big Texan felt a wave of guilt pass through his soul. More people were dying because of his creative mind. More widows and orphans. More destruction.

Then another emotion took over. Dusty felt the taste of satisfaction welling up inside. *They've ruined my life,* he thought. *Those government bastards have fucked with me and my friends since this whole nightmare got started. Now they're on the short end of the stick. Now they're the ones being hunted like dogs. I wonder how they like it?*

An exceptionally loud explosion snapped his attention back, a column of flame and smoke filling the sky above the ridge. He turned to Penny and said, "If I were you, I'd take the girls back to the barn and lock yourselves in the gun room. Don't come out for a while. I don't know what else to tell you to do."

Penny nodded, the proximity of the violence next door making her nervous. She reached out and touched Dusty's shoulder. "Be careful... and good luck."

She turned to leave when Dusty had a thought. "Hold on a second. I want you to take Mitch with you."

And then he was gone, running back their observation point, where he found his brother still mesmerized by the distant conflict. Dusty quickly explained Penny's news and then voiced his theory.

"Mitch, I want you to go back to the farm with Penny and girls," he announced with a stern voice.

"You what? I'm not going anywhere."

"Yes, you are. You've got a wife and family to think about. Besides, you're my best hope for eventually clearing up this whole mess. You've got to survive... if for no other reason than to clear the Weathers name. Now go, and don't give me any shit about it."

"Come back with me. I have a car, and we can run. I can get you out of here."

The older brother wouldn't hear of it, "There's only a single road out of here. We've got Laredo on one side, the cops on the other. Laredo has fallen into the hands of what I bet is a drug cartel after the rail gun. From what Penny heard on the news, it's the biggest battle on American soil since the Civil War. There's no place to run... no way out. Penny has a safe place for you guys to hold up. You can sneak back home after it's all over."

The Professor knew his brother. He'd seen the look of determination in the man's eye a hundred times and knew it was pointless to argue. "And what are you going to do?"

Dusty really didn't know. There was a voice inside... a line of reasoning that demanded he do nothing. If the FBI took a serious ass-kicking, it might just allow him to slip through and escape.

Maybe they'd think twice about offering him a pardon and dropping all the charges.

Then the patriot's voice made itself heard. The concept of foreigners invading Texas didn't sit well with the gunsmith. When he weighed in the fact that the interlopers were criminals and had probably killed dozens of innocent Americans, a strong urge to fight began to emerge.

Dusty lifted his gaze from the battle below and then turned to his brother. "I don't know, Mitch. I really don't know. One thing is for certain. The confusion of that war down there is my best chance of escape. Now you think about your wife and my nieces and nephews. You think about the name mom and dad made for our family… a reputation you've carried to even higher levels of respect. It doesn't matter if I survive or not – what I want is the world to eventually know that I wasn't some madman. I want the Weathers name to go forward untarnished. For my kid and your children. Now go."

Shultz dove behind the storage tank, rolling away as a string of bullets slammed into the earth where his body had been just a moment before. Bits of soil and rock stung his cheeks as the bullets cracked past. He rolled again, coming up prone and aiming the AR15 rifle at the men that were trying to kill him.

He fired three shots, one of the cartel goons falling as the rest dove for cover. The FBI man's rifle locked back empty. Rolling quickly behind the cover, Shultz slapped his last magazine into his weapon and then chanced a quick peek around the corner. That last burst had given them something to think about. It would be a few seconds before they tried to rush him again.

He was exhausted, out of breath and now, almost out of ammo. This was all going to be over soon. He glanced behind him and identified the last six remaining lawmen. Two of them were hurt, one bleeding badly. "Anybody got any ammo?" he shouted.

The look on their dirty, fatigued faces answered the question.

They had been pushed back, again and again, retreating toward the big factory that dominated the landscape. It seemed so odd to the FBI man... that word retreat.

Since he had joined the bureau so many years ago, his side had always been the strongest. When the FBI conducted operations, they were always the overwhelming force. They always had the most guns and men. Today was the first time he'd felt the bone chilling fear of death and defeat.

In the last 20 minutes, he'd watched comrade after comrade fall. Withering fire, belt-fed weapons, and the foe's overwhelming superiority in numbers had made the outcome of the engagement inevitable. Still, the American men had fought hard. They had taken down so many of the invaders... but wave after wave kept coming at them.

Shultz had initially joined with the cartel army to buy time. He had visions of hundreds of reinforcements marching over the horizon – the cavalry saving the day. When the first helicopter had been destroyed by a ground-to-air missile, that hope had been shaken. When the cartel forces had started firing RPG rockets into the midst of his defenders, any realistic thought of rescue had been lost. Shultz and his men had shotguns and pistols – no match for hand grenades and machine guns.

There was no place to go... nothing else to be done. They had fought like cornered animals, and now the end was near.

He took a moment and assessed the situation. The handful of surviving lawmen was huddled in the midst of pipes, liquid storage tanks and other industrial equipment. Spread around a perimeter of less than 20 yards, they had good cover, but he knew it wouldn't help much.

There was no way they could withstand the next assault.

Tio strolled through what had been the main battleground just a few moments before. He glanced down at the two dead Americans and grunted with satisfaction when he noticed the bloody initials "DEA" on the back of a dead man's jacket.

Whiffs of smoke drifted past the cartel boss as he passed, burning police cars, and the cordite from ammunition creating a surreal fog of death and destruction. He felt at home here, relishing in the atmosphere of violence and carnage.

He was within a mile of the objective. They would mop up the last few remaining Yankees and then roll into the farm where he knew the man with the rail gun was hiding. Already he'd sent men to seal off the road. There was no way Weathers could escape.

Approaching footfalls brought his attention back, a trusted lieutenant hustling up. "The Americans have taken cover by the main building. We are gathering for the final push," the winded man reported.

"Good," Tio replied. "Let's hit them from two sides and be done with this. We are running behind schedule."

The man nodded and then trotted off, waving for another group of cartel shooters to join him. Tio followed, wanting to make sure this last step was properly executed. None of the Americans were to survive.

Shultz could tell what they were doing. He could spot the occasional enemy soldier running here and there, most of them heading to an area hidden from his sight. They were gathering for the final push.

"I've got movement over here," shouted one of the agents from Corpus. "They're forming up on the east side. They're organizing in order to hit us again - any minute now."

"I've got at least thirty more over here," Shultz replied. "They're going to rush us from two sides."

"Where the fuck is the help?" one of the lawmen asked, his voice near panic. "Where the hell's the Army? The Air Force? We're dying like dogs out here, and no one is going to fucking help?"

Shultz was surprised it had taken so long for his men to feel the sting of overwhelming fear. "We've got to hang on just a little bit longer," he reassured. "Remember your training, and let them get close enough so that every shot counts. Help is on the way. Think about it – you know it's true."

"I'm down to four shells for this 12-gauge," another chimed in. "Danny's laying here bleeding to death, and I can't do shit about it. This sucks."

"Just hang in there," Shultz replied.

"There's no place to go anyway," someone said. "They've got us completely cut off. Why don't they just come in and get it over with?"

As if on cue, Shultz spied several of the cartel thugs rise in the distance. *Gawd, there's a lot of them*, he thought, flicking off the safety and bringing his weapon up.

"Incoming!" screamed one of the lawmen on the other side, just before an explosion ripped through the air less than 10 feet away.

The pings and thwacks of incoming rounds began sounding off the surrounding machinery. Shultz instinctively ducked lower as bits of metal stung his flesh like a swarm of angry bees. One of his comrades began shooting – a clear sign the assault was getting close.

Shultz aligned the front post of the AR15's sight on the closest enemy and moved his finger to the trigger. "Just a little closer, pal," he whispered, wanting to hold off until the last possible moment to ensure a hit.

A prayer his mother had taught him began echoing inside the FBI agent's head. Shultz whispered the words as more and more bullets impacted around him. He finished the verse and then squeezed the trigger.

A wall of earth and pavement erupted, slashing through the advancing line of attackers. A blast wave that rocked the ground beneath the FBI team instantly followed. Soil, blacktop, and sand rose 100 feet into the air as a thunderous clap echoed past. Instinctively ducking, Shultz covered his head as an avalanche of dirt, sod and debris rained down all around the lawmen. Even after the deluge had ceased, it took Shultz a moment to clear his vision and focus. He managed to look up as the cloud started to dissipate. Where were the cartel troops? They were gone – simply vanished. A smoldering trench slowly appeared through the haze… scorched, barren earth where once his formidable foe had been standing.

His first thought was that the Air Force had dropped a bomb. He quickly scanned the sky, looking for any sign of a jet or bomber. *Maybe it was a missile*, he thought.

The sound of gunfire overwhelmed the ringing in his ears, reminding him that the fight wasn't over. He managed to crawl across their narrow perimeter to reinforce the other side.

There were dozens of cartel raiders rushing the lawmen's position. Reinvigorated, Shultz shouldered his rifle and began firing at the attackers. The trespassers were within 75 yards and closing fast on the American position.

"Who's that?" the man beside him shouted, pointing toward a lone figure running across the lane to the south. Whoever it was wore a distinctive cowboy hat. Had help finally arrived?

Shultz watched in amazement as the newcomer raised what was an odd-looking rifle. "What the hell is he doing?"

Before any answer came, the senior FBI agent felt a sense of weightlessness as he was picked up and tossed through the air - the momentary defilement of gravity soon replaced by the bone-jarring impact with the ground. Shultz's vision blurred grey, white squiggly lines vibrating through the void.

The world went black.

Dusty watched the last of the invaders sprint toward the main Tri-Materials building. As he had approached the battlefield, he'd noticed a large group of employees fleeing from the facility and into the adjoining field, obviously evacuating due to the raging firefight occurring immediately in front of their workplace.

He calmly dropped another ball bearing into the breach of the rail gun and continued his deliberate trek toward the huge structure. He stepped through the area where the lawmen had been making their last stand, noting the dazed and moaning defenders strewn haphazardly across the ground. "Sorry about that," he whispered. "They got in too close before I could take them out. But you'll live."

He kept walking until he was almost to the road. Now a safe distance away from the the big plant, Dusty paused, observing through the rail gun's scope as the last of the cartel men scrambled inside. He hadn't had a chance to ask Mitch if the facility were to blame for killing the chickens, but he had no doubt the company was responsible for the arrest and hassle of the Boyce family. Maybe even murder.

Glancing around one last time to make sure he was in the clear, Dusty then checked the green LED. One of the shortcomings of the rail gun was the recovery time between shots. It took a while for the ultra-capacitors to recharge after each discharge. "I'll have to work on that," he calmly noted.

As if on command, the small dot illuminated green – ready to fire.

He adjusted the power setting, increasing the reading from 02 to 05. "That should do it," he stated coldly.

He shouldered the weapon, centered the aiming laser, and mumbled, "Take this job and shove it."

He squeezed the trigger.

For a brief millisecond of time, it appeared as though nothing happened - almost as if the super-weapon had failed. But this was an illusion. The lower walls of the massive building expanded outward, swelling like a balloon being filled with water.

And then the architectural integrity of the supporting walls succumbed. Chunks of structural steel and concrete accelerated outward, tossed through the air like sheets of paper blown by a strong wind. Dusty watched as entire sections of the roof rose high into the air.

Like a knife through butter, the base of the towering smoke stacks was sliced by the blast wave. They wobbled for a moment and then began their long descent, eventually collapsing on top of the imploding building. The ground shuddered with their impact, more debris rising into the already darkened air.

Dusty watched as the final bits and sections of walls collapsed inward, sure none of the criminals seeking shelter inside could have survived.

He glanced around at the devastation that surrounded him, shaking his head at the waste and carnage. Bodies littered the ground, strewn in the unnatural positions of death. Scattered among the now-scrap law enforcement vehicles, a few wounded men moved, twitching or thrashing in pain. His first thought was to render aid to the causalities.

For a brief moment, Dusty considered surrendering. He and the rail gun had caused enough slaughter. It was time to end this episode of viciousness, turmoil, and butchery. Anywhere he ran, the reaper of life was sure to follow.

"But would it stop?" he asked, surveying the fatalities as black smoke and flame rolled across the landscape.

"No," he whispered, "it wouldn't stop. Another finger would find this trigger. Another man would hold this gun. Another man who might make it worse."

He forced his mind to concentrate on the list of constructive advancements that could be gleaned from his invention. Grunting, Dusty whispered to the battlefield ghosts, "Now I need to see the positive come from my work... now more than ever. I need it just to break even for all of the evil I've caused."

Agent Shultz felt like he had a bulldozer sitting on his head. Even the feeble attempt to roll onto his side initiated waves of torment through his abused body.

It all came rushing back... the firefight... the few remaining men and the retreat... struggling to hold their position until reinforcements could arrive... and then the rail gun. He conjured up the image of Durham Weathers, complete with western hat, raising the rifle-like device to his shoulder.

He managed to move, tilting his head to spit a mouth full of grit. The effort was exhausting. His mouth was full of cotton and every fiber of his being protested even the slightest movement. One leg was definitely broken. And judging from its lack of movement and unnatural positioning, he was pretty sure his left arm was going to end up in a cast as well. He fought his way through the pain, the fact that the man responsible for all of this was nearby. Or at least Shultz thought he was close. That all depended on how long he'd been out.

Several blinks cleared some of the fog, vague images barely visible through the smoke and cordite haze that had shrouded every major battlefield since the invention of smokeless powder.

"Where are you?" Shultz whispered, his eyes searching the area.

Instead of finding Weathers, his gaze fell on a corpse lying across the field. The man's neck was bent at a funny angle, his arms and legs at odd degrees. For some reason, the dead man's face held Shultz's attention, the lifeless eyes staring directly back.

For a moment, he thought he was looking at one of his fallen comrades. There was a familiarity in the cadaver's profile... something about that face.

It then occurred to the FBI man – he was looking at Tio, one of the bureau's most wanted men. Memorized from countless bulletins, case files and inter-agency operations conducted with the DEA, Shultz was sure. The leader of the Gulf Cartel was lying dead just 40 feet away.

"Well, I'll be damned," Shultz managed to mumble. "At least something good has come from this."

Moaning distracted the agent, diverting his attention back to the men who were fighting alongside him before Weathers had fired his gun. Realizing they might need medical attention, Shultz summoned all of his strength and rolled over. Nausea surged through his torso, but he somehow kept it together.

He looked up to see Dusty kneeling beside one of the fallen deputies, holding a bottle of water to the wounded fellow's lips.

"You're under arrest," Shultz managed to gasp.

Weathers looked up, the sound of a voice startling him. Shultz noticed the man's expression was serious for just a moment, and then a grin formed on his lips.

"It's good to see you haven't lost your sense of humor," Weathers replied. "Most guys are a little sour after getting their asses kicked as badly as all this," he continued, sweeping an arm to indicate the carnage that surrounded the two men.

Shultz had to admit, the man had a point. He wasn't capable of taking in a stray dog at the moment, and it probably showed.

"I thought about letting them kill all of you," Dusty admitted. "It crossed my mind, if only for a moment. But I couldn't let that happen."

"Are they all dead?" Shultz asked, making a weak effort to look around.

"Yes, they're all dead."

There was a hint of sadness in the man's voice Shultz realized, almost as if he regretted killing the invaders. "You brought this on," the agent stated. "All of this is on you, and you know it."

Dusty stood and squared his shoulders. He stepped closer, towering over the prone agent, who for a moment thought the Texan was going to finish him off.

Instead, Dusty smiled and said, "No, it's on your head Mister FBI man. I didn't want any of this. My conscience is clear."

Shultz grunted, "How can you possibly think that? You've left nothing but a path of destruction and death in your wake since College Station. I'm only trying to stop the killing. That's all we've been trying to do."

It was Dusty's turn to laugh. He knelt down and handed Shultz the bottle of water before responding. "I didn't initiate any of the gunplay, sir. It was you and your kind that fired the first shot every time. If you and your law dogs had backed off and let me be, none of this would've happened."

"You know we couldn't do that... that was never in the cards." Shultz took another sip of the drink and then nodded at the rail gun slung across his adversary's shoulder. "You're holding a weapon of mass destruction. We can't let people walk around controlling that sort of power. Look around if you need proof. Durham Weathers may be the nicest guy in the world, but that's not going to stop every power-hungry megalomaniac on the planet from trying to get his hands on your damned invention. That dead man over my shoulder... the one with the broken neck... he's one of the most ruthless men in the world. That's Tio, the leader of the Gulf Cartel. He's no doubt the guy who wanted your invention bad enough to invade a country. That's why we've been trying to arrest you and seize that fucked-up piece of technology you've got hanging from your neck."

Dusty glanced up at the corpse, his eyes taking in the now-dead criminal. "What's your name?"

Shultz didn't answer for a moment, the question taking him by surprise. The lack of response didn't deter the man beside him. Dusty reached down and flipped the agent's ID badge over so he could read the name.

"Thomas Shultz. Well, Tom, it's the power-hungry megalomaniacs in Washington that I'm most worried about. Think about it for a minute. Every invention, creation, and device that can be used as a weapon *has* been used as a weapon. Chemical, biological, nuclear... you name it. When my brother informed me of the potential power within my little discovery, the last people on earth I wanted controlling it were politicians. Handing over something like this is, has been, and always will be a receipt for human suffering. The difference with this little baby is that there's no second chance. It can end it all if a mistake is made, and that scares the shit out of me."

"How's that high and mighty philosophy working out for you?" Shultz asked, his good hand motioning toward battlefield. "Sure looks like it's already being used as a weapon to me."

"I'm not going to debate you on this. This isn't the place or the time. What I do want is for you to take a message back to your superiors. Tell them to set up something... anything that keeps this technology from being used in warfare. I don't care if it's a collation of universities, a specially created commission, or a remote Pacific island that is guarded by aircraft carriers. Convince my brother that my rail gun will never be weaponized, and I'll gladly hand it over in a heartbeat. Oh, throw in a presidential pardon for yours truly as well. I want to go back to my ranch and enjoy the company of a pretty girl I know back home."

"That's never going to happen, Weathers, and you know it."

Dusty frowned, his eyes moving off to the pile of smoldering rubble that had just a few minutes ago been a huge industrial complex. "Then perhaps I should visit Washington with my little invention. Maybe our illustrious elected officials will give my proposal serious consideration after I demonstrate a money shot into the Potomac. The tsunami shouldn't wipe out too much of DC."

Down the Tri-Materials lane, one of the burning police cruisers picked that moment to explode. The event caused Weathers to stand quickly and scan the area for a potential threat. After observing nothing that concerned him, Dusty glanced down at Shultz and continued, "You can stop this madness. It's all so pointless. Deliver my message, Mister FBI Tom. Let them know I'm growing tired of playing cat and mouse. If they don't come to their senses soon, I'll be forced to get mean, and we all know where that will end up."

And with that, Dusty turned and began walking away. After two steps, he paused and looked over his shoulder, "Oh, and by the way, you're welcome."

"Welcome for what?"

"For my saving your life, Mister Tom. I could have let those thugs roll over your position and then toasted their asses. Think about that."

As Weathers continued on his way, Shultz reached inside his jacket and pulled his pistol. He flicked off the safety and managed to steady his shaking hand long enough to center the sights on Dusty's back. His finger slowly put pressure on the trigger - but then he stopped.

He couldn't do it, and he didn't know why. Did he feel a debt? Was it something the man had said?

The effort drained the last of his energy, and he let the weapon slip to the ground and lowered his head. He watched Weathers trek away until the Texan had disappeared from his view. Shultz closed his eyes, wondering why he couldn't put a bullet in the most wanted man on earth.

An idea came to Dusty as he walked toward the road. His instinct to get away from the battlefield was overridden by the FBI agent's words. He was a target, first for the Russians and now a drug cartel. Anger and frustration began to override the commonsense of escape. Maybe the elected leaders of his own country weren't the only ones who needed a clear message.

He changed course and returned to Tio's dead body. Fueled by an ever-increasing rage, Dusty bent and lifted the drug lord's body, hefting the lifeless form over his shoulder.

He proceeded to one of the police SUVs, a large Suburban that appeared unharmed. He unceremoniously dumped Tio's corpse onto the hood and then rummaged inside until he found a roll of duct tape in the back. A few moments later, Tio was secured to the front of the vehicle like a trophy deer being taken down from the mountains.

Dusty hopped inside his newly requisitioned ride and headed from Laredo.

Colonel Zeta examined the roadblock with a critical eye. It was the third such formation he'd inspected in the last 15 minutes.

All of the main roadways into Laredo were now home to such obstacles. The nationalist inside of the colonel was proud that his men had fought so well. The military man within him knew their glory would be short lived if Tio didn't return soon with the promised super-weapon.

"You have too many men huddled too closely to this barricade," he chided the inexperienced officer in charge. "The Americans will put a Hellfire missile up your ass if they catch you bunching up like this. Spread your men out and keep them out of sight."

The nervous leader seemed confused, looking around as if trying to identify suitable cover for his squad.

Frustrated, Zeta pointed at a corner gas station. "Use that structure over there. Keep two men here and shelter the rest inside of that building. They'll have plenty of time to react if there is a counterattack."

Without waiting for any response, the colonel leapt back into the idling Land Rover and sped off.

As he drove to the next roadblock, Zeta couldn't help but gaze up at the sky. He knew it was a worthless use of time as the odds of spotting any American aircraft or drones were low. Still, his eyes drifted skyward.

They had lost over 350 men taking the city. After recovering from the initial shock of the assault, the American law enforcement officers had fought bravely, vicious pockets of the men that took time, ammunition, and casualties to overcome. While this stubbornness had been somewhat anticipated, the reaction of the local population had not.

The response from the citizens of Laredo reminded the colonel of the quote, *You can never invade the American Mainland – there will be a rifle behind every blade of grass.*

Zeta grunted, now having had firsthand experience with those rifles. The Mexican officer didn't know who had coined that little bit of wisdom. Many believed it had been Admiral Yamamoto of Japan, but that was incorrect. No matter the source, the adage had been proven accurate in Laredo that afternoon.

While 350 causalities were still considered acceptable losses, Zeta's forces had been surprised by the ferocity of the common civilians. It seemed that every shopkeeper, bartender, and housewife possessed a weapon of some sort. Once word began to spread of the invasion, the police were often joined by everyday men and women, firing everything from deer rifles to old revolvers at his men.

The entire situation had hurt the morale of his troops. Killing uniformed, armed government servants was one thing. Taking down older men barricaded inside the local VFW was another. Worse yet, his men considered themselves liberators of a sort. The commander had overheard more than a few rumblings from his men – his troops amazed by the hostile reception they had received from the local Mexican Americans.

Some of his men had been motivated by what they saw as a long history of abuse and discrimination against their countrymen. While no one had envisioned joyful parades celebrating the liberators, they definitely hadn't anticipated having to kill so many members of their own race.

Zeta was himself shocked by the reaction of the local Latinos. They had resisted his efforts with as much grit and determination as the Anglos. He recalled coming across one injured man, lying in the street and bleeding out. A rusty relic of a shotgun was lying nearby, evidence that his men had taken fire from the old man.

At least sixty years old, the leathery hands and wrinkled face were those of someone who labored outdoors. For some reason, Zeta had paused, bending down next to the old fellow and asking in Spanish, "Why did you fight us? We are your countrymen."

"You are from the old world," the man sputtered, anger resonating in his voice. "I came here twenty years ago to find a new life. You bring the rotting decay of the old world with you. This is a better place, and you shouldn't be here."

Zeta shook his head, wondering why his thinking was so far off from the reality on the streets around him. It was troubling.

And now Tio was late.

Zeta had estimated it would take four to six hours for the Americans to respond. It would be growing dark in another two, and he wanted to be either back across the border or on the offensive before the light faded. It all depended on Tio and the actual power of the super-weapon. If it were even half as effective as some claimed, they would expand their beachhead on U.S. soil and rally the rest of the Mexican army to join their cause.

But now he was beginning to have doubts. It had been two hours since the syndicate boss had taken his handpicked soldiers and charged forward to capture the prize. With his typical overconfidence, Tio had commented, "I'll be right back," before pulling out of Laredo.

Parking the SUV at the next cluster of his men, Zeta found this group was better prepared. He was met by a serious-looking young officer who saluted smartly.

"Sir, how long before the Americans start dropping bombs on our heads?" the skittish man asked.

Zeta managed to keep the grin off his face, happy that the young soldier was thinking ahead. "They won't use bombers. As long as we are integrated tightly with the civilian population, they won't risk killing their own people. When they come, they'll use conventional ground forces."

"Armor?"

The colonel shook his head, "Unlikely. It takes longer to arm, fuel and transport heavy armor. The worst thing we'll see in the next 10 hours will be helicopter gunships. We have a ready supply of ground-to-air missiles if that's the case."

The kid didn't seem convinced. "Are we here on a suicide mission, sir? We caught the Americans off guard, but that element won't last long. My men are becoming concerned. We feel like sitting targets just mulling around, waiting to be attacked."

"I'm concerned as well," Zeta admitted. "We should know the outcome of Tio's efforts shortly. If he has not returned here by dusk, I'll pull us back over the border and into our native land. We can deal with the Federales later."

The mere fact that the colonel had a plan that didn't involve certain death seemed to settle the younger man down. Zeta was about to move on when excited voices began shouting at the roadblock.

Just as he'd expected, the invaders had barricaded the road at the onset of Laredo. Dusty pulled the SUV to the side and stepped from behind the wheel. The rail gun's scope provided an excellent view of the armed men scrambling into positions. For a moment, Dusty was tempted to fire the weapon, the concept of anyone holding American soil offending to the Texan.

"But that's not what I'm here for," he whispered as he lowered the rail.

Walking beside the open door of the SUV, he reached inside and pulled the transmission into gear. The engine's idle was enough to move the heavy vehicle forward at a snail's pace.

Twenty steps later, Dusty felt like the he had the slow rolling Suburban headed in a reasonably straight line. He took his hand from the wheel and stepped aside, watching his message as it headed toward the roadblock just over 500 yards ahead. The terrain on both sides of the road was flat and featureless, so even if his aim was off, he was sure its meaning would be understood.

He watched the SUV travel for a few moments, and then he proceeded south, trotting through a new subdivision, toward the Rio Grande.

Zeta lowered the binoculars and ordered, "Hold your fire! Hold your fire!"

He turned toward the lieutenant and instructed, "Send a man out to retrieve that truck. There's a body taped to the hood, and I want to verify its identity."

The Suburban had rolled off the road, coming to a stop against the curb some 200 yards shy of the cartel's barricade. Still, it was close enough for Zeta to view the corpse secured to the hood. A feeling of fear began to rise in the officer's gut.

A few minutes later, one of his soldiers drove the police SUV to the barricade. Zeta walked over, holding up Tio's head by the hair.

"You failed... you incompetent son of a bitch... you failed. Now we all may die," the frightened officer hissed.

Pivoting on his heel, Zeta shouted, "Everybody back across the bridges! Now! Hurry! Tio is dead, and the Americans will be coming for our heads!"

Radio broadcasts sounded throughout Laredo, the military walkie-talkies carrying the order to withdraw. The meaning was clear to even the lowest private – something had gone badly wrong, and it was time to flee.

Men began scrambling, trying to carry looted booty and their weapons at the same time. Commandeered trucks and cars raced through the streets of the town, tires squealing as their engines raced south... to the bridges... to safety.

Colonel Zeta tried to maintain order and discipline, but it was nearly impossible. His men were frightened, the flush of the easy victory suddenly replaced by the enormity of their foe. The U.S. military forces would be coming, and they would be pissed. Not a single man expected anything less than a merciless, crushing response.

Toward safe passage on the other side of the Rio Grande they fled, bustling, shouting groups of men who acted as though they were being chased by Satan and an army of demons. Zeta followed, a zombie-like trance replacing the enthusiasm of a dream fueled by revenge. Not only had he allowed his sister to perish horribly, now the souls of all of these men would haunt him forever.

Despite the profane deflation engendered by their failure, Zeta's training refused to abandon discipline. Passing a squad that was trying to hotwire a flatbed truck, he ordered them to cease the effort and retreat. Another group, intent on one last looting pass at a jewelry store, was shouted into submission. His radio transmitted stern orders to maintain a rear guard.

Zeta continued driving slowly toward the south, his last mission in life to save as many of his men as possible. Deep down inside, the colonel was a defeated man. He no longer feared death, no longer cared about himself. Glancing down at the pistol he had used to execute the insubordinate ass at the jail, Zeta smiled. He'd use the same weapon to end his own life as soon as his men were safely across the border.

Dusty pulled down the fire escape ladder and climbed. He found himself on the roof of a two-story building overlooking the valley and downtown Laredo. The fiery red of the late afternoon sun colored the great river's water with a dark crimson hue, a stark contrast to the pale steel and concrete structures of the five paths crossing over the waterway.

He lifted the rail gun and studied the scene below, noting clusters of armed men here and there. They all appeared to be hurrying – in a rush toward the south. It dawned on Dusty that they were trying for the bridges. He noted the still-smoldering booths of the border patrol, the pillars of smoke thin and anemic compared to other, larger infernos raging across the skyline.

Sighing, he realized there wasn't anything he could do about the destruction to the city itself, the carnage of its citizens, and pillaging of its assets that had befallen the innocent south Texas town. There wasn't any doubt her populace had been devastated by events that he felt were somehow related to his presence. He cringed when he noticed two bullet-ridden police cars, the bodies of the officers still lying where they had fallen. *Those men probably had families, wives and children who will be shattered by the loss,* he observed.

His remorse was cut short by a rumbling roar overhead. Dusty looked up to see two fighter jets screaming down the river, small American flags discernable on their tails. "Those look like the same ones that shot at me," he mumbled. "This is madness... pure insanity."

With bright fire trailing from their engines, the two fighters passed low over the bridges and then executed a gradual turn to the north. Dusty watched in horror as a ball of flame appeared at the base of one of the spans, the eruption soon followed by the smoke plume of a missile arching toward the sky and chasing the planes.

White-hot puffs of flares began spitting from the jets as the pilots hit the afterburners and launched decoys. Dusty held his breath as he watched the pilots bank hard in an attempt to distract, avoid, or outrun the incoming projectile. He exhaled in relief as he watched the warhead miss the two planes, its exhaust spiraling out of control into an empty sky.

Returning his attention to the ground below, he detected what clearly were officers trying to organize the panicked invaders. Men were pointing, shouting, and hustling everywhere. The flurry of activity appeared to be absolute bedlam.

"Why aren't you going across the bridges?" Dusty whispered. "Why aren't you running back home?"

A quick scan of the nearest crossing answered the question, two large military helicopters visible on the Mexican side of the bridge. "They don't want you back home," he mused. The trespassers on the U.S. side were pinned between a rock and a hard place.

"I'd choose the hard place if I were you," Dusty smirked. "One hell of a rock is about to fall on your head."

No sooner had the Texan made that observation, than a deep rumble sounded from the north. Dusty could perceive several small, black shapes as they appeared on the horizon, their number increasing with every passing second.

Evil looking attack helicopters darted over Laredo, their wasp-like bodies bristling with rockets and guns... nothing short of delivering gory revenge in a hail of firepower on their agendas.

They swooped over the city low and fast, over a dozen of the heavily armed war birds acting as if they were daring anyone to shoot at them. They got their wish.

Three trails of white smoke whooshed up from the city streets, each shoulder-fired anti-air missile arching toward one of the gunships. But the helicopters didn't try to outrun the incoming warheads; instead they maneuvered in a manner opposite that of the fighters. Going low and barely skimming above the urban landscape, the darting craft sought to confuse the incoming seekers.

Two of the three shots missed their targets, but a third found its mark before the pilot could react. Shaking his head in sorrow, Dusty watched as the burning hulk of machinery impacted the ground and exploded in a huge fireball.

The surviving birds didn't retreat. Before their dead comrades had even made contact with the Texas earth, they turned and began to unleash a relentless and unforgiving hailstorm of rockets and chain-gun fire.

A wall of soil, blacktop, and debris erupted from the ground, the entire area housing the anti-air teams avalanched with incoming fire. There was no way anyone could have survived the counterattack.

More noise from the north drew Dusty's gaze away from the battle below. He sat in awe of what appeared on the horizon.

The sky grew dark with incoming helicopters. There was no way to count them all; Dusty was absolutely convinced that the entire U.S. Army was on its way to Laredo.

He watched, fascinated as a formation of four Blackhawks landed in a low, grassy knoll in a schoolyard, their open bay doors disgorging a steady stream of infantry. More and more of the copters appeared, their wheels barely touching the ground before discharging their heavily armed cargo and then lifting off to make room for the next wave.

Again, gunfire drew his attention away from the spectacle of the assault, the distant drifts of shouting and shooting men adding to the orchestra of helicopter turbines.

Dusty focused his optic, quickly realizing that the invaders were now shooting at their own countrymen across the open expanse of one of the bridges. They were trying to fight their way back into Mexico and escape the full anger and might of the United States military.

Colonel Zeta stared across the bridge at the stubborn, pig-headed captain in charge of the small blocking force that was preventing the cartel's mercenaries from returning to Mexico. Already his rearguard had reported that advancing elements of the 1st Cavalry were approaching the outskirts of town. He had trained with the troopers based in Fort Hood and had no intention of facing them in battle. He needed to get across that river... and needed to do so right now.

He'd tried to negotiate with the man across the river, but there was no chance. The scared officers controlling the Mexican side of the border had obviously been threatened. They refused to allow his men to cross, regardless of any bribe, inducement or plea he offered. Evidently, Washington had pressured Mexico City to block their retreat – an unexpected turn of events. And that is how Zeta suddenly became a man without a country.

Turning to his second in command, Zeta barked, "I want everybody forming up on this one bridge. We're going home, either in a box or on our own two legs."

It took 15 minutes for his men to arrive, only a few of their original over-the-road trucks having survived the battle of Laredo. It was one of these behemoths that Zeta positioned at the front of his formation.

On both sides of the oversized vehicle, he placed a number of men equipped with rocket propelled grenades. He was going to blast and shove his way through.

"Everyone's accounted for," someone reported. "The rearguard is falling back to our position now."

"Good," Zeta whispered. "We may pull this off just yet."

He verified one last time that all of the drivers and men on foot knew their orders, and then turned to the RPG shooters. "On my command," he ordered. "Fire!"

Dusty was keeping a close eye on the U.S. troops from his perch. He had selected the overlook because it struck a balance between his need to be as far away from the area as he could to avoid capture without compromising his vantage of the battle before him. He was torn between cheering for his countrymen as they kicked the invaders' asses and his own safety... *Now, I have reached a new low; I am just like those danged rubberneckers gawking at the roadside wreckage,* he mused.

Finally believing his intervention was no longer warranted, the gunsmith began to rise when complete chaos erupted on the Mexican side of the bridge closest to him. Several balls of red and white flame appeared, soon followed by the reverberations of explosions rolling across the river.

Dusty's first instinct was that the U.S. Air Force had dropped bombs on the wrong side of the border, but no sooner had the racket died down he recognized the racing of several engines and then a volume of gunfire.

A quick look through his optic explained what was going on. Whoever was leading the invaders was smart, grouping all of his men at one bridge and attacking the authorities on the other side. Evidently, they preferred to face the Mexican government rather than the infantry that was advancing closer by the minute.

And it appeared as though the retreating Mexicans were going to succeed.

Dusty watched the line of vehicles slowing crossing the span, both sides of the bridge filled with riflemen firing bursts of automatic fire into the defenders' now-burning roadblock on the south side of the river.

"Nooooo!" Dusty yelled over the ruckus. "No. No. No. You are *not* going to get away."

His head pivoted back and forth between the retreating army that he loathed so deeply and the U.S. Army that was still a fair distance away. "They're not going to catch those bastards," Dusty said. "I can't let that happen."

The green LED glowed brightly in the late evening light. Dusty dropped the ball bearing into the chamber and flipped on the aiming laser. He shouldered the rail gun and centered the red dot directly in front of a large semi that was leading the charge across the bridge.

He pulled the trigger.

The Texan's aim was true, a 20-foot wide expanse of the bridge evaporating into thin air as the pipeline to an alternative reality expanded at the speed of light. A few thousandths of a second later, it closed, leaving a pure vacuum in the space and time it had previously occupied... a blankness that demanded to be filled for the law of this universe's physics to remain true.

A fountain of concrete, rebar and blacktop shot into the air, the concussion crushing bone, metal and sinew for the unfortunate men and machines on the bridge. The blast wave expanded outward in all directions, pulverizing everything in its path.

The lead semi-tractor was obliterated almost instantly, its trailer flung over 200 feet through the air.

The row of buildings closest to the river was blown flat, appearing as though a tornado had magically formed and swept the structures away. For miles in every direction, windows on both sides of the Rio Grande were shattered by the resulting shock wave.

Dusty watched from his elevated vantage, his eyes maintaining a tight focus on the bridge. It was like watching a children's cartoon as the few surviving sections wobbled, shook, and then began collapsing into the river below. Displaced water shot high into the air as huge chunks of the span were consumed by its depths, others peeking from the water's surface. It was all over in a few seconds, nothing but open air where a mammoth 8-lane structure had serviced traffic just a few moments before.

"That road to Mexico is closed," Dusty whispered, bending to return the rail gun to his duffle. He rearranged the contents and then stood, casting one last glance at the town below. He turned to make for the ladder and found himself staring directly into the barrel of rifle.

Zeta pushed a small portion of rubble away, the effort providing some relief from his crushed chest. He wiped the blood from his eyes, trying to raise high enough to get a glimpse of the bridge beyond. It was a wasted effort, his body completely unresponsive.

Letting his neck relax, only the sky appeared in his view. He knew it was over; his time had come.

An aroma fought its way through the waves of pain and fear that consumed the colonel's mind. A sweet smell that reminded him of lilac. Consuela. The homemade shampoo she used on her hair.

The light grew brighter and music filled his ears. The sounds of guitars in perfect pitch. Consuela dancing to the music, a smile of joy painted on her beautiful face.

Then the rhythm changed, the melody switching to a hymn he sang at mass so long ago.

The light became dim around the edges of the sky, fuzzy clouds closing in on the dark blue of the late evening. And then it went dark as the music faded away.

Dusty raised his hands high into the air. There weren't any theatrics in the look of fear that encompassed his face.

"Who are you?" barked a gruff voice.

"My name's Dusty," he stuttered, trying desperately to recover from the shock of the soldier's appearance.

"Where are you from?"

"West Texas," he answered honestly.

The older soldier continued the interrogation. "What are you doing up here?"

"Hiding from the Mexicans," was all Dusty could think to say.

That must have been the right answer because the next words carried an almost friendly tone. "Go hide someplace else. We're setting up here, and you don't want to be around."

Before Dusty could respond, the two men were moving past him, hustling to set up a large bore rifle with the biggest scope the gunsmith had ever seen. He realized he'd bumbled into a two-man sniper team seeking a good position to cover their unit as it advanced through town.

Dusty didn't waste any time, quickly climbing down the ladder and scurrying off. His first instinct was to head away from the city center, but a line of advancing U.S. military quickly reversed his course.

"Shit," he mumbled as he jogged through an alley. "I fucked around for too long, and now I'm pinned."

He ventured onto a street, scanning all directions for some place to lay low. He judged most of the buildings were occupied by frightened, confused citizens huddling in the safety of their homes. If he tried to break in, he most likely would be met with a shotgun blast. Not an option.

Down the street, less than a block away, he spied two shot-up police SUVs. Both units were punctured with bullet holes and surrounded by piles of spent cartridges and glass. There were three dead men still lying in the street.

He walked over to the wreckage and bent to check the body of a man lying nearby. There was no pulse or respiration.

Dusty inhaled, and with a scowl of distaste, scooped up a handful of bloody mud pooled next to the body. He rubbed the copper-smelling goo on his face and neck. He then rolled the body over and quickly removed the man's jacket.

Noting the "ATF" initials on the back and breast, Dusty put the windbreaker on and then removed the neck-chain containing the deceased man's badge and ID. It soon joined his disguise. The corpse's baseball hat and broken sunglasses soon rounded out his costume.

Checking his appearance in the closest SUV's mirror, Dusty inhaled sharply at his image. The side of his head appeared burned and bloody, the red stains on the jacket adding to the charade.

He ambled over to another destroyed cruiser and sat down, leaning his back against the wheel. "Time to watch the show," he whispered.

And what a show it was.

He sat and observed the Apache gunships circling in advance of the ground soldiers. Flinching as they roared overhead, Dusty watched as the apocalyptic war birds patrolled, each bristling with missiles, rockets and cannons. Coming from two different directions, the nose-down attitude and crisscrossing pattern seemed as if the pilots were flirting with the enemy, hoping some foe was stupid enough to rise up and take a shot at them. Dusty smirked, knowing any such action would be met with a hailstorm of lead and explosives.

As the airborne predators circled the area, the sounds of grunted orders and rushing bodies soon filled the air. He spied soldiers in full body armor, scanning right and left with weapons shoulder high. They were looking for work.

Dusty watched as they progressed toward his position, impressed at their coordinated movements. Teams of troopers swept up the street, clearing every opening and potential enemy position as they advanced.

He heard the impact of combat boots nearby and immediately focused his eyes on an empty point in space.

He sensed more than saw the soldier nearby. Without warning, a hand reached for his neck, quickly finding his pulse. "I've got an injured man over here," a voice shouted as streams of troopers flashed by.

A heavy bag marked with the red cross of a medic landed on the ground next to Dusty's leg, and then a kind, concerned face was in his vision. "Hey! Hey, buddy! You okay? You hit?"

Hands felt up and down Dusty's torso, the medic searching for wounds.

"I'm... I'm... I'm okay," the gunsmith managed weakly, not wanting the soldier to find the rail gun or cut away his duffle. "There are some guys on up that street that are hurt worse. Go help them," he weakly protested.

Another soldier appeared, an older man wearing an officer's rank. "He's in shock," the medic reported. "Other than that and the burns on his face, I think he's okay."

Pretending to have trouble focusing, Dusty blinked several times and finally found the officer's face. "I'm okay," he whispered. "Go kill those sons-ah-bitches."

"Get him to the triage area and then rejoin the squad," the captain ordered. He then reached over and touched Dusty's shoulder. "We'll take care of them," he promised.

A short time later, two men appeared with a stretcher. When they bent down to load Dusty, he weakly pushed one of them away. "I can walk, damnit! I can walk. Please, let me walk away from this. I have to walk away... I won't be carried."

The two troopers looked at each other, impressed by the old cop's determination and honor. "Let us help you. Okay?"

A short time later, Dusty was being lead to another spot, a young Army private under each arm.

As they moved through the battlefield, Dusty spied a solid line of blue and red lights coming up the road. Dozens of fire trucks, police cars, and ambulances were converging on Laredo, following the military forces as they swept through the city.

Dusty eventually found himself riding in an ambulance and keeping up his act of confusion and shock. It seemed like they rode for hours, the EMTs busy with the two other more seriously injured patients that shared the tiny space inside. He was taken to a hospital, the facility in an absolute state of bedlam.

A compassionate aide showed Dusty into a waiting area, the large room filled with badly hurt people from both Laredo and the battle at Tri-Materials. He waited patiently, sitting quietly in a corner and trying not to attract attention.

Nurses, doctors, and orderlies rushed back and forth, moving the wounded and treating some right in the middle of the waiting area. When the mayhem began to subside somewhat, Dusty rose and blended with the remaining crowd, finding a restroom away from the emergency area.

He pulled several paper towels from the dispenser and soaked them under the sink water. Entering a stall, he spent a considerable amount of time cleaning both his face and clothing of the clotted blood and soil.

When he emerged, a quick check in the mirror revealed a harried-looking, but unscathed ATF agent. He exited through the front door, unnoticed amid the urgent rush of friends, family and law enforcement bustling around the facility.

As he bounded down the front steps, Dusty read the large sign on the medical building. "Central Hospital – Victoria, Texas."

"At least I know where I am," he whispered.

Dusty walked three blocks before ducking behind a dumpster and changing his outfit. It felt good to don his normal western hat and be rid of the badge, jacket, and sunglasses.

Feeling more like himself again, he continued walking, unsure where he was going. He thought about the bus station, but wasn't sure the tiny town had such a thing. Renting a car was obviously not a viable option. No, he needed to get away from the quaint, pintsized Texas berg as soon as possible. If anyone came looking for him here, it wouldn't take a whole lot of effort to trace where the ambulances had deposited their cargo.

After several minutes, the forlorn sound of a train bellowing its horn gave him an idea. Following the thundering rhythm of the locomotive as it meandered across the tracks, he cut through a residential area and then a thin wood. He soon located the tracks, complete with an engine pulling a long line of boxcars. He was in luck – it was moving slowly.

Glancing around to make sure no one was in the immediate area, he took off at a fast sprint, racing to catch the northbound freight. Dusty had to really push hard to catch his ride. Like a hobo from a time long ago, he finally closed the gap, grabbed the rail of an open, empty boxcar and pulled himself aboard.

He quickly rolled out of the opening, puffing hard to catch his breath. It wasn't long before he was leaning back against the wall and watching the lights of the Texas night scroll by.

Mitch motioned for Penny to stay put. Shouldering his deer rifle, the professor chanced a glance outside the cracked door of the barn apartment.

He and the girls had heeded Dusty's advice, hiding in the cramped confines of the reinforced storage area, barely able to move. The distant thunder of explosions and gunfire had kept them there, no one complaining about the cramped accommodations.

Twenty minutes after hearing the last, distant sound of violence, Mitch had thought it safe to exit the claustrophobic hide. The smallish apartment was a huge relief as compared to the gun closet.

Another hour passed, Penny doing her best to keep the girls quiet while Mitch remained vigilant at the door. He could detect nothing outside, only the occasional, faraway siren reaching his ears.

"I'm going to take a walk, have a look around," he had finally announced. "You guys stay put and let me make sure it's safe."

He found the barn's interior undisturbed, the lack of any villains or intruders reassuring. The next step was the check of the great outdoors.

Caution ruled his actions as he pulled the sliding barn door open, the noise of the rusty rails causing him to jump. Again, no thugs, criminals or dope fiends descended on his position.

The light of dusk illuminated the barnyard, enough so that he verified Penny's property wasn't housing a small army of invaders from the south. Still, Mitch remained cautious, weary of stragglers or others with ill intent.

He decided to check on the house, scanning right and left as he made for the abode. He was just about to step onto the back porch when the sound of footsteps stopped him cold.

He shouldered the rifle, wondering if he could really shoot anybody. As the shadow of a man appeared around the corner, Mitch decided he could indeed pull the trigger.

"Who the fuck are you?" the professor challenged, trying to make his voice sound as menacing as possible.

"I own this place," the surprised man responded. "Who the fuck are you?"

Mitch took a few steps closer to the guy. Whoever it was, the stranger looked like shit. He was wearing a filthy, torn and tattered jumpsuit that had once been a bright, fluorescent orange. Mitch's first thought was the guy had been out hunting, the highly visible clothing worn for safety. It then occurred to him that the man before him wasn't a hunter; he was an escaped prisoner!

The click of the rifle's safety froze the stranger, Mitch taking another half-step forward. "Get off this land! Right now, or I'll blow your head off."

"But… but… I own this place, Mister," the guy protested.

Before Mitch could respond, Penny's voice rang out from behind. "Mike! Mike! Oh my God!" the woman yelled, rushing to jump in the trespasser's arms.

The girls followed, each competing with their mother to hold, hug and kiss their father.

Mitch lowered his weapon, relieved that he hadn't had to shoot the guy. "How in the hell does Dusty do this sort of thing," he mumbled, watching the joyous reunion.

Day Ten

Agent Shultz thought he was dreaming again. The scuffle of shoe leather had forced open his eyes, but the vision that filled his narcotic-fogged mind didn't make any sense.

Surely, he was dreaming, because there was no way the director of the FBI would be standing next to his hospital bed.

"Hello, Agent Shultz," the somewhat familiar voice said gently. "How are you feeling, son?"

Why not talk to my dream? Shultz thought. "I'm doing well, sir. As best as could be expected. Are we still being invaded or did reinforcements arrive yet?"

A grunt from the nation's top lawman was the initial answer, quickly followed by a flat, "No, all of the rogue Mexican military units are either dead or have been apprehended. The same can be said of the private army assembled by the Gulf Cartel. Our nation owes you a debt of gratitude."

The painkillers circulating through Shultz's body lowered his inhibitions while enhancing his sense of humor. "Our nation doesn't owe me squat, Director. It was Durham Weathers who saved the day. Did we catch him?"

The frown on the director's face was clearly visible. "No, Weathers is not in our custody. He's either dead or has escaped. But I'm not sure what you mean when you say he saved the day?"

Shultz blurted out the story, repeating the conversation between Weathers and himself as best he could. The director listened, his face remaining expressionless as his subordinate made the report.

Without a word, the senior man moved to the hospital window, his mind clearly trying to digest Shultz's words. The injured agent couldn't help himself, violating all the rules by offering an opinion.

"Why don't we consider his offer, sir? It seems reasonable to me. I've studied the man for weeks now, and I don't think there's a criminal bone in his body. I've seen that weapon in action four times, and I now appreciate why he's so desperate to keep it out of the wrong hands."

There was a hint of anger in the director's voice, his abrupt spin to face the bed accenting his displeasure. "Because that's not the way our country works, Agent Shultz. Our government is of the people. We are a representative democracy. Just because one man doesn't trust or respect our authority doesn't mean we cave in to his wishes. If we give in to Weathers, that sets a precedent. What happens to the next guy who claims he has a nuke... or the home chemistry guru who mixes up a batch of some super-germ? The majority of the people elected our boss. The majority has spoken. We can't allow one man to supersede the rest of our citizens just because he doesn't like how the vote turned out."

Shultz clearly understood the argument, his ex-boss Monroe and he having debated the topic numerous times. "He's not going to give up, sir. He believes that his position is in the right, and that we're wearing the black hats. He's smart, creative, and very adaptable. A lot of pain, suffering, and destruction are in our future if we don't figure a way to end this soon."

Smiling, the top FBI man bent and patted Shultz on the shoulder. "We're working on it, Tom. You focus on healing and getting back to your desk. Again, I wanted to thank you for your brave actions. It was above and beyond."

Shultz watched him leave, still having some doubts concerning the reality of the whole visit. As he thought about their conversation, he decided he didn't care very much for his boss.

I wonder if working for Durham Weathers will be better? he mused.

The duffle didn't make a good pillow, but Dusty was so exhausted he didn't care. The gentle sway of the rail car and constant rhythm of the wheels had overridden the discomfort of the hard floor and lack of facilities. He'd actually managed to sleep through most of the night.

While he had no idea of the rail line's destination, his general sense of direction told him they were heading north. He didn't care, as every mile between him and the events in South Texas improved his odds of avoiding capture.

Light flooding into the boxcar rousted the Texan, his sleepy eyes taking note of a completely different landscape passing by the open door. There were trees, green plant life, and much denser vegetation than the arid area he'd last seen during the day. North it was.

As the new day progressed, he'd had to switch trains. After a bumpy stop in a marshalling yard thick with tracks and cars, Dusty had waited almost an hour for his transportation to start moving again. When it became clear that wasn't going to happen anytime soon, he'd hopped out of his coach, made sure no one was around and then boarded another train that was moving out. The accommodations varied little from his previous lodgings.

He had a bottle of water and a little beef jerky in his bag, the light meal leaving him still hungry but not desperate. There was little else to do but think and plan... and capture the occasional catnap.

Small towns passed by his transport's door. Keeping back and out of sight, he been tempted to disembark at a couple of the communities that laid along the rail line. Sometimes the engine up ahead slowed considerably; sometimes the locomotive rolled right though at a speed that made jumping out potentially lethal.

For what seemed like hundreds of miles, Dusty didn't mind his method of touring. A sense of progress building with each passing mile, he was content to appreciate the fleeting scenery and think. It was therapeutic in a way, helping him reconcile the death and carnage from the previous day.

But eventually hunger, boredom, and stiffness began to take hold. Two railroad employees had almost discovered him at the last yard, and he couldn't stow away on the locomotive forever.

An hour before dusk he felt their momentum slowing. Packing up his belongings, Dusty moved to the door and chanced a peek ahead.

Sure enough, there was a settlement on the horizon. He didn't know where he was, but there were lights, buildings and hopefully somewhere to find a bed. As was custom, the engine slowed considerably as it approached the maze of crossings and intersections.

Dusty didn't want to leap right in the middle of downtown wherever-he-was, so he watched as civilization meandered by. It certainly was not a metropolitan area, but there was a main street, several stores and a few cars waiting at the signal.

He spotted an opportune, grassy-looking patch of earth ahead and steadied himself. The landing jarred him to his core, and he rolled several times, the train's speed much faster than he'd anticipated. He was going to be sore tomorrow.

After brushing himself off as best he could, Dusty stretched his aching muscles and began hiking toward town.

The trek was less than a mile, but it took its toll as the gunsmith was dog-tired. He hadn't eaten a proper meal in 24 hours and could recall at least four energy-draining adrenaline surges in the last couple of days. He craved the kind of cuisine that did not lend itself to his duffle bag and a hot shower to ease his aching muscles while purging his skin and hair of the layer of Texas grit that currently covered him. And while he was creating his wish list, at least 10 hours of sleep in a bed would go a long way to his recovery.

The blinking light of the hotel indicated a vacancy. Dusty knew his fake Canadian passport was probably compromised from the rental car company back in Houston. He recalled the motorcycle chase through the Bayou City's suburbs – it all seemed like a lifetime ago.

Deciding to bluff his way into a room, he entered the small lobby and asked for a room.

The lady behind the counter was watching a small television and barely looked up. "I've got two queens or a single king – which do you want," she said, never taking her eyes off the game show.

"The king will do just fine," he responded, unzipping the duffle to put on a show of looking for his ID.

"That will be $89 with tax," she announced, pushing a yellow registration form across the counter.

As Dusty looked inside his bag, he spied the ATF badge and ID he'd removed the previous day. He pulled it out and showed it to the clerk. "I'm working undercover," he stated with a clear voice. "I'd prefer that no one knows I'm in town."

The woman glanced at the badge and then handed it back. "No problem, officer. We don't have feds staying with us often, but I'll keep it between you and me. You'll want the government discount I assume?"

"Yes, of course."

The lodgings were several levels below the luxury accommodations Grace and he had enjoyed in Kemah Bay, but Dusty was satisfied. The bed included a mattress that in itself was nothing to brag about, but it beat sleeping on the moving wooden floor pulled by a locomotive. Realizing that his rumbling stomach would not be compatible with a good night's sleep, he set out in search of food.

There hadn't been any restaurants close by, and he doubted the availability of delivery in such a small town... except... maybe... pizza.

A moment later, he searched the yellow pages and was soon to be the proud owner of a large, thin pepperoni and green pepper pizza pie with double cheese. After disconnecting the call, he closed the phone book at looked at the cover.

Dusty grunted, finding it funny that he hadn't even wondered where he was until just now.

According to the bold print on the directory before him, he was now a resident of Pikesville, Kansas.

Mitch grabbed the large section of sheet metal with both hands and pushed it out of the way, a puff of dust and low thud signaling its impact with the ground. He stood and studied the storage tank revealed by his action, reading the numerous warning signs, specifications and operational instructions plastered on the container.

"This has got to be it," he whispered.

Twenty feet in diameter and just over ten feet in height, the object of his attention looked like a short, stubby grain silo. Steel rivets dotted the exterior, their patterns indicating a stout structure designed to withstand significant pressures.

The professor paced around the perimeter, finally arriving at a complex maze of pipes, valves, and pumps attached to the tank. Again, he focused his attention on the hardware's specifications, rubbing dust and grime from the myriad of plates and badges attached to the equipment.

Pulling out his tablet computer, he browsed two manufacturer's websites, gathering additional specifications and quickly reading the details regarding the intended use of the apparatus.

The labels, declaring the tank was filled with an innocent cleaning solvent, were incongruent with the hardware used to pump the contents into what was once the Tri-Materials facility. "Gotcha," he said, looking up at the now-destroyed facility.

The pumps and valves were designed specifically for corrosive liquids with a dense viscosity. No plant manager in his right mind would have such expensive, extreme-duty equipment pumping cleaning solvent. It would have been an unfathomable waste of resources.

Mitch turned away from the reservoir and scanned the ex-factory's grounds. There were dozens of people shifting through the rubble and examining what had been a battlefield just a few days ago. Most were law enforcement, several agencies dedicating forensic teams to try and piece together or document exactly what had happened. A few were no doubt insurance examiners, the Tri-Materials executives having promised their shareholders that the facility would be back in business as soon as possible.

Ignoring all but one individual, Mitch inserted two fingers into his mouth and sounded a shrill whistle. The noise caused several heads to pop up, but he was only interested in Randy. When his friend looked up, Mitch waved him over.

"Whatcha got?" Randy asked as he stepped around a pile of rubble.

"Check this out. I think I've found the smoking gun."

"I sure as shit hope so, buddy. I'm probably in enough trouble already."

Mitch grinned, "Oh hell, Randy, the Houston EPA office can do without you for a couple of days."

"That's not what I'm worried about. I told those cops down at the road that you were my assistant. When they find out you're not a government employee with a damn good reason to be here, my retirement will vanish in a whiff of vapor."

The professor shook his head, knowing his worry-wart friend was exaggerating. "Check out this tank. We've got a containment and pumping system designed to handle anything up to nuclear waste, and yet the hazard tags suggest it contains nothing more than dish soap. Seems kind of odd to me."

The EPA troubleshooter repeated Mitch's earlier investigation, first scanning the signage and then the hardware. "Hmmm," he sounded, "I think you might be right. Seems like a lot of overkill. I'm going to pull the van up here and see if I can test a sample."

Forty minutes later, Randy removed his protective mask and motioned to Mitch that it was safe to approach. He lifted a small glass tube of yellow colored liquid that had been extracted from the tank's testing tap and declared, "This is the smoking gun. Your farmer friend was right – this shit is about as toxic as I've seen in the last ten years. Nasty, nasty stuff here."

"I thought so," Mitch replied, eyeing the tank with a hint of disgust in his eye.

"I'll have to take this back to the lab and have a full analysis performed, but my little mobile chemistry set indicates the presence of cyanide and at least two other banned substances."

Randy secured his equipment and then proceeded to scan the area for the nearest cop. He finally spied the man he was looking for and nodded to Mitch. "I've got to go tell the authorities to rope this area off. We've got to get all these guys out of here before they start getting sick, or we have an accidental spill. There's probably enough poison in that tank to sterilize the entire Rio Grande River from here to Brownsville."

Mitch glanced at the tank again, this time with a hint of fear in his eyes.

Randy removed a cell phone from his jacket, sighing deeply as he speed dialed. "I'm declaring this location as a level two contamination site," he declared. "I want a full hazmat investigation team down here pronto. We need soil and water samples at a three, five and ten mile radius."

After listening to the response, Randy replied, "I don't care how pissed they are going to be – I've got several thousand gallons of deadly shit right next to me. We're damn lucky this tank didn't get punctured during all the gunplay."

Hanging up the call, Randy glanced up and prompted, "Come on – let's go tell the cops they have to leave. This is going to be the highlight of my day."

And Beyond

The newshounds were having a field day. America had been invaded – or had it? Mexico had declared war – or had it? It was terrorists. It wasn't. The bedlam and confusion made for good ratings, salivation glands working overtime in every major media outlet around the world.

Rumors, exaggeration, innuendo, and partial facts provided a nearly endless stream of fodder for reporters everywhere. Not since 9-11 had there been anything like the events in south Texas.

The authorities tried desperately to keep the media away. Using every excuse in their well-practiced book, they cited an active crime scene, ongoing military operations, live ammunition, and unexploded ordnance as reasons why the reporters should keep their distance.

It didn't work.

The savvy editors knew that speculation and deductive reasoning would only hold their viewing audiences for so long. They needed facts, hard evidence, and on-site documentation. Immense pressure was repeatedly heaped upon the men and women trying to cover the story and explain to the American people what had happened.

The politicians weren't about to let such a watershed event pass by without their participation. Every pet project, political angle, and fringe value was pushed to the forefront in order to take advantage of the publicity frenzy.

Oddly enough, the truth of the story mattered little as the few facts that were known were rather deftly twisted in such a way to support either side of any issue this event brought to light.

Congressmen who wanted immigration reform attempted to leverage the events in south Texas as a harbinger of the future and justification for why their position should be supported.

Hawkish legislators decried the need for more military spending and extreme border enforcement. Dovish Senators blamed the violence in Texas on a lack of U.S. foreign aid and underfunded social programs at home.

Labor unions weren't to be denied their moment in the sun. They and their supportive Washington legions emerged with messages relating the job-killing NAFTA treaty to the disaster du jour.

On and on went the parade of spin, propaganda, and positioning.

By late in the day, a new trend began to emerge in public opinion. One by one, the theories used to explain the events in Laredo began to fall victim to the truth. Little tidbits of genuine information eventually eked out of the region, often to the chagrin of those in charge. An interview with an FBI agent off the record, an unauthorized report from a military unit, and an eyewitness account by a citizen of Laredo... all seemed to contradict what the authorities were reporting.

Video images taken by cell phones began to appear on the internet, social media postings flying in the face of the "truth" being spouted by some member of Congress just a few minutes before.

Members of the Tri-Materials Board of Directors demanded to know what had happened to their facility, miles away from where the battle supposedly took place. Two networks managed interviews with surviving employees, both of whom described a major battle taking place in front of their plant.

For a few hours, it looked as if the poor, distraught, victimized corporation would contribute to the growing public outrage. Jobs had been lost. Workers would go without paychecks.

That sub-plot of the tragedy quickly reversed course when Tri-Materials was presented with a slate of subpoenas from the EPA. Salt was thrown into an already festering wound of the region when it became known that the now-destroyed manufacturer had been poisoning everyone's air. One radio commentator observed that at least one thread of silver lining had been identified in the dark cloud shrouding the happenings in southern Texas – the exposure of a corporate bully.

Americans began to sense a cover-up, the movement initiated by the conspiracy theory buffs and their multitude of forums and bloggers. Fringe websites began seeing more visits and readers than the mainstream media outlets. This forced the big boys of the news world to seek deeper truths in order to maintain their share of advertising revenue.

It was through this fog that a reporter happened to bumble into one Mrs. Penny Boyce. Shy at first, uncomfortable with speaking to anyone about the events of the last few days, her story eventually began to unfold.

The reporter was talented, projected an air of trustworthiness, and was skilled at her craft. Her report back to New York rocked the newsroom like an earthquake.

Mrs. Boyce's facts were undeniable. Her tale of a fugitive, the already well-known Durham Weathers, and the events of the past few days all made sense. The explosion on the Lexington, the obvious firefight at Tri-Materials and most important of all, an explanation for why a small army of armed men would invade America from the Mexican border.

The deception-onion served by the government spin doctors began to lose layers, peeled away by the sheer number of people involved in the incidents.

Even when the truth was told, it often served to degrade the public's perception of the authorities. The Air Force stated unequivocally that no bombs had been dropped, yet several eyewitnesses described an explosion at the bridge. Where had the bridge gone? If no bombs had been utilized, what the hell happened to the Tri-Materials plant? The government was lying!

By dinnertime of the second day, even average Americans were getting a sense that their elected officials weren't being forthright. The center-mass of public opinion shifted, accelerating in velocity toward a cover-up.

Mrs. Boyce's explanation opened doors, explained oddities, and allowed bright people to connect the dots. One network managed to get overhead views of the Tri-Materials facility. Within fifteen minutes, retired military men were on the air, all projecting credibility with years of experience performing bomb damage assessment. Unanimous in their claim that no known weapon could have caused the visible damage to the factory, one man even went so far as to compare the odd patterns of destruction at the plant with the damage at the Houston Medical Center. Those dots were being connected all over the region.

Penny's tale served a secondary purpose. The story of corrupt local officials, at best looking the other way while Tri-Materials filled their campaign coffers, shed an equalizing light on Dusty's activities. While no one was calling him Robin Hood just yet, the "bad" of his actions was somewhat offset by the "good" that had resulted from the violence.

While they didn't receive page one space, more than a few media outlets covered the promised investigations into what many claimed was a plague of graft along the border. A few more minds were swayed to Dusty's side of the ledger.

The more the authorities tried to squelch the girth of the story, the more fuel they threw on the fire.

Then the political in-fighting began to dominate the airwaves. The inaccuracies put forth by a Republican earlier in the day were used by a Democrat that afternoon. "Proof," claimed the liberal, "that the gentleman from the other side of the aisle was purposely deceiving the American people."

It seemed that anything stated by the government was either a deliberate lie or proof of ignorance. Neither helped the authorities or their images. Back and forth the rhetoric flew, both sides of the political spectrum trying to jockey for an advantage. The average Joe Nobody citizen quickly tired of the whole thing.

Within hours of the Boyce interview, the populace began to get a more complete picture of Durham Weathers. Fort Davis again experienced an invasion of strangers, reporters arriving in droves to investigate the mysterious figure's background.

Old stories were dug up, one of the main contributors being the *Houston Post*'s article titled, "God's Gun." That article, once shunned nationally as speculation and hearsay, was reanalyzed in a new light.

Every time a government official or law enforcement officer would characterize Dusty as a black hearted criminal, a segment of the population would immediately consider that he might instead be a hero. After all, statement after statement concerning Mr. Weathers had been false – why should anyone believe what was being said about the man?

Accelerated by social media, round the clock news coverage, and an unprecedented amount of internet traffic, Durham Weathers began to develop the genre of a folk hero. A news station in Wyoming carried an interview with a local militiaman who said his organization would welcome the fugitive with open arms. The well-armed fellow went on to claim that Weathers was a patriot and should be protected against the overreaching government cronies.

Other elements of the nation arrived at a completely different perspective, one fringe group demanding nothing short of Dusty being shot on sight.

As the days passed, and more and more information became known, a growing segment of the population began to wonder about the real story concerning the man from West Texas.

There was a hunger across the land... a strong desire for someone to explain all of the holes, meaningless doubletalk and misstated particulars surrounding the gunsmith, Durham Weathers. It didn't help that no one knew the whereabouts of the fugitive, that fact leading to an even deeper current of mistrust and speculation.

Some people subscribed to the theory that the government had indeed captured their man. Others claimed that Dusty had been assassinated by teams of black ops shooters. Law enforcement was inundated with reports of sightings, people claiming they had spotted the Texan everywhere from New York City to Singapore.

The governor of Texas was quoted as saying, "I don't know if Mr. Weathers is a bad man or a good guy; I don't know if he's dead or alive. It he's still among the living, I pray he's left our state. We can't handle any more of his tourism."

Plans for a rail gun were published on Amazon, the author claiming he had helped Dusty design the all-powerful weapon years before. The device did function - firing a steel projective with the equivalent kinetic energy of a BB gun.

Defense lawyers from all over the nation made public appearances on whatever media would carry their words. They pleaded for Durham Weathers to come forward so they could represent him.

Hank and Eva Barns appeared on several news specials, recalling the story of how the federal government arrested Mr. Barns and held him without due process or trial. It only added to the growing shadow of conspiracy surrounding the entire affair.

Before long, the name Dusty Weathers was being used alongside other men of lore. John Dillinger, Butch Cassidy, and even Robin Hood were common comparisons.

By the end of the first week, America had pushed aside the fear of a war with Mexico, cartels or another barrage of terrorist attacks.

Once the security of the nation was no longer in question, public opinion began to gather in camps.

A small, but growing contingent believed Durham Weathers was just another example of government overreach and abuse of liberties. Others disagreed.

Dusty was labeled with practically every term, both flattering and derogatory, in the English dictionary. A zealous minister determined that the Texan was the Antichrist, the seed of Satan come to destroy the earth. One member of Congress labeled him as "the prince of darkness."

The NY Times editorial board judged Weathers a radical, far-right lunatic. They justified their harsh verdict by the fact that the gunsmith didn't trust the U.S. government and should have immediately surrendered his technology for the good of all.

Dusty's wishes for his invention became known as well. Offers surfaced, quite often associated with fantastic fanfare. One oil company ran a 30-second commercial during primetime television, the message detailing a plan to meet Dusty's demands by building a super-secret facility where the rail gun technology could be matured and developed.

Several foreign countries hopped on the bandwagon, with Dubai, France, Canada, and even North Korea offering Dusty political asylum. Cuba topped them all, buying a full-page ad in the Miami Herald. The three-color fold displaying a man in a cowboy hat, sitting on a pristine beach, holding a large cocktail and being adorned by two beautiful, bikini clad girls. The title read, "Come on down – we'll treat you right."

A deluge of solutions began surfacing, university students offering up proposals to crowd source enough funds to purchase a private island where the rail gun's secrets could be redirected into creating free, clean energy and to reverse global warming.

Several large companies made it clear that they had the wherewithal to protect Dusty's technology, some even posting 800 numbers where he could call and be escorted into their protective custody.

Mainstream America listened to it all with an intelligent ear. The obvious untruths and deceptions surrounding the tale of the West Texas man were receiving more and more attention every day. The feds had been playing games with the facts, and that was troubling.

People started asking questions, directly worded inquiries pinging all levels of government. What had Durham Weathers done that prompted such a heavy-handed response? Why wasn't his powerful new discovery being explored, expanded, and utilized for the good of all? Why isn't the man being treated with the respect due such an intellectual giant?

From the White House press corps to town hall meetings with legislators, people began posing such questions to their representatives. Pressure was building, and it was clear that there were some in government who didn't like it.

Washington was a city that thrived on power, and it became obvious that Durham Weathers was siphoning some of that drug-like influence from those that ran the country. A series of counterattacks soon began, officials and experts from numerous government agencies warning that the rail gun might not be a safe form of energy while others expressed doubts that the technology could be commercially developed.

Dusty's mysterious whereabouts and silence allowed for the general public to hear only one side of the story. At 10 days after Laredo, the Texan's popularity began to fade.

Grace knew all of this, monitoring the news cycles with a keen eye while she tried to rally support for her cause.

No one wanted to help her. She pleaded, begged, threatened, and flirted with the powerful people in her rolodex – all to no avail.

Dusty was poison. An unknown. A hot potato that no one wanted to handle.

Frustrated and feeling the momentum draining away, she decided to declare war in her own way. She didn't have a rail gun to shoot, but she was armed with knowledge. "I'll let Dusty handle that rail thingie. I'm going to pull out the big guns."

Grace smoothed the front of her skirt for the third time. Following a hastily established routine, she checked her makeup, hair and watch in quick succession. She had ten minutes before it was her segment.

The "green room" of the cable news network was well furnished. Along one wall was a large section where those waiting to appear on national television had signed their names. Henry Kissinger, two presidents, the king of Saudi Arabia and countless movie stars had left short messages or signed their names.

A small tray of cheese, crackers, and dip sat on a nearby table, pitchers of iced tea, spring water, and some sort of fruit drink available as well.

In addition to the flat screen monitor displaying live images of the network's broadcast, a long table was equipped with a computer and a keyboard. The hostess had informed her it had unhindered access to the internet. Burning nervous energy, Grace decided to check her gardening forum one last time before making her debut on national television.

It took a few moments for her to log in. She noticed on the initial screen that someone had posted a new message on her thread.

Moving the mouse with anxious hands, she smiled when the screen refreshed. "I'm seeing similar colors blooming here in Kansas," someone had posted. "I agree with the previous post about the Canadian cold fronts being the cause."

Dusty was alive! He was in Kansas.

She read the message over and over, hoping there was some other small hint or piece of news hidden inside the simple text.

"You're on, Mrs. Kennedy," a voice interrupted.

Grace walked to a staging area just off camera, most of her nervousness overridden by Dusty's message.

She could hear the host's voice. "In our next segment, we have an exclusive interview with Ms. Grace Kennedy, the attorney representing Durham Weathers, the most wanted man in the world. Can she give us some insight into the man behind this weapon of mass destruction? Please stay tuned – we'll be right back after these messages."

Grace was shown to a seat, the famous commentator reaching across the small desk and shaking her hand. It seemed like only a few seconds passed before the red light on the television camera began to blink.

For the first ten minutes, Grace responded to basic background questions. How did she meet Dusty? What type of man was he? Simple, easy to answer inquiries that she'd fully anticipated. After another commercial break, the newsman got down to business.

"Why do you think the United States government is trying to suppress the technology behind this invention?"

Grace smiled, finally getting the opening she'd been waiting for. "Obviously I can't speak for our government, but there are many entities who would *not* benefit from its development. Oil and gas companies come to mind, as a source of free, renewable energy would eventually put them out of business. The defense industry is another example. Why would any nation buy a billion dollar weapon that can be easily defeated by a handheld device? The list could go on and on."

"So you're saying that current-day commercial interests are the reason why our federal officials are keeping a lid on this entire affair?"

"I don't know that for a fact, Bill, but it seems a reasonable explanation. There is no negative that I, or anyone else, has found with Durham's device If used for the safe, peaceful generation of electrical energy. There's no pollution, residual waste, or known danger. Why wouldn't our government and scientific community embrace such technology? Why paint him as a criminal and destroy his public image? I can't find another explanation for the actions of our government."

The host considered the attorney's answer for a moment and then countered. "I had the director of the FBI on this show a short time ago. Many law enforcement professionals claim that this device meets the description of a weapon of mass destruction and is extremely dangerous. They cite several attacks purportedly initiated by your client."

Grace waved off the question, her expression making it clear that such claims shouldn't be taken seriously. "Are these the same law enforcement personnel who originally claimed that the invasion of Laredo was nothing more than a large gang intent of robbing local businesses? Are these the same men who told our nation that the two fighter jets in Texas went down due to a mid-air collision? Or what about the purported bomb scare in College Station, which we soon learned was nothing but a cover story? If the American people want to continue to believe these men, that's their right. But frankly, if they tell me it's raining outside, I'm going to pack a picnic. Their credibility is low."

The lawyer's verbal volley drew a chuckle from the host. Checking the sheet of paper in front of him, he retorted, "But he *has* broken the law."

Grace nodded, "Yes, there's little doubt of that. But I could say the same for 99% of our viewers. There are over 27,000 pages of federal laws, which reference over 10,000 federal regulations. These numbers don't count Internal Revenue Service codes or state and local laws. The Congressional Research Service recently admitted that they could no longer even count all our laws, much less document them. Other institutions have asserted that the average American breaks three laws every day. Any of us can be labeled a criminal, prosecuted, and have our lives devastated while fighting the charges. Obviously, our law enforcement agencies must allocate available resources according to the greatest threats to our nation. My client was simply trying to defend himself from an overbearing government, yet he is the subject of such incredible scrutiny. So, why wasn't the government investigating that company down on the border instead? The one dumping cyanide into the environment? Their deliberate actions outside the confines of the law knowingly endangered thousands of people with the potential to cause more economic damage than Durham Weathers ever has. Why hasn't there been public outrage over the corruption that allowed that poison into the very air we breathe? In an odd way, my client has done the country a service..."

Bill nodded and then said, "I'll give you the last word, Mrs. Kennedy."

"Thank you," Grace responded and then looked directly into the camera with her most sincere expression. "Out there, hiding, alone and scared is a good man who any of you would welcome as a friend or neighbor. He wants nothing more than to help humanity. He has committed violence only as a last resort and only in self-defense. He is being persecuted for demanding that his discovery is never used as a weapon. Is this the intent of a madman? Are these the wishes of a terrorist? He wants nothing more than to elevate the quality of life for every person on the planet. Is this the mark of a dangerous person? I ask my fellow Americans to rally to his cause, which is just and humane. I ask everyone watching this telecast to ask themselves if they would have acted any differently than Durham Weathers. Help me bring him in from the cold. Demand the truth from our government so that he can be judged in the light of day by his peers, just as our constitution demands."

The camera again went dark and Grace relaxed momentarily against her seat, catching her breath before rising to leave. "Mrs. Kennedy, you realize what you've just done, don't you?" the host asked.

"I hope I've helped my client and informed the general public of the truth," she said.

A grimace came across the newsman's face, his eyes both sincere and yet sad. "Perhaps. But to be blunt, I think you just fired the first shot of what could be our country's second revolution."

The End

The Olympus Device: Book Three will be released in late 2014

Made in the USA
Lexington, KY
19 July 2014